THE
BOMB
MAN

ANDY GREENAWAY

Dedicated to the Major.
Dearly loved, sorely missed.

The events depicted in this book took place in Londonderry in 1973, at the height of The Troubles. The people in the story are based on real characters. But to keep their identities secret, and to protect them from reprisals, their names have been changed.

ONE

A milk churn had been placed upright by the side of the road. In any other country, no one would think anything of it. Just a harmless aluminium vessel, they would think. There would be no thought of how it got there. Why it was there. Or who put it there. In any other country, passers-by would have more important things to worry about than an out-of-place milk churn. Are the kids doing okay at school? Can the husband hold down his job? How are we going to make the mortgage payment this month?

But this wasn't any other country. This was Northern Ireland. 1973. And a milk churn standing on the side of the road wasn't an ordinary occurrence. It was to be viewed with instant suspicion.

A local farmer from Magherafelt called it in. 'There's a bomb on the side of the road,' he said. 'They must have put it there late morning. Because I drove past there in the tractor at around six, and it wasn't there then. And then I drove by there again at eight, and it wasn't there then either.'

The farmer's wife, who was busy making a pot of tea while her husband put in his complaint, was agitated. Why was he making such a fuss about an old milk churn? The old fool was worrying about things that were not his problem. Wasting a poor police officer's time.

'Can you describe it, Sir?' the police sergeant on the desk asked.

'A milk churn,' the farmer said.

'A milk churn?'

'Yes. A milk churn. Standing where it shouldn't be standing.'

An hour later, the army set up a blockade at each end of the small country road and Ron Bristow, Ammunition Technician with 321 Explosive Ordnance Disposal, was walking toward the suspect device with wire-cutters in his hand. 'In and out,' he muttered to himself. 'In and out.'

Bristow reached the milk churn and knocked the side with a knuckle. The vessel was full. Fuel oil and fertiliser, no doubt, thought Bristow. The Irish Republican Army's readily available ingredients for making a bomb. The solar glint from the churn dulled as thick, grey clouds rolled over and blocked out the sun. A blustery wind was blowing the thick billows of cumulus to the North. The sky was threatening to open up and release a torrent of water.

'Don't rain,' said Bristow to himself as a few droplets of water hit his face.

He looked over his shoulder at the group of soldiers two hundred yards up the road. Keeping a safe distance. Watching. Waiting. Some biting their nails. Not the first time he had been the centre of attraction that day. The jobs had been coming in thick and fast. Each one, so far, a hoax. Was this another one? Maybe not. But it was most likely a simple device made from simple materials and by unsophisticated bomb-makers. Of that he was convinced. *In and out.* Get this one done and move onto the next.

The bomb disposal man slowly lifted the lid.

TWO

They sat on the edge of the settee, their eyes fixed on the TV. A grim-faced newsman announced the plight of the eighth bomb disposal expert to die in Northern Ireland in the past six months.

Jean Thomson spoke first, 'Did you know him?'

'Yes, I did.' Dave Thomson had met Ron Bristow at Catterick Camp in North Yorkshire during an instructors' training course. More of an acquaintance than a friend. A quiet man who didn't mingle well. While the other course participants would meet up at the Sergeants' Mess every evening for a few drinks, Bristow would excuse himself and go back to his room. To study. No one believed it. He was an introvert who was awkward in social situations.

'But I didn't know him well,' said Thomson.

'I feel sorry for his wife.'

'He wasn't married.'

'Oh good.' Jean quickly realised that didn't sound right. 'I mean it's good he wasn't married, because that means, you know. Not good that he died.'

Thomson chuckled, 'It's okay. I know what you mean.'

'It's getting worse.'

'They've had enough.'

'But we went there to protect them, didn't we?'

'Yes. But we didn't do a very good job of it.'

They sat quietly for a while as footage from a helicopter showed the crater created by the explosion. Jean had a question on the tip of her tongue, but she was finding trouble getting it out. It was a question she desperately wanted to ask but didn't necessarily want to hear the answer to.

'Do you want a cup of tea?' she asked.

'I can make it.'

'No, no,' said Jean as she jumped to her feet and headed for the kitchen. As she put the kettle on the gas stove, she caught her own reflection in the kitchen window. She hadn't realised it, but her face looked drawn and etched with worry. Could he see that? God, I hope not. I don't want to add to his stress. Ron Bristow flashed into her mind. Another one dead. The bodies were mounting up. Couldn't the army be doing more to protect them? A knot tied itself in her stomach. She was too young to be made a widow.

Thomson appeared in the frame of the kitchen door. The kettle was whistling. 'The water's boiling.'

Jean was immersed in her own world. She hadn't heard the high-pitched noise that would normally make her hair stand on end. 'I've got it,' she said as she switched off the gas and poured the water over a Tetley teabag she'd dropped in a mug. She squeezed out as much tea as she could with a teaspoon and added three sugars and a drop of milk.

Thomson returned to his armchair and continued to watch the news. But his mind was racing. It was only a matter of time before he was sent to Northern Ireland and he wasn't looking forward to it. Too many ammunition technicians were losing their lives. Unprepared and inadequately trained. The army had been caught off guard by the IRA's tactics. They'd never faced a conflict like this before. Wars were usually fought with guns and bullets. This one was being fought with bombs and timers.

The role of an ammunition technician had literally changed overnight. His usual job was to inspect, store, test and ship ammunition. But now he had been given the additional responsibility of bomb disposal expert. And it was a problem. The ammunition technician was far from expert.

The rule book on how to dismantle a terrorist bomb hadn't been written. The techniques hadn't been developed. The protocols were still in incubation. Like every other ammunition technician, Thomson had been thrown into a job he hadn't signed up for.

Thomson was worried about how his wife would take the news when the day came. *Not well*, he thought. And his kids? Would they even understand?

Jean came back into the room with a mug of tea and a side plate with three McVitie's digestive biscuits on it. She handed them to her husband and took a seat on the settee.

Army life had been good to Jean. She'd gotten used to the middle-class living: a spacious house with a garden, a car and holidays abroad. It was a far cry from the small, mildewed terraced house where she grew up, in the slums of Sankey Bridges, a downtrodden part of Warrington in the North West of England.

But despite all the luxury, life would be worth nothing without her husband. She looked over at him as he sipped his tea and, at that instant, built up enough courage to ask the question. 'Will you have to go there?'

Thomson was caught by surprise. But it didn't show. It never did. 'Most likely,' he replied as he dunked a biscuit in his tea and took a bite. Her eyes welled up.

Thomson reached out and put his hand on top of hers. 'Don't worry. Everything will be okay.' The words sounded hollow. But they were the best he could find.

She knew the answer would be yes. So she didn't fully understand the emotions rising inside of her. Why the tears were sprouting out of her tear ducts and down her cheeks. Perhaps it was because he was so accepting of his fate. Obedient to the powers-that-be. Unquestioning of the sacrifice that was expected of him. But what about her? Did she count for nothing?

THREE

The clanging from the alarm clock filled the air, as it did every morning at 6 a.m. Even though electric clocks were now the rage, Thomson preferred the old-fashioned wind-up with two bells on top. It was loud and annoying. The perfect wake-up call.

Thomson opened his eyes, silenced the clock with his palm and rolled out of bed on autopilot. He put on his dressing gown and slipped downstairs to the kitchen to complete his daily pre-breakfast routine. First, he ironed his shirt, spraying starch on the collar, making it rigor mortis stiff. Then he moved onto the trousers, steaming the seams until the creases were sharp, like the edge of fine paper. And finally, his shoes, which were assailed intermittently between Thomson's spittle and a duster. Spit, polish, spit, polish. By the time Thomson put the shoes down on the floor, he could see his face in the leather shine.

Jean trundled downstairs half an hour later, pulled a frying pan from the cupboard and put it on the gas stove. She threw a large chunk of lard in the pan and, as soon as it had melted, filled it with bacon, eggs, tomatoes and half a slice of bread. She wouldn't be eating any of it herself. It was too greasy for her liking. She'd just make herself a slice of toast. But for Thomson, it was part of a ritual. It was the same breakfast he'd eaten every day since he joined the army as a boy soldier at the tender age of fifteen, always washed down with a cup of sweet tea.

Jean scraped the food out of the pan with a spatula, piled it on a plate and placed it in front of her husband. As he ate, Jean chatted away to him about the latest gossip from Warrington. Her sister Margaret had been evicted from her home. Turned out her husband was a compulsive gambler and had racked up a debt of ten thousand pounds without her knowing.

'They've got to leave that beautiful house and move into a council flat,' said Jean, a hint of outrage in her voice. 'I told her he was a rotten apple.'

Thomson didn't get much of a chance to talk when she got started. But he didn't mind. He liked hearing her ramble on.

Thomson finished his breakfast, stood up from the kitchen table and put his black beret on his head, adjusting it so it was perfectly placed at forty-five degrees. Jean took his empty plate and put it in the sink. He gave his wife a kiss and stepped out into the fresh air. Unlike most of his neighbours, who drove their cars the short distance to camp, Thomson preferred to walk. It was only a short walk. Three-quarters of a mile. But it gave him time to clear his head.

As Thomson neared the camp, he thought how nondescript it was. Horse chestnut trees had been planted on the inside of the perimeter fence, exactly ten feet apart. They partially obscured the facilities inside: one-story brick huts dotted around a large spacious area.

Thomson reached the gates. Security was tight. Two infantry soldiers from the Gurkha regiment stood guard at the entrance. Nepalese men no taller than five foot three. Each wore a wide-rimmed terai hat, had a SLR rifle in their hands and a large, curved Kukri attached to their belt. They'd seen and greeted Staff Sergeant Thomson every morning for the past year. But he still had to show his proof of identity.

He flashed his ID card and the white-and-red barrier was lifted to let him through. One of the Gurkhas broke into a grin as Thomson passed by, his crooked white teeth gleaming in the sun. I wonder if that's the smile they give their enemies just before they cut their throats with a Kukri, thought Thomson as he smiled back.

From the gates, he turned left and came to a large patch of neatly mown lawn. A small wooden sign had been hammered into the ground, standing military straight. The sign wasn't there yesterday. It had appeared overnight.

Thomson stopped and looked down at the small placard, inspecting the hand-painted words. Neat and precise. KEEP OFF THE GRASS. Across the sea of green, beyond the sign, was the school. And by cutting across the lawn, Thomson could shorten his walk by a minute. Maybe a bit more. But that would go against his principles. He loved the army because of the discipline it imbued in people. The self-regulation it imbued in *him*. Rules were rules. And he followed them without question. Even small instructions on a sign like this had a role in shaping the world-renowned discipline of the British Tommy. He had walked across that lawn every day since he'd been posted here. But no longer. Instead of walking across the precluded space, he decided to walk around it. Like the good soldier he was.

As he made his way to the halfway point, two crows landed on the grass and started pecking at the ground. Bloody crows, thought Thomson. They don't care for rules. They do what they please. They live by crow rules. The two birds, parading around on the forbidden patch of grass, somehow tampered with the order of the camp, which agitated Thomson's sense of disciplinary harmony. The staff sergeant clapped his hands loudly and the two birds flew off into a nearby tree, finding a perch from which they could spy their harasser.

It was a small victory he knew would be short-lived. As soon as he walked away, the crows would get back to their worm hunting. Thomson watched them for a while before moving on, navigating his way around the lawn and on to the school.

As he walked into his office, Thomson was greeted by the department's clerical assistant who had a hot mug of tea waiting for him. The frumpy middle-aged mother, with a penchant for Laura Ashley, beamed a generous smile. She liked Thomson. He had a good heart and, although he was a grumpy bugger at the best of times, treated her more like a friend than a subordinate. Thomson sat down behind his desk and sifted through a pile of mail.

'Your first class is in fifteen minutes,' said Agnes.

'Any biscuits?' asked Thomson.

'Better than that,' replied Agnes as she placed a Tupperware container on Thomson's desk and removed the lid. Inside was a large slice of chocolate cake. Thomson's eyes widened and a smile arched across his face. 'Are you trying to get me fat, Agnes?'

'Had some left over.'

Thomson picked up the slice of cake and took an oversized bite.

'I see another one's gone,' said Agnes casually. 'I hope they catch who've done it, string them up by the neck and cut their balls off with a blunt axe.'

Thomson choked on his cake.

* * *

The students dutifully scribbled notes on foolscap writing pads to the sound of Thomson's monotonal words. Ammunition storage and inspection was today's topic. The subject was dry. But it was at the heart of what an ammunition technician did. If the students didn't get their heads around this, they wouldn't pass and would be reassigned to another part of the army – a more mundane existence as a cleric or general storeman, packing away blankets and cans of beans.

But today the students were distracted. News of Bristow's demise was on everyone's lips. Terrorism, bombs and death were at the top of their mind. A student put his hand up.

'Yes?' asked Thomson.

'Staff, how do you handle a mercury tilt?'

'You mean if it's attached to an explosive device?'

'Yes.'

'You smash it to pieces with a disruptor.'

'But what if you have to get up close and get your hands dirty?'

'It's not a position you want to get into. You should always use a disruptor.'

Another student, a tinge of excitement in his voice, jumped in. 'But if you *had* to use your hands, what would you do?'

'Call my wife, tell her where the will is and say goodbye.' The students' enthusiasm was deflated by Thomson's answer. 'Look, I know you all think it's a heroic endeavour to dispose a bomb. But it's not. It's a job. And if you keep that in mind, and treat it as such, you'll live. If you start thinking you're a hero, you're doing exactly what the IRA wants you to do. The terrorists *want* you to take risks. Because then, the chance of killing you goes up. They're relying on your bravado.'

'So is that why so many ATs are dying? Because they're taking chances?' asked a student at the front.

The bell rang. The loud, annoying clang announced the end of the lesson and an end to the probing questions.

'Was that what happened with Staff Sergeant Bristow? Do you think he...'

'Let the dead rest in peace,' said Thomson.

'But…'

'Focus on your work. We'll pick up where we left off in our next lesson. And remember, you're not here to learn about bomb disposal. You're here to learn about ammunition inspection and storage. Dismissed.'

The students in the room stood up and walked out of the classroom in an orderly fashion. A corporal, who was walking against the flow, was bumped around like a ball bearing in a pinball machine.

'You're going the wrong way. Lesson's over,' advised Thomson as he collected his lecture notes.

'Major Owen wants to see you, Sir.'

The uttered name caught Thomson off guard. His body stiffened. Major Owen was in charge of deploying ATs to Northern Ireland. He alone decided who went and who stayed, who would face death and who would stay safe on the mainland. The major's nickname among the men was the Grim Reaper. And today, this man, whose long, invisible shadow stretched across the camp, had summoned Staff Sergeant Thomson.

* * *

The major sat behind his large oak desk, writing notes in the margins of a report. There was a knock on the door. 'Come in,' he answered without looking up.

Thomson opened the door and stood to attention. 'Sir, you wanted to see me.'

Owen looked up. 'Ah, Thomson. Take a seat, won't you?' Thomson sat in the wooden chair on the opposite side to the major. The same chair numerous other men had sat in. The same conversation. The same outcome. The same feeling of inevitability.

Thomson spotted a Clarksons travel brochure placed neatly next to a pile of military documents. He couldn't hold back the wicked urge to ask, 'Going on holiday, Sir?'

The major looked down at the brochure and replied without hesitation. 'Yes. Driving the family down to France next week. Found a lovely cottage in Provence.'

'That's nice.'

'You should try it yourself one year. Beautiful.' The major, the bubble of his conscience unpoppable, picked up the brochure and slipped it into the top drawer of his desk. 'Now, back to business. An opening has come up in Ireland.'

'You mean Staff Sergeant Bristow?'

'Yes, Bristow.'

'It was on the news last night.'

'Most unfortunate. He'd only been there for two weeks.'

'What happened?'

'The bomb went off,' replied the major glibly. Thomson wanted to tell the major what an arsehole he was. A pen-pusher who put good men in danger from behind the safety of his administrator's desk. But he decided to keep his mouth shut.

'He left a vacancy in Londonderry,' continued the major. 'And you'd be the perfect candidate to fill it.'

'Thank you for thinking of me, Sir,' replied Thomson with uncamouflaged sarcasm. 'How long's the tour?'

'Four months,' said the major. 'You need to pass a psychology test first, mind you.'

'A what, Sir?'

'A psychology test.' The major tapped his temple with his forefinger. 'Make sure you're all okay up there.'

'Why wouldn't I be?'

'I wouldn't know. Beyond my pay grade. A psychologist is coming in this afternoon. Some woman from the university. You're on the list of victims.'

'Anything else, Sir?'

'No, I think we're done.' There was no emotion in the major's voice. He was matter of fact. He'd had this conversation so many times, thought Thomson, it had become second nature. No remorse. No worry. No guilt. Just words. Just part of the job.

FOUR

A tall, studious major from the Army Medical Corps was sitting behind a desk at the front of the classroom. Sitting next to him was a petite woman in her late forties wearing a grey cotton dress and silver wire-framed glasses. She had a thick pile of papers in the grip of her long, bony fingers.

The major cleared his throat and addressed the twenty or so ATs sitting at their desks. 'Morning everybody. My name is Major Hartigan. This is Doctor Ford. Doctor Ford is a psychologist from the University of Warwick.' The ATs fidgeted in their seats, a sense of paranoia creeping into their psyche.

'As you all know,' continued the major, 'the job of an ammunition technician in Northern Ireland is a difficult one carried out under extremely intense conditions. Our aim is to make sure you're not only physically fit, which I'm sure you are.' The major let out an awkward chuckle. When he realised everyone in the room was straight-faced, he continued. 'But that you're also free from any serious personality weakness or disorder.'

Thomson smiled at the major's ungainly delivery. He was probably a public school boy. Eton, perhaps. Or Harrow. His voice lacked empathy. And to make matters worse, his plum-in-the-mouth accent lacked authority.

The woman stood up and took over. 'We're going to hand you each a paper.' She strolled around the classroom handing out multichoice questionnaires. 'Remember, there isn't a right or wrong answer. Just choose the option that feels right to you.'

A sergeant from the back of the room stuck his hand up.

'Yes?' asked the major.

'Why are we doing this test?'

'As I said, to see if there is any serious personality weakness.'

'What does that mean?' asked a stroppy warrant officer.

'To put it plainly, we want to see if you're all mentally fit to go to Ireland.'

'What if we fail the test? Is it going to affect our careers?' asked the sergeant.

The major wasn't expecting a question like that. Soldiers were normally compliant. Unquestioning. But ATs were taught to probe. Be curious. Their lives quite often depended on it. 'I can't tell you.'

'So it could? Is that what you're saying?' asked the warrant officer.

'Look, I think we should move on.'

'It's a fair question,' said Thomson.

'It may be a fair question,' replied the major tautly. 'But it's not my concern. If you have questions, you can raise them with the CO.'

The ATs in the room murmured and shuffled in their seats.

'You have thirty minutes to complete the paper,' said the woman as she examined her watch. 'Starting now.'

Thomson turned to the first page of the paper and was faced with a barrage of strange questions. *Do you like putting your feet into furry slippers? Is a white circle the light at the end of the tunnel or a train heading toward you? Do clouds make you feel happy or sad?*

There was no point trying to figure out the right answers. Most of them seemed so ludicrous that it was impossible to figure out the intent. Thomson ticked the boxes he felt most comfortable with and hoped he'd picked enough of the right ones to pass.

After thirty minutes, the major collected all the questionnaires and plonked them in a pile on the table at the front. The psychologist sat in her chair with a stony expression, arms folded across her chest.

'Thank you, gentlemen,' said the major. 'We'll let you know the results by the end of the day.'

'Is that it?' asked the warrant officer.

'Yes, that's it.'

The ATs got to their feet and slowly shuffled out of the classroom, a low hum of gossip permeating among them. Thomson didn't hang around to chatter. He made his way back to his office where a pot of tea had been prepared by Agnes. 'How was it?' she asked.

'Very strange,' replied Thomson.

'I hear they're doing it because too many of your lot are getting blown up. They think some ATs might have suicidal tendencies. They *want* to die.'

'Is that right?'

'Yes.'

'Where on earth did you hear that from?'

'Susan.'

'Susan?'

'She's the CO's secretary. Overheard him having a conversation with another officer.'

'She shouldn't be eavesdropping.'

'Just saying.' Agnes disappeared into her area and started organising files. Thomson shook his head. Typical. The secretaries and clerical assistants knew more about what was going on around the camp than he did.

* * *

The results of the psych test arrived on Thomson's desk just before 5 p.m. All it said was PASS. No explanation of what the tests were trying to determine and no insight into his character. Nor, for that matter, any opinion about his mental state.

According to Agnes, who had heard the gossip through the secretary grapevine, eight of the twenty ATs in the class had failed the test. Thomson was trying to work out who they were. Every man in that room seemed normal, calm-headed and professional. He'd worked with most of them at one time or other.

He didn't want to think about it and put it to the back of his mind. All that mattered right now was that he'd passed and had been given the green light to serve in Northern Ireland.

FIVE

Thomson normally walked home at a brisk pace. But today, he walked slowly. He needed time to gather his thoughts, to work out in his head how he was going to break the news to her. Should he let it out the moment he got home? Or should he wait until the children had gone to bed? She was bound to be teary and he didn't want the children to see her crying. It would only upset them. Yes, after the children went to bed. That would be best.

He would have to update his will, of course. And make sure she knew where to find the life insurance policy.

But then what? Just carry on as normal for two weeks? What if he went over there and never came back? Good, capable men were getting killed. There was every chance he could get killed too. Two weeks wasn't a long time to sort out things that needed to be sorted. He needed to see his mum. See his dad – who he'd fallen out with many, many years ago – and maybe try and make up with him.

There were lots of places he wanted to travel to. Canada. Hong Kong. New Zealand. No point thinking about that right now.

Thomson reached his house. He opened the front door and walked in. Jean was in the kitchen preparing supper. Braised beef, boiled potatoes and cabbage, with a thick, meaty gravy bubbling away in a pan.

Jean turned to greet him with her warm smile. But as she looked into his face, the smile dropped into a sullen arc.

'What's happened?' she asked.

Was it that obvious that something was up? He thought he was good at hiding his feelings. But obviously not with this woman. 'They're sending me to Ireland.'

'Oh,' she replied. 'When?'

'Two weeks from now.' He was surprised at how calm she was. He expected more emotion.

'Well, we knew it was coming, didn't we?' She moved close to her husband and hugged him. He hugged her back.

Andrew, their nine-year-old son came running into the kitchen. 'Is dinner ready?' He stopped like a freeze frame in a movie as he saw his Mum and Dad hugging. 'What are you doing?' he said with a frown.

'None of your business,' chided Jean. 'Go and get your sister.'

Andrew ran to the bottom of the stairs and shouted, 'Karen, dinner's ready.' Karen, his four-year-old sister, toddled down the stairs, ran into the kitchen and took her seat. The one she always took, right next to Thomson. 'Hello, Daddy.'

'Hello, sweetheart.'

Jean's stomach was churning. This was the moment she'd dreaded. She knew it would come. But it was still a surprise when it finally did. She wanted to cry. Not today. Some other time, when the kids were at school, when Dave was at camp and she was alone.

The kids scoffed their dinner. Thomson left some of the potatoes and cabbage. Jean hardly touched her food at all. 'Any pudding?' asked Andrew.

'What do you think?'

'Pudding,' replied Karen.

Jean got up from her chair and walked to the oven. She picked up a thick tea towel from the counter, opened the oven door and pulled out a baking dish.

'What is it?' asked Andrew greedily.

'Bread and butter pudding.'

'Not for me, thanks,' said Thomson. Jean didn't want any either. So she served up the pudding just for the two kids.

The adults watched patiently as Andrew and Karen munched through their dessert like human locusts, leaving the baking dish stripped bare of any visible victuals.

'Those dishes are so clean I could put them in the cupboard without washing them,' said Jean with a smirk.

The humour was lost on the children. 'Please may I leave the table?' asked Andrew.

'Please I leave the table?' quickly followed Karen, copying her brother as closely as she could. Jean had trained them well. Manners were very important to her. And she was a stickler for them.

'Not yet,' she said softly. 'We've got something to tell you.' She passed the oral baton to her husband. He paused for a short while, looked at his wife, thanked her for her support with a smile and turned to his children.

'I'm going to Northern Ireland for a short while.'

Andrew was old enough to know what was going on. He'd seen the news. The kids at school had talked about it. 'Are the IRA going to try and kill you?'

'They can try,' laughed Thomson, suddenly realising it wasn't the time to joke around. 'No,' he said seriously.

'But people are getting killed,' continued Andrew.

'I'll be careful.'

'I'm sure those dead soldiers were careful too.'

'Look, Andrew, some people take chances they shouldn't. I'm not going to take any chances. I'm going to be safe.'

'I don't want you to go.'

Those words were like a knife through Thomson's heart. He didn't know what to say. Jean squeezed his forearm and stepped in. 'It's your dad's job, Andrew. He doesn't have a choice.' A tear started rolling down Andrew's cheek. Jean got out of her seat and gave him a big hug. 'Come on, there's no need to cry. Go upstairs and do your homework. I'll be up in a minute.' Andrew climbed off his chair and walked out of the kitchen.

Karen didn't know what it all meant, but she knew something wasn't right. 'Why is Andrew crying?'

'He doesn't want me to go to Northern Ireland,' said Thomson.

'Why?'

'Because he's worried.'

'I'm worried too.'

'And why's that?' asked Jean.

'I don't know.'

'Come on, you,' said Jean. 'Let's go upstairs and get your pyjamas on.'

SIX

It was the big day. A strange day. It wasn't sad and it wasn't happy. Just somewhere in the middle. A day of warm smiles and cloudy hearts. The two weeks Thomson had been given to sort out his affairs and say his goodbyes had passed far too quickly.

He'd managed to zip down to Croydon with his family for the weekend and spend some time with his mum and dad. He had intended to make it up with his father, but there never seemed to be a right moment to talk. So they both endured each other's company, hiding behind a façade of warm smiles and polite chat.

He'd tried to strike up a conversation with his wife about what she should do if he was killed. Move up north with the kids. Buy a house with the insurance money. Find another man. Get on with life. She would have none of it though. 'You're not going to die,' she said. 'So there's no point talking about it.'

There were many things he had hoped to squeeze into his last two weeks. Meet up with close friends. Take the kids to the seaside. Take his wife to London to watch a West End show. But the days had run out. The hours had run out. And now the minutes were running down too.

Thomson was dressed in civilian clothing. Pale blue jeans, a beige open-necked shirt with a huge collar that poked over the top of a white

navy jumper, a grey raincoat his wife had bought him from Marks &
Spencer and brown Hush Puppies on his feet. Orders had come from
the top. Army personnel were not to wear their uniform while travelling
to Ireland. Or any other apparel that would give them away as a British
soldier. There was only one exemption to that rule. He was required to
carry a service pistol. A Browning L9A1. Thomson kept it hidden in a
holster under his jumper.

He lugged his suitcase through the front door of their house, walked
up the small path that cut through a patch of lawn and planted it onto
the street next to where the Q car was waiting for him. A covert vehicle.
Nothing fancy. Just a white Ford Escort. A military vehicle camouflaged
as civilian. The driver climbed out, grabbed Thomson's suitcase and
shoved it in the boot. 'Ready when you are, Staff.'

Jean and the kids huddled around Thomson, fencing him in. Or at
least that was what Jean wished she could do. Stop him from leaving.
Keep him tethered right there in front of the house.

As Thomson kissed his wife goodbye, as he ruffled his son's hair,
as he took the limp daisy out of his daughter's raised hands, he wanted
to say something meaningful. Something reassuring. But all he could
muster was, 'I'll see you soon.' He wanted to say more. Promise he'd
return. Kneel down and beg the gods to spare his family and himself
from the worst. But that would be tempting fate in every sense of the
word. It would be better if the celestial lords didn't notice him. If they
simply ignored his movements and left him out of their deliberations.

Thomson kissed Jean again, got into the passenger seat of the car and
waved. Jean, Andrew and Karen waved back as the car pulled away.

'Bye-bye, Daddy,' shouted Karen. Jean watched the car turn a corner
and disappear. She waited for a couple of minutes. Maybe it would come
back. Maybe he'd forgotten something. But it didn't.

Jean looked up. Thick, dark clouds, swirling in the wind, blanketed the sky. A few droplets splattered on the pavement. It was going to bucket down. She hoped it wasn't an omen.

Andrew took her hand and squeezed it. 'He'll be okay,' he reassured her, not entirely convinced of his own words. Jean squeezed back and smiled.

Andrew could see the effort it took. He prayed to God there and then. In his head. So only the Almighty could hear him. Keep my dad safe, God. Don't let the IRA kill him. I mean it. You better look after him. Or else…

SEVEN

Thomson had a two-hour wait before the ferry to Belfast departed, so he had some time to kill. He weaved his way through the crowd, found a newsagent and bought a copy of *The Times*. He parked himself on one of the benches that lined the walls of the drab terminal. The front-page news was dominated by the Cod Wars between Britain and Iceland. Three Royal Navy frigates had been sent to protect British trawlers from aggression by Icelandic patrol boats. A squabble over fish, it seemed, was more interesting to the British public than a war where lives of British citizens were being lost every day. Thomson flicked through the pages of his newspaper. It wasn't until page six that he found news about The Troubles. The Royal Ulster Constabulary had shot a man dead in County Fermanagh. It was a small piece. Easy to miss. Disrespectfully unimportant.

Thomson read the parts of the newspaper that interested him and, after twenty minutes of browsing, turned his hand to the crossword. He was quite good at solving the paper's famous cryptic clues. It was a slow process, though. And after he'd solved the third clue, he looked up at the clock hanging on the terminal wall. It was time. He folded his newspaper, picked up his suitcase and headed for the gate. He flashed his ticket to the ticket inspector who waved him through. There was a hum all around him as people happily chatted away. He could hear a Liverpool accent one moment and an Irish one the next.

Once on board, he made his way to the third level and found his berth. It had four beds crammed ergonomically into a box. He had no idea who his roommates would be. Maybe he'd be lucky. Maybe he'd be the only one occupying this berth. He hoped so, but knew it was wishful thinking. The ferry was an oversized sardine can.

He felt a pang of hunger in his stomach. He needed food. So he parked his suitcase on the bed next to a porthole and headed upstairs to the ferry bar on the fifth level. The place was already busy, a steady flow of people quickly filling the place up. Thomson found a stool at the bar and claimed it.

'What can I get you?' asked the young barman with a thick Irish accent.

'Ham and cheese sandwich and half a lager.'

'Half?' asked the barman, checking to make sure he'd heard correctly. Men on this ferry didn't order halves. They ordered pints. Halves were reserved for the women.

'Just a half.'

The barman pulled a sandwich from a shelf laden with other work-ing-class bar food: pickled eggs, crisps, pork scratchings and pork pies. He placed the ham and cheese sandwich, still wrapped in its paper, on the bar in front of Thomson. He then got to work on the half pint of lager and, a moment later, placed it, almost with a sense of loathing, alongside the sandwich. 'That will be sixty pence.' Thomson pulled some change from his pocket and counted it out on the bar. He slid it across to the bartender who picked it up, deposited it in the till and moved onto the next customer.

As Thomson took a bite into his sandwich, he could feel the ferry moving. He was on his way. Ten hours from now, he'd be in Northern

Ireland. He looked around the room. There were a lot of Irish people on this boat. How many of them were Protestants and how many of them were Catholics? It wasn't a question he would normally ask himself. He didn't give a damn about religion. People were people. But where he was going it *did* matter.

His gaze caught that of a hard man sitting with some of his friends. Labourers with thick callouses on their hands. Brick layers and hod carriers. They seemed to have settled in for the night and, by the amount of empty pint glasses on the table, had already sunk two or three pints each. The hard man took a swig from his glass as he locked eyes with Thomson. It was a silly game and Thomson wasn't in the mood to play it. He turned to his sandwich and gobbled it up. He washed the meal down with his lager. It tasted good. Perhaps he should have had a pint after all.

'Another?' asked the barman.

'No thanks,' replied Thomson, as he climbed down off his stool. The ferry was rocking in the rough sea, rain lashing against the glass. It was going to be a rough crossing. Thomson tried to walk straight but instead lurched to the left. He quickly found his sea legs and made his way down to the third level. He was tired and looking forward to his bunk.

As Thomson approached his berth, he heard voices chattering away inside. Irish voices. He lingered outside for a while, listening to their conversation. The men were blathering about work things. The low pay. The long hours. The shit weather. The bastard English foreman.

Thomson opened the door and entered. The men stopped talking. It was as if he'd interrupted a secret meeting with secret topics and secret plots.

'Evening,' said Thomson, as he lifted his suitcase off his bunk and placed it underneath.

'Evening,' replied an abrasive middle-aged man with large, tattooed forearms and a craggy face.

The three men eyed Thomson suspiciously. He wasn't one of them. His hands were too smooth. His physique too slight. His clothes unmistakably middle class. This man hadn't seen a hard day's work in his life.

The rain thrashed against the porthole of the ship. The vessel was now in open sea and was being rocked in twelve-foot waves.

'Going to Ireland?' asked the man with the craggy face. *What a stupid question*, Thomson thought. He was tempted to crack a joke – No, I'm going to France. But thought better of it.

'Yep,' he replied in a tone that made it clear he wasn't interested in starting a conversation.

'What are you going for?'

'Fishing.'

'Fishing? Whereabouts?'

'Does it matter?' Thomson didn't like this man and his probing questions.

'Are you English?' Another stupid question. 'The English aren't that welcome in Ireland these days.'

'That's news to me?'

'You should pay more attention to the telly. There're bombs going off. Killing people. English people.'

'I've heard they're killing Irish people too.'

'Not everybody in Ireland is a true Irishman.'

'And you are?'

'Aye. You better believe it. I'm the real deal.'

'Good for you.'

The attempts at baiting the Englishman were not working. The man with the craggy face looked Thomson up and down with contempt.

'You're not a fisherman.' Thomson ignored the accusation. 'Are you an army boy?'

And what the hell has that got to do with you, Thomson wanted to say. But he thought better of it. His orders were to travel incognito. Thomson hung up his coat, kicked off his shoes and laid down on his bunk fully clothed. He put his hand on his Browning. The hardness of the pistol under his jumper gave him comfort. His eyes closed, but beneath the lids his mind was fully alert.

The man with the craggy face could smell army. He wanted to punch the cocky Englishman in the nose. Skinny runt. I could tear that snotty bastard to pieces. But as much as he was up for a fight, his mind wandered back to another time. A punch-up with another skinny soldier boy two years earlier near Hereford. Turned out the fucker was an SAS sergeant. That was the day he'd got the pummelling of a lifetime. Broken nose. Broken cheekbone. Broken thumb. *Besides,* he thought to himself, *if I get into a fight on a boat, I'm going to get arrested by the coppers and locked away.*

'Time for lights out, lads,' scoffed the man with the craggy face. The other two, who hadn't squeaked a murmur during the exchange of words, had taken off their boots and were lying on their bunks. They were more interested in getting some shut-eye than taking part in a pointless argument.

The man with the craggy face switched off the lights, got onto his bed and noisily shuffled around until he was comfortable.

Thomson put his arms behind his head. The room was in darkness except for the fragment of light that seeped through the porthole window. One of the Irishmen in the room was snoring. Thomson wished he could drop off like that. He watched the rain smashing against the porthole glass. The patterns of water running down the outside had hypnotic power. Thomson needed some sleep. He wished he wasn't in this room, with these people. His eyelids felt heavy. He let them close and drifted off into a deep sleep.

* * *

The sunlight seeped through the porthole into the room and touched Thomson's face like an angel's fingers. Thomson opened his eyes. He stared at the ceiling for a while before he lifted himself up and sat on the edge of his bunk. The Irishmen were still asleep. He quietly put his shoes on, grabbed his coat, plucked his suitcase from under the bunk and headed for the cabin door.

'See you around, soldier boy,' muttered the man with the craggy face. Thomson ignored him and slipped through the door, closing it softly behind him.

Desperate for a pee, Thomson made his way to the toilets. The queue was long. He waited patiently as men with hangovers slowly emptied their bladders. The stench of urine floated down the corridor. People in the queue were scrunching their faces up, trying to withstand the assault on their noses. Thomson held his breath as much as he could. And when he had to breathe, he did it through his mouth. He finally got to a urinal and relieved himself. He would have liked to have brushed his teeth, but all the sinks were taken with men washing and shaving their faces. He wasn't going to queue. Not in that putrid air. He could freshen up once he got to base.

He made his way up to the bar area, which in the mornings was converted into a breakfast room. There was another long line of people queuing up for their fried breakfast. Thomson wasn't in the mood for queues this morning. Breakfast would have to wait too. Enjoying some fresh air seemed a better way to spend his last hour on the ship. He broke ranks, climbed up to the top floor of the ferry and walked out onto the empty deck. The wind was cold and blustery. Thomson emptied the stale air from his lungs and inhaled fresh air laced with sea salt. He stood at the bow of the ship and grabbed the railings. The grey skyline of Belfast was visible. It was a low-rise city with church spires breaking above the terraced houses.

Thomson saw a plume of smoke rise into the sky from somewhere in the city centre, slowly blooming into the shape of a mushroom. A few seconds later, he heard a faint rumble. Was that what he thought it was?

EIGHT

Thomson disembarked from the ferry and shuffled down the gangway, hemmed in by an impatient, murmuring crowd. Ten minutes later, the horde of passengers dispersed as it entered the spacious main hall. Thomson looked around for a man holding a sign with his name on it.

'Staff. Staff.' Thomson swung right toward the sound of the voice. A short, pudgy man, dressed in jeans and a zipped-up leather jacket held up a piece of cardboard in the air with the name THOMSON written on it. 'Over here, Staff.'

Thomson made his way over to the pudgy man and shook his outstretched hand. 'How did you know it was me?'

'The suitcase.'

Thomson hadn't thought about it before. But his suitcase was a dead giveaway. A civilian wouldn't know it was military. But anyone in the Forces would instantly recognise the army-issue luggage – always a light-green canvas outer and brown leather corner guards.

The pudgy man led Thomson outside into the carpark and toward the Q car, a dirty white Ford Escort. Within five minutes, the two men were driving down the M2 toward Thiepval Barracks at Lisburn, the HQ for the British Army in Northern Ireland.

'What's your name?' asked Thomson.

'Private Morby,' replied the pudgy man from the Pioneer Corps, the labourers of the army. Pioneers did repairs on buildings, built roads, looked after stores and did all sorts of other menial tasks, such as driving people around. The ATs called them 'chunkies', the kind of name you'd give to someone who was more at home using his hands than using his mind.

'Mind if I put some music on?' asked Thomson.

'Go ahead.'

Thomson pushed a button on the radio and music blared out through the speakers. It was the pop band Dawn with their hit song, 'Tie A Yellow Ribbon Round The Ole Oak Tree'. It was a catchy tune and, as Thomson listened to the lyrics, his mind wandered to Jean. He worried about her. More than he worried about himself. Which he knew didn't make sense. She was home safe. He was about to walk into the middle of a war. But even so, he couldn't help but think that her situation was tougher than his. Waiting. Worrying. Counting the long, slow, endless days.

The song petered out and a news bulletin took its place. A man with a clipped English accent and a deep baritone voice read the report. *In Belfast this morning, a bomb exploded in a car showroom. It is the third time the showroom, located in the Lower Falls area, has been targeted. The IRA called in the bomb half an hour before it went off. No one was killed or injured.*

'I saw that from the ferry,' said Thomson.

'That's Northern Ireland giving you a warm welcome,' chuckled Morby, tickled by his own joke.

In other news, Billie Jean King has reached the final of Wimbledon. She will face either Chris Evert or Margaret Court.

* * *

Thiepval Barracks was like a meat plant. Newbies like Thomson
would arrive and be processed: briefed, equipped and shipped out to
their mission in double-quick time.

First, Thomson made his way to the orderly room where a clerk
asked him to fill out several arrival forms. From there, he was taken
to see Major Braithwaite, the SATO (Senior Ammunition Technician
Officer) for Northern Ireland. The discussion was brief. The major
welcomed Thomson to Northern Ireland, officially assigned him to the
EOD section in Londonderry, told him to be careful and then sent him
in the direction of Lieutenant Colonel Wilkinson, the CATO (Chief
Ammunition Technical Officer) of Northern Ireland. Wilkinson was a
bit warmer than the major and asked the staff sergeant about his family.
Thomson appreciated the concern. It wasn't often a senior officer took
the time to show a bit of empathy. The expected demeanour of the
military ruling class was to be direct, cool and distant.

After the pleasantries, the lieutenant colonel took Thomson through
the operating procedures in the province and gave him an update on
some of the latest tactics the IRA were starting to employ: mercury tilts,
double circuits and radio control.

From the CATO's office, Thomson made his way back to the orderly
room where the clerk issued him his kit: two sets of combats, a wind-
breaker, a helmet, a flak jacket and a pair of Wellington boots.

'Good luck,' said the clerk.

'I don't believe in luck,' said Thomson as he made his way to the
carpark outside.

Private Morby was standing outside the car smoking a cigarette. He
threw it to the ground, stamped it out and opened the boot of the car.
'That was quick, Staff.'

Thomson threw his new gear into boot. 'How far to Ebrington Barracks?'

'Two and half hours. We'd better get going though. It's nearly witching hour.'

'And what would that be?'

'When the naughty boys come out.'

* * *

The Ford Escort chugged northward up the A6. The road cut through a part of the country that was staunchly Catholic. The British Army was not welcome around the sparsely populated area inhabited mostly by farmers.

Thomson looked out the window. He was struck by the wild and beautiful scenery. On the left side of the road was long grass and clusters of heather, disappearing down the hill into crags and crevices. Windswept trees dotted the landscape, gnarled and bent like calcified old men. To the right of the road was a rocky slope. Grey and dreary, casting a gloomy shadow over the road.

'This is the Glenshane Pass,' said Morby. The private put his foot on the pedal until the car was cruising at eighty miles per hour. He seemed a little anxious. Thomson didn't mind the speed. It meant they would get to base quicker and he could jump into a hot bath. He was tired and starting to smell.

All of a sudden, the pudgy private took his foot off the accelerator.

'What's up?' asked Thomson.

'Have you got your pistol on you, Staff?' replied Morby as he slowed the car down to forty.

Thomson patted the Browning under his jumper. 'Yes.'

'Good. There's a car up ahead parked on the side of the road.'

'Is that a problem?'

'If it's an IRA checkpoint, it is.'

'Why would there be a checkpoint?'

'They've been trying it on lately. Setting up roadblocks. Stopping cars. Got into a firefight with a couple of squaddies a few weeks back.'

'Who won?'

'A draw.'

'Anybody shot?'

'One of their lads got a bullet in the leg. Then they scarpered.'

The Ford Escort edged toward the car on the side of the road. Both men had their hands on their pistols, ready to pull them out at the slightest sign of trouble.

The car was a green Austin A30 from the 1950s. An old woman had opened the bonnet and was standing by the front fender. Steam was pouring out from the radiator. The woman looked into Thomson's eyes. A silent appeal for help.

Morby glanced at the woman over Thomson's shoulder. He briefly eyed her up and down before putting his foot on the accelerator and speeding away from the scene.

'Shouldn't we help her?' asked Thomson.

'Not on my watch,' said Morby. 'As far as I know, she could be a decoy. I'm not getting shot for trying to be a gentleman.'

* * *

The two men had to show their identity cards before they were allowed through the sandbagged front gates of Ebrington Barracks. Ten infantrymen, wearing full combat gear and carrying SLRs, lingered on either side of the road that snaked into the camp while one of their comrades manned a heavy machine gun that had been mounted opposite the guardhouse. *The IRA wouldn't dare launch an attack on this place*, thought Thomson. They'd be torn to bits by the firepower.

Morby pulled up outside the main building of the camp, jumped out of the car and grabbed Thomson's suitcase from the boot.

'Where to now?' asked Thomson.

'I was told to drop you off at the main building, Staff. The brigadier wants to see you.'

'What?' Thomson was caught off guard. Brigadiers didn't make time for lowly staff sergeants. They were too busy with important matters. Too busy with the bigger picture. Why would a brigadier want to see him, a ranker?

'He's got a thing for you bomb disposal boys.'

'Are you pulling my leg?'

'Nope. Every AT who comes through here gets an audience. He's on the top floor.' Morby jumped into the Ford Escort, hooted the horn and drove off. The car disappeared into the heart of the camp. Morby would no doubt be heading for the NAAFI for an early afternoon pint, his day's work done.

Thomson walked into the main building with a suitcase in hand and climbed the four floors to the top. He stopped for a moment to catch his breath and gather his bearings. To the left, he spied an office with a wooden plaque outside the door. The words 'Brigadier W. MacIntyre' had been printed in gold across the varnished oak. Thomson made his way along the corridor and knocked on the door.

'Enter,' said a female voice. Thomson pushed open the door and stepped inside an outer office. Sitting behind the desk was an attractive blonde woman in her early forties. 'Staff Sergeant Thomson?'

'That's right. The brigadier wants to see me.'

'Yes, he's just on a call right now. He'll be done soon. Can I get you a cup of tea?'

'That would be lovely.'

As Thomson took a seat, the blonde woman stood up and made her way to a small kitchenette. Thomson couldn't help but notice her figure. Slim yet curvaceous in all the right places. The woman turned to ask a question, the cleavage of her large breasts catching Thomson's eye. 'Sugar?'

'Yes, three.'

The blonde woman smiled to herself. She'd spotted the staff sergeant's roving eyes. He was a good-looking man. Looked like a decent chap. But that wasn't necessarily a good thing. Decent people in this city quite often ended up dead. It was the indecent people. The cunning, the conniving, the immoral who usually made it out of Londonderry alive.

'Here you go,' said the blonde as she placed the cup of tea in front of Thomson and took her place behind her typewriter. 'My name's Dorothy.'

'Dave.'

'How was your trip over, Dave?'

'Not exactly a pleasure cruise.'

'I've heard that boat stinks to high heaven.' The two laughed.

'That's an accurate description.' Thomson took a sip of his tea. 'So are you from Londonderry?'

'Born and bred.'

'Must be hard seeing all this violence and destruction in your hometown.'

'It's been brewing for a long time. The Catholics have been treated badly.'

'No excuse for bombing the hell out of a city.'

'I agree. But what would *you* do if you were pushed into a corner?'

'I'm not sure what you're getting at.'

'Imagine being treated like a third-class citizen. Your family of eight forced into a tiny shithole of a house. No job prospects. Constant intimidation from a police force. And Orangemen beating up your best friend for walking on the wrong side of the street.'

'Sounds like a shit deal.'

'And there's not a thing you can do about it. You're not even allowed to vote.'

'That can't be true. Everyone has the right to vote in this country.'

Dorothy laughed at the staff sergeant's naivety. 'I'm sorry,' she said as she regained her composure. 'That was rude.'

'Am I missing something?'

'This isn't the mainland. This is Northern Ireland. The voting system here is rigged.'

'I don't believe you. We're not a tin-pot dictatorship.'

'You put too much faith in the government.' Dorothy put her elbows on the desk, clasped her hands together and leant forward. Thomson pushed his back against his chair as the space between them narrowed. 'This is how it works, Dave. You can have four adult Catholic males in a council house and only one gets a vote. That's the law the politicians have put in place. And it's designed to keep the Catholics under the thumb. But if you're a rich Protestant man with four properties, you get four votes.'

'Are you serious?'

'Yes, I am. The population of Derry is eighty percent Catholic. And not one of them sits on the council.'

'Are you Catholic?'

Dorothy laughed again. 'No. I'm Protestant. Not that I'm religious, mind you.'

'You sound sympathetic.'

'Don't get me wrong. I feel for the mothers and the kids and the ordinary working men. I understand why the IRA came about. But if the movement started out with good intentions, it isn't that way anymore. It's filled with a bunch of sadistic bastards.'

'You seem to know a lot about it.'

'If you live here, you know enough.'

The phone on the desk started ringing and Dorothy picked up. 'Yes, Sir. I'll send him in.' She replaced the receiver on its hook. 'He's ready for you.'

Thomson stood up and placed his empty teacup on its saucer. 'Thanks.'

'No worries. Just a cup of tea.'

'For the other stuff.'

'Not that it will help.'

'Guess not.' Thomson walked to the door of the main office, tapped it twice with his knuckle and walked in. The brigadier had risen from behind his desk ready to receive his guest. Staff Sergeant Thomson stood to attention.

'At ease, Staff Sergeant Thomson,' said Brigadier MacIntyre. He held out his hand to a wooden chair on the visitor's side of his desk. 'Please.'

Thomson settled into the seat as MacIntyre planted himself in a plush, upholstered, green leather chair.

'A bloody mess, isn't it?' said MacIntyre. It was a question designed to put the staff sergeant off balance.

'Beg your pardon, Sir?' replied Thomson, uncertain of the question.

'This whole situation,' continued MacIntyre. 'We're in our own country fighting a war against our own people.'

'I haven't thought about it much, Sir.'

'Do you think it's a war we can win?'

'I'm not sure I'd call it a war, Sir?'

'Well, what would you call it?'

Thomson pondered the question. He wasn't quite sure what the brigadier was trying to get at. Top brass didn't normally ask staff sergeants questions like this. 'I would call it domestic unrest.'

The brigadier let out a chortle. 'I like the way you put it. Not many people around here would agree, unfortunately. To the Protestants, it's an insurrection. To the Catholics, it's a war against injustice. And we're caught in the middle.'

'I thought we'd already chosen a side, Sir.'

'Indeed. You can't sit on the fence for ever, Staff. It makes for an uncomfortable seat. The Catholics have turned The Troubles into a revolution against the queen. And that makes you, as a British soldier, the enemy. If you don't watch your back, you'll find a knife in it.'

'I've got eyes in the back of my head, Sir.'

'You look like a decent bloke, Dave.'

'I would like to think I am, Sir.'

'Don't be too nice. Nice guys get sucker punched. A lot of stupid squaddies, even though they've been warned, get lured by a pretty girl. And guess where they end up?'

'In trouble?'

'Worse. Dead in the gutter.'

'Don't worry about me, Sir. I was born in Croydon. We don't trust anybody. Not even the local priest.'

'Good,' said the brigadier. 'How you feeling about the tour?'

'A little nervous to be honest,' replied Thomson.

'If you wasn't nervous, I'd be worried.' MacIntyre tapped his fingers on his desk. 'You boys have got the toughest job out here. I have a lot of admiration for the work you do. But let me give you some advice. Be patient. The ATs getting killed out here are the ones who are in too much of a hurry.'

'Does that include Bristow, Sir?' The question clearly took MacIntyre by surprise and his jovial eyes turned unfriendly for a fraction of a second. Thomson realised he'd edged over the line. 'Sorry, Sir. That wasn't very tactful.'

'It's okay, Staff. You have a right to ask. Was Bristow unlucky or was he careless? I don't know. Maybe he was a bit too hasty in his work. Maybe he didn't respect the bomb-maker enough. But I have a question for you. Will you make it out in one piece? Or will you be another statistic just like Bristow?'

NINE

The brigadier walked Thomson over to the ops room. He was a fast walker, and Thomson, who thought of himself as a fast walker, struggled to keep up as they made their way across the quad.

'Here we are,' said McIntyre as they reached the one-story red-brick building. *The army must use a template*, thought Thomson. It was exactly the same as the building he worked in every day at Kineton, back in England.

MacIntyre skipped up the three steps to the front entrance of the ops room and barged through the double swinging doors. Thomson followed him along a corridor fitted out with worn linoleum flooring. The walls were painted eggshell white, with old prints hanging from them in crooked frames. Images of famous battles from the British Army's glorious past: Rorke's Drift, Lucknow and Waterloo.

MacIntyre opened a door to a small office. Captain Granger was sitting behind a desk writing up a report.

'Morning, Captain Granger,' said MacIntyre.

'Morning, Sir,' replied the young officer as he stood up and saluted.

'Staff Sergeant Thomson,' continued MacIntyre.

'Ah, you've arrived. Good to have you on board.'

'Thank you, Sir,' said Thomson.

'I'll leave it to you to show him the ropes,' said McIntyre.

'He's in safe hands with me, Sir,' replied Granger.

'I'm sure he is,' said MacIntyre as he turned to Thomson. 'If you ever need a chat, Staff, don't hesitate to come and see me.' MacIntyre threw a lazy salute and left the room.

As soon as the brigadier was out of earshot, Granger's sprightly demeanour fell away, replaced by a more solemn disposition. 'You may have noticed, Staff Sergeant Thomson, that Brigadier MacIntyre has a way of being familiar with rank-and-file soldiers such as yourself.'

'I noticed that, Sir.'

'I do not afford the same latitude. I expect our relationship to be as it should be. Formal. Is that understood?'

'Understood, Sir.' The words pompous bastard flashed into Thomson's mind. Men like Granger relished the elitist distinction between a commissioned officer and a mere rank-and-file soldier. He was a snob.

'Good. Now, how much has the old man told you?'

'Not much, Sir. Just a bit of advice on being patient.'

Captain Granger shook his head dolefully. 'Bloody old fool. He hasn't got a clue what's going on out there. Take that advice with a pinch of salt, Staff Sergeant Thomson. He's not an AT. These jobs come in fast and furious. We don't have time to mess about. We're in and out. Like a breeze.'

'In and out, Sir?'

'That's right, Staff. In and out,' reiterated Granger.

Thomson was unsettled by Granger's flippancy. Too many ATs were dying in Northern Ireland. As such, instructors back at the school, like himself, had been directed to train ATs to be cautious and patient when dealing with an explosive device. A sentiment that had just been echoed by MacIntyre. But here was an officer, an arrogant pillock, serving up a very different kind of advice. He was one of those officers, in the heat of battle, that would end up being shot in the back by his own men.

'Has anyone told you how we operate?' asked Granger.

'No, Sir.'

'Okay. Here's how it works, Staff Sergeant Thomson. Listen carefully. Because I don't like repeating myself. There's five of us. But we have only four ATs on standby at any one time. If there's a call, Duty-One takes it. When there's another call, Standby-Two takes it. A third call, Standby-Three takes it. And a fourth call Standby-Four takes it. The remaining operator stays off.'

'What if there's a fifth call, Sir?'

'If everyone's out, that job has to wait until a duty AT becomes free. The off duty stays off duty. Standing orders from CATO. Not that I agree, mind you. I think we could all do a bit more. But I'm not in charge.' Granger picked up a report from his desk and shoved it in a drawer. 'Any further questions, Staff Sergeant Thomson?'

'No, Sir. I've got it.'

'Right, I'll introduce you to the rest of the unit.' Granger brushed past the staff sergeant and strode out of the office. Thomson followed him, suitcase in hand. The door to the ops room was right around the corner. A large poster of a light-brown cartoon cat, with a bomb disposal helmet on its head, was stuck on the outside of the door. Felix, the name of the cat, had become the unit's call sign. No one was quite sure of where the name came from. But one rumour persisted. When 321 EOD was first formed in the Province back in 1970, the officer commanding had the idea of giving it the call sign 'Phoenix,' to symbolise the unit rising from the ashes to conquer Irish terrorism. However, the young signaller that he told this to misheard him and thought he'd said 'Felix', the famous cat from Hollywood. The name stuck and, soon afterwards, the light-brown cat with the bomb disposal helmet was born. To many in the unit, it seemed an appropriate symbol. Cats have nine lives. If an AT was lucky, he'd have nine lives too.

The ops room was old and tired. Once-white walls were yellow from years of nicotine building up on them. The brown Chesterfield furniture was worn, the leather cracking like a Renaissance oil painting. A sagging settee had been squeezed into an alcove, with an old TV and video player planted in front of it. A stocky man, with a bushy moustache, had sunk into the cushions and was watching *Dirty Harry* starring Clint Eastwood. Thomson spotted a large hunting knife strapped to his thigh. This man didn't fit the mould of your usual AT. He was too muscular. Rough around the edges. At first glance, more brawn than brains.

Thomson took a few steps inside. The grainy floorboards creaked with every step. He spied a small bar at the far end of the room with four high stools lined up along the wooden top. Military plaques, from regiments who had served with 321 EOD, had been put up on the wall. A single tap, serving Carlsberg lager, stood tall in the middle of the bar like a beacon, beckoning men with dry throats. Sitting on one of the stools, hunched over a writing pad and furiously scribbling away, was a short, slightly pudgy man with three stripes on the arm of his khaki shirt. The man caught Thomson's gaze, climbed down off his perch and walked buoyantly toward him.

'This way,' said Granger. He led Thomson to a long refectory table in the centre of the room where a slender man was sitting drinking tea, smoking a pipe and reading a thick book. 'Morning, men,' said Captain Granger. 'We have a new member of 321 EOD. Staff Sergeant Thomson.'

The pudgy man from the bar reached Thomson first and stuck out his hand, a cheery grin spread across his face. 'Keith Cooper.'

Thomson took it. 'Dave Thomson.'

Cooper continued speaking, words firing from his mouth like a Gatling gun. 'We've been expecting you. Great to have you on board. Good trip over? I hate that blooding crossing. They pack people in like sardines. Weather here is bloody awful, isn't it?'

The slender man who had been absorbed in his book seemed to have been taken by surprise and struggled to get to his feet. 'How do you do? Alan Sutton.' Thomson shook his hand. It was a gentle shake. The man was awkward, gangly and scholarly. Someone who would be more at home in a grand lecture hall than a squalid military outpost.

Thomson caught a glimpse of the book cover he was reading. *Iliad* by Homer. 'That's a bit heavy.'

Sutton smiled. 'A scholar, perhaps?'

'No, I prefer Robert Ludlum.'

'Not to worry. Welcome *ad obscuri lateris*.'

'*Gratias*,' replied Thomson.

'You know the ecclesiastical language?'

'A little bit.'

'A grammar school boy!'

'Yes.'

The stocky, muscular man put his movie on pause and sauntered over from the alcove with a swagger. 'Enough of that froggy stuff, Alan.'

'It's not French, it's Latin,' replied Sutton with a touch of disdain.

'Whatever. Who do we have here then?'

'Staff Sergeant Thomson,' said Granger.

'Dave,' added Thomson.

The stocky man held out a large, calloused hand. Thomson took it but soon regretted the decision as the man gripped his hand tightly, squeezing out the blood until it turned white. 'The name's Rip Kersey.'

'Good to meet you, Rip.' Thomson tried to squeeze back. But it was no use. Rip Kersey was too strong. His hand too big. The grip was painful and Thomson wanted to let out a yelp. He managed to keep it in, determined not to show any sign of weakness. Kersey finally released his grip and gave Thomson a hard slap on the back. A greeting from Kersey was akin to a beating by thugs in an alleyway. Thomson noticed a tattoo on his forearm. A dagger, with the words 'By land and by sea' inked underneath. 'A marine!'

'That's right, Dave,' said Kersey with a grin. 'A real soldier.'

'How did you end up here?'

'Just like you. Terrible luck.'

'We should get you out of those civvies, Staff Sergeant Thomson,' said Granger.

'Yes, Sir,' replied Thomson, who was still wearing his clothes from the day before. He was starting to smell like an unwashed sock.

'You'll be staying in the Sergeants' Mess. Sergeant Cooper can show you the way.'

'Happy to. Shall we head over there now?' said Cooper in a loud, speedy voice.

'I could get out of these clothes. Getting a bit whiffy,' replied Thomson.

'Thought I could smell something,' laughed Cooper. 'Thought maybe a rat had crawled in here and died somewhere. It's only around the corner. We can pop by the mess and get you a sandwich if you like. They do a mean egg mayonnaise sarnie.' Cooper came from a conservative middle-class family. His parents didn't talk much to others or to each other. To their surprise, Keith did. He was a natural chatterbox. Being an only child, and with the solitude that such a child can experience, he'd become brazenly forward. He made friends easily and would talk to anybody, quite often giving the impression that he'd known them for a lifetime. Family. Friends. Strangers. Even pet cats and dogs. The running joke on camp was that he could start a conversation with a broom.

'Let him get a word in edgeways, Keith,' said Kersey. 'If he was a donkey, he'd have no hind legs by now.'

'Hey, just having a conversation.'

'It takes two people to have a conversation.'

'Show him to the mess, Sergeant Cooper,' interrupted Granger with an irritable clip.

'Yes, Sir. This way, Dave. I'll show you a shortcut.'

As the two men headed for the door, a phone started ringing. To the left of the room was a small wooden table. Innocuous but, as it turned out, the most important corner of the room. The only items on the desktop were a notepad, a mug full of yellow pencils and a red and black telephone. It was a direct line from the control room, where signallers received calls from the police, or army commanders on the ground, when a suspect package had been found.

Granger picked up the receiver. 'Yes?' He grabbed a pencil out of the mug and started writing furiously on the pad. 'Thanks.' Granger put the receiver back on its hook and turned to Staff Sergeant Thomson. 'Get into your combats.'

TEN

Dismantling a bomb in Northern Ireland was not a simple, straightforward process. Protocols had been put in place by army brass. And they had to be followed to a tittle.

The vast army machine would lay dormant until activated by a seemingly ordinary event. An old man, perhaps, would make a call to the police. Always from a public phone box so there could be no trace of who he was or where he lived. The last thing he needed was the coppers turning up at his door, signifying his involvement. That would cause the nosey neighbours to natter and perhaps the news would get back to some vindictive IRA thugs, who would no doubt pay him a visit. No, just to be safe, always from a public phone box. And when they asked for his name, he'd hang up.

The old man would have seen something suspicious. A shopping bag most likely, conspicuous by its abandonment. Like an unwanted baby left on a doorstep. From that one tiny call, from a shrinking old man, about that little shopping bag, the cogs of the giant machine would be put into motion.

The police sergeant who received the call would pass the tip-off up the ladder to the Police Liaison Unit. They in turn would report the bag to British Army HQ at Thiepval Barracks in Lisburn. Office-bound soldiers, with university degrees and shiny pips on their shoulders, would scour wall charts and maps saturated with red, blue and white pins. Tiny markers that informed them of which units were out on the road – and which were still in the barracks. After some calculus by the academicians, a regiment would be assigned to the task. And from there, the baton would continue to be passed on in a lengthy relay.

A signaller from army HQ would call a signaller at a command centre, one of many dotted around the province: Drumadd, Shackleton or maybe Abercorn Barracks. From there, the orders would be passed up to the regiment's commanding officer, usually a brigadier cossetted from the action on the ground. From his high tower, he would instruct a lower-ranking officer, a captain perhaps, to deploy a platoon. The captain would call upon his NCO to rustle up twenty-five infantrymen from their barracks and herd them onto a Bedford troop carrier. The grumbling truck would ferry the compliant squaddies to the precise location of the shopping bag. Once there, they would cordon off the area around the suspicious item with red-and-white tape. As soon as the shopping bag was isolated, the platoon's radio operator would call the Ebrington barracks command centre, where a signaller would receive the details of the operation and then make several calls of his own. To the escort, to the driver, and lastly, to the 321 EOD ops room.

And after all the to-ing and fro-ing, and the immense human resources assigned to the operation, an AT would pick up the phone and receive his instructions, oblivious to the vast criss-cross of communications that had formed a web with him at the centre of it. The AT, with his unique knowledge of explosives, would be called out to take care of the suspicious item that may or may not be a bomb.

Thomson was now a part of the vast, bureaucratic machine. A small, but vital cog. At the brunt end of a long, circling chain of command. On his first day in Northern Ireland, he was making his way to check out a suspect device, which would most likely be a shopping bag called in by a shrinking old man.

* * *

The aggravatingly noisy Saracen, with the four-man escort inside, wound its way through the streets of Londonderry. Tucked in safely behind was Granger's Land Rover. They were heading for Ewing Street, a Protestant pocket on the North side of the city. It was early afternoon, but the light was fading.

'Thought it was supposed to be summer, Sir,' joked Thomson from the back of the Land Rover.

'You get the occasional day of sunshine, Staff,' replied Granger. 'But it's generally bloody miserable.' The front wheel of the Land Rover hit a cavernous hole in the road sending the occupants of the vehicle upward, their heads banging against the roof. 'Bloody hell, Corporal. Are you trying to kill us?'

'Sorry, Sir,' replied Jock Henderson, Granger's driver and number two. 'Didn't see the hole. Probably put there by the IRA.' Thomson laughed at the cheeky remark, but Granger didn't see the humour in it.

'Just keep your eyes on the road, Corporal.'

Henderson straightened his lips. 'Yes, Sir.'

He's a cocky little bugger, thought Thomson to himself as he steered his eyes away from the black tarmac and toward pedestrian life on the streets. It seemed no different to a scene you'd see in an English town. More reminiscent of the North than the South. It could be Warrington, where Jean was from. Old women with scarves on their heads walking home with shopping bags filled with fresh vegetables from the grocer and fresh meat from the local butcher. Men with flat caps walking their dogs. Kids in school uniform walking home with satchels slung over their shoulders and footballs tucked under their arms.

'Things look pretty normal around here,' said Thomson.

'This is a Protestant area,' replied Henderson. 'Wait until you see the Bogside. Looks like a warzone.'

The Saracen turned into a cobbled lane lined on either side by small backyards hemmed in by high red-brick walls. Narrow and insulated, the alleyway was normally used by the rubbish collection trucks. But today it was an artery that was clogged up by a small convoy of military vehicles.

Dogs started to bark as the Saracen grumbled down the lane, purring like a dying cat. A corporal from the Green Howards put up his hand, bringing the iron-plated vehicle to a halt. Before the wheels of the Saracen had stopped moving, the four Welsh Fusiliers inside scrambled out of the back, rifles at the ready and eyes darting around looking for something dangerous to lock onto.

The Land Rover pulled up behind. Thomson, Granger and Henderson stepped out onto the permanently puddled lane. Ninety-Nine, the self-pronounced leader of the four-man escort, stood to attention in front of Captain Granger and saluted. 'Usual routine, Sir?'

'Yes, Ninety-Nine,' replied Granger.

Ninety-Nine organised the escort. Two behind the party and two in front. It was the job of the escort to protect the ATs from attack. From snipers, who would hide behind bedroom curtains with their rifles, waiting for an opportunity to take a shot – or potential assassins, pistols hidden in their trousers, who would mingle in the crowds of onlookers who would habitually gather to watch the ATs do their work.

'Okay, lads,' shouted Ninety-Nine. 'Keep your eyes peeled.' People from the terraced houses had started to flow out onto the street. The neighbours were chattering away with each other, excited by the presence of the army.

'Get them back inside, Private,' shouted Granger to Ninety-Nine.

The private turned to the crowd. 'For your own safety, please go back inside your houses.' Curiosity got the better of the residents and they were reluctant to move. 'Come on, shift it!' shouted Ninety-Nine aggressively. The people took notice of the bark and slowly shuffled back into their backyards, peeping above the brick walls to get a view of the drama unfolding.

A major from the Green Howards approached Granger. 'Afternoon, Felix.'

'Afternoon, Sir,' replied Granger.

'There's a suspicious package in the outhouse of number 37,' said the major as he pointed out the location with his finger a hundred yards along the road.

'Any witnesses, Sir?'

'Mr MacAteer, owner of the property.'

'Can I speak with him?'

The major walked Granger and Thomson to a makeshift shelter that had been set up a safe distance from the house. Underneath the tarpaulin was a wiry old man smoking a cigarette and drinking tea from an army-issue metal cup.

'Mr MacAteer,' said the major.

'Yes?' replied the Irishman.

'This is Captain Granger. He's from our bomb disposal unit and wants to ask you a few questions.'

'Right you are,' replied Mr MacAteer.

'Maybe you can start with how you found the package,' said Granger.

'Shopping bag,' said Mr MacAteer.

'What?'

'It's a shopping bag. Those IRA bastards put it in there. I was in the kitchen and I heard a noise in the backyard. I looked out the window and two men were messing about in the dunny. Well, I opened the door and shouted at them.'

'Do you know the men?'

'Never seen them before in my life. Anyhows, as soon as they see me, they scarper out the gate and down the road. I walked over to the dunny and I sees this plastic shopping bag. And I think to myself, those bastards have put a bomb in my backyard.'

'Did you look inside the bag?'

'No bloody way. I went straight to the phone box down the road and called you fellas.'

'What time was that?'

'Around 12.30.'

'Thank you, Mr MacAteer,' said Granger politely as he looked at his watch. The time was now 3.30 p.m. The danger period had passed. The IRA used parking meter clocks as timers in most of their bombs. The pocket-sized alarm clocks were designed specifically for motorists. Parking meters on the streets of Londonderry only lasted two and half hours, so if you were parked up and didn't want to get a ticket from a traffic warden, you needed to get back and feed the meter on time. The parking meter clocks were essentially a two-and-a-half-hour timer. Every motorist had one. And so did every IRA bomb-maker.

If an AT was unsure about a bomb, he'd let it 'soak'. If the device hadn't gone off within two and half hours, it was probably safe to handle.

'No problems,' replied the Irishman. 'Just make sure me house doesn't get blown up.'

'We'll try.'

'Anything else, Felix?' asked the Green Howards major.

'No, Sir,' replied Granger. The captain made lengthy strides back to the Land Rover, with Thomson matching him step for step. 'It's a hoax.'

'And what if it isn't a hoax, Sir?' asked Thomson.

'It is. My gut tells me so, Staff. They do this kind of thing just to waste our time.' Thomson wasn't about to argue with an intransigent superior and decided to keep his mouth shut. 'Hook and line, Corporal Henderson,' shouted Granger.

'Yes, Sir,' replied the wiry corporal, who rushed to the back of his vehicle and lifted a giant metal spool, mounted on a metal stand, and placed it on the ground. A two-hundred-yard-long rope was wrapped around the spool's core with a small grappling hook attached to its end. Henderson grabbed the hook and presented it to Granger.

'Staff, take that will you?' said Granger. Thomson took the hook and yanked on the rope to give himself some slack.

Granger, with a touch of excitement in his voice said, 'Right, let's go.' The captain steamed ahead toward number 37, propelled by unfettered enthusiasm. Thomson followed, a tight grip on the hook. Henderson let the rope run through his fingers as it unfurled from the spool, controlling the run of the line to prevent any snagging.

All eyes were on both men as they walked toward the danger zone. The incessant murmuring from the people hiding behind their walls stopped as soon as the show had begun. Thomson could hear his own breath. It was becoming heavier as they approached the old wooden gate. His heart was beating a little bit faster than usual. His mind starting to work overtime. What if the bomb was radio-controlled? What if an IRA man was hiding somewhere nearby? In a car. In a bedroom. On a roof. Waiting for them to get close. Waiting for the right time to activate the detonator and blow them to smithereens? Stop thinking. Focus on the job. If it happens, it was meant to be. No point worrying about it. Just do your job.

Granger reached the gate first and seemed irritated that Thomson was straggling fifteen feet behind him. 'Hurry up, Staff. We haven't got all day.'

Thomson caught up with Granger and knelt down behind him, his breathing heavy from anxiety. Granger took no notice of Thomson's panting and pushed the gate open. He crept inside the sparse back-yard. The ground had been concreted over. Three orange clay pots, with roses growing in them, were lined against the wall of the house. An old, rusting bicycle rested against the wooden fence that separated Mr MacAteer's yard from his neighbour's. The outside toilet was a small wooden shack nestled in the corner at the back of the yard. The wooden door was rotting and, as soon as Granger opened it, the smell of stale urine hit his nose. 'Phew.' His nose wrinkled up with disgust.

'I can smell it from here,' added Thomson, who was standing outside in the street.

Granger looked past the dunny door and spied a plastic Co-op shopping bag standing upright on the toilet seat. He gently opened the top with his index finger and looked inside. A brown paper package lay at the bottom. 'Pass the hook, Staff.'

Thomson handed the iron hook through the back gate. Granger took it and slipped the iron barbs through the shopping bag handles. 'All secure. I'm coming out.' As soon as Granger reappeared, Thomson made a beeline toward the Land Rover, running the line through his fingers. 'Where are you going, Staff?' shouted Granger.

'Walking back to the Land Rover,' replied Thomson, a little confused at the question.

'Give me the rope,' demanded Granger. Thomson complied with the order and handed over the rope. Granger knelt down next to the backyard wall, the outhouse a mere three inches on the other side.

'What are you doing, Sir?' asked Thomson.

'Seeing if it's a bomb, Staff,' replied Granger as he wrapped the rope tightly around his hand and gave it a good old tug.

ELEVEN

Eoin Twomey was banging her hard from behind. Every thrust seemed to pump out a raspy grunt from Sheila Docherty's mouth. Her buttocks were translucent white and large. And every time Twomey banged his pelvis against her buttocks, the flesh would ripple like wobbly jelly.

'Harder, you fucker,' mumbled Sheila. 'Come on, show me what you're made of, man.'

That kind of language got Twomey excited. He pushed into her faster and harder now. He could feel the orgasm rising like an awakened volcano. His rapture had reached a tipping point. He couldn't stop now even if Sheila's husband walked through the door and caught them red-handed. He exploded just as Sheila reached a climax of her own. 'Fuck me,' said the forty-year-old mother as she collapsed on the bed, Twomey falling on top of her.

'What, again?' said Twomey with a chuckle.

'Bet you could too.'

'Keep talking like that and Little Eoin will be hard again in no time.'

'I wouldn't call Little Eoin little.'

Sheila rolled over onto her back, uncoupling herself from her lover. Twomey fell on his back next to her and reached for a packet of cigarettes. They smoked in silence, savouring the post-orgasmic serenity.

Sheila took a long drag and eyed Twomey up. He wasn't the best-looking man. His nose was a bit crooked and his eyes a bit too close together. He wasn't the smartest, either. She'd had more meaningful conversations with her Border Collie. But one thing was for sure. God had blessed Eoin Twomey with a heavenly body.

One of her friends had said he was Adonis. Sheila didn't have a clue what she was on about. But if they were looking for someone to play the new Tarzan, Twomey would have the perfect physique for it. Shame about the face. And the accent.

'What?' asked Twomey as he caught Sheila studying him.

'Nothing,' replied Sheila as she sat up in bed and pulled her bra on.

'What do you mean nothing? I saw you looking.'

'You'd better get going. My kids will be home in an hour and I've got to clean up.' Sheila liked being fucked by Twomey. It was fantastic sex. More than she got from the old man. All he could ever muster, when he could be bothered, which was about once every two months, was a couple of thrusts and a couple of groans. It was like making love to limp lettuce. Whenever her husband wanted sex, she would make sure they did it during the ad break in *Coronation Street*. That way she wouldn't miss the second half.

'When's the old man back?'

'Tomorrow.'

'Dundalk again?'

'I guess so. He doesn't really tell me much.'

'He's a miserable bastard.'

'Bet you wouldn't say that to his face.'

'You're right there. He'd crack my skull in half.'

'He's a twat.'

Sheila playfully slapped Twomey's organ. 'Come on. Get dressed and fuck off. And make sure nobody sees you.' *If Steve Docherty ever found out about the affair*, thought Sheila, *Twomey would be a dead man.* She'd be okay. The wives always were. Her punishment would be a black eye and a bust-up lip.

Twomey pulled on his clothes and gave Sheila a peck on the lips. 'Next week then?'

'I'll call you when he's out of town.'

'Right you are, my lovely. I'll be waiting for that call.' The man with the Adonis body ran down the stairs, popped his head out of the back door and, once he was sure no one was watching, slipped out of the house into the alleyway. He was happy with himself. That was a good session. Always was with Sheila. She knew how to hit all the right buttons. He strutted happily down the street, unaware of eyes watching his every move.

* * *

The house, which had been home to a low-level IRA operative, had been firebombed six months earlier by the Proddies. The structure was still standing but the place was inhabitable. The living room was sooty black and part of the outside wall, weakened by the kiln-like heat of the fire, had collapsed.

It would be bulldozed at some point, but not anytime soon. The council were in no hurry to set aside time or resources. It was a Catholic slum and the council's priorities lay with their Protestant constituents.

The undercover Special Branch man settled in on the charred beams in the loft. A couple of tiles had slid off the roof leaving a spyhole. It was an ideal lookout over the Bogside.

He had snuck in the night before, lugging his Nikon F with its heavy tele-zoom lens attached to the front. Of particular interest, and in direct line of sight, was Steve Docherty's home. He was suspected of being a high-ranking IRA henchman. And Special Branch wanted to know who was coming in and out of his house.

The spy was chronically bored. His mind anaesthetised by the tedium of his mission. All he'd seen in the morning was Mrs Docherty ferrying her kids out of the house in school gear and frog-marching them down the street, giving them an earful about something or other. Late morning, she put out the laundry in the tiny, terraced backyard. Early afternoon, he saw her again when she ventured out with a couple of empty shopping bags. She returned an hour later with them full of groceries. Then nothing for two hours. At 3 p.m., a twitchy man in a denim jacket walked to the back gate of the house, looked around nervously and then scurried into the yard. Mrs Docherty opened the back door. He couldn't help himself and planted his mouth on her lips. She was visibly annoyed by the ill-conceived act. She shuffled him inside, looking around to see if any nosey neighbours had caught the indiscretion. Click, click, click. The undercover man had got it all on film.

TWELVE

Detective Inspector Jonny McGuigan was in a bad mood. The powerful men upstairs had screwed him over again. The IRA bomb factory he'd uncovered was going to be raided that evening against his advice. That would put his source at risk of detection. He couldn't let that happen. The source was close to the inner circle of the IRA command. A highly prized asset that he'd groomed painstakingly over two years. But that didn't matter to the short-sighted, grey-haired egoists that ran Special Branch. They were sycophants to Whitehall and the pompous politicians that ran the country. They would prefer short-term results to appease their masters, it seemed, over long-term intelligence success. And if they were lucky, they'd be rewarded with shiny tin medals to hang on the chests of their uniforms.

The car was parked across the road from the run-down bookies. McGuigan wound down the window to let the stale air out and let some fresh air in. They had staked the place out for three hours, watching sad old men go in with hope in their eyes and come out a couple of hours later with embittered faces, ready to look for solace in their losing ways by squandering the little money they had left on a couple of pints. 'Where the fuck is he?'

'He'll be along,' replied Detective Sergeant Drew McBride as he plucked a paper bag full of bon-bons from his coat pocket. 'Want one?'

'What flavour are they?'

'Lemon.'

'I fucking hate lemon.'

McBride picked a powdery ball from the brown paper bag and popped it in his mouth. He grimaced as the sourness swarmed his taste buds. 'That's horrible.' He opened the car window and spat the mangled sweet onto the pavement.

'Watch what you're doing, fella,' said an agitated pedestrian who, if he'd been walking a little bit faster, would have been hit by the sugary projectile. 'What are you doing spitting sweets about?'

McBride craned his neck to get a view of the walker and apologise. 'Twomey?'

'Who's asking?'

The two Special Branch men climbed out of the car and flanked Twomey from the front and the back. McBride pulled his badge and flashed it in the IRA man's face. 'We need a bit of your time.'

Twomey wanted to run. But thought better of it. If one of the coppers pulled a gun he could end up with a bullet in his back. No, he'd get in the car. Listen to what they had to say. But keep quiet all the same. Like he was trained. And if they gave him a good beating, so be it. It wouldn't be the first or the last.

Twomey slipped into the back seat where he was joined by McGuigan. McBride turned the key in the ignition and the engine roared to life.

'Where you taking me?' asked Twomey.

'Do you really need to ask?' replied McGuigan. Of course he didn't. He knew exactly where he was being taken. Strand Road police station.

McGuigan eyed Twomey up and down, like an undertaker measuring a corpse for a coffin. This man didn't realise it, but he was key to McGuigan's plans.

* * *

The interview room was oppressively small and excessively bright. Twomey was sitting at a flimsy wooden table impatiently drumming his fingers on the surface. He'd been left in the claustrophobic space for more than two hours. No water. No food. No cigarettes.

The door flung open. McGuigan and McBride bristled into the room. McGuigan planted himself in the seat opposite Twomey while McBride remained standing, looming over him, a little too close for the IRA man's comfort.

'How long have you been a member?' asked McGuigan.

'I wouldn't know what you're talking about,' replied Twomey.

'Steve Docherty.'

'Who?'

'He's your boss, isn't he?'

'I don't have a boss. I'm unemployed. Get a cheque every week.'

'What about Mrs Docherty?' For the first time, Twomey flinched. Ever so slightly. Almost imperceptibly. McGuigan picked it up. 'You know Mrs Docherty, don't you?'

'Never heard of her.'

McGuigan placed a dossier on the table and opened it up. Inside were photographs. Twomey's jaw stiffened, his eyes bulging involuntary out of his head.

'So who's this woman you're mushing with?'

Twomey remained tight-lipped.

'Got a furball in your throat?'

'I've got nothing to say.'

'What do you think Steve Docherty will do when he finds out you're shagging his wife?' Twomey fidgeted in his seat. 'I think he'll smash your fucking head in with a hammer.'

'I'm not working for you,' said Twomey, his voice trembling.

'Well, you don't need to make a decision right now,' said McGuigan, leaning back in his chair, combing his bright orange hair with his white pasty fingers. 'We'll give you some time to think about it.'

'I'm not doing it,' said Twomey, his voice cracking with anxiety.

'We'll see,' said McGuigan, standing up. 'You can go.'

'Serious?'

'Yes. I'm serious. You're free to go. Detective Sergeant McBride will show you the way out.' Twomey stood up and followed McBride out of the room. 'We'll be in touch.'

* * *

Four teenage boys were loitering across the road from Strand Road police station. They weren't ordinary teenage boys. They weren't the type that go to school, do homework, go to church on a Sunday. No, these were Dickers. Kids from the slum who worked for the IRA. Sometimes for free. Sometimes for a pack of cigarettes. Sometimes, if they were lucky, for a couple of quid. Their job was simple. To stake out certain areas. Like police stations. Or army barracks. And pubs. 'Dick that junction,' their handler would say. Or 'Keep your eyes peeled on that house.' And so that's what they did. Just idle the days away hanging around the streets looking for something out of the ordinary. Something to report.

Jason McEvoy was the eldest of the group. He'd been a Dicker for three years and had become adept at picking up on things that weren't quite right. He was a master of spotting people who looked out of place. Especially Special Branch or Military Intelligence. A car that didn't fit. Or someone he knew who was in the wrong place.

Jason kept his eyes trained on the entrance of the police station. A man walked out. A man he knew. Eoin Twomey. They were literally neighbours. What the fuck was he doing in the police station? And why is he looking so agitated? He may have been picked up. A lot of IRA players were. All the time. In which case, there would be nothing to worry about. Twomey would call it in. Tell his IRA masters everything about what happened.

But just in case, Jason would inform his handler.

* * *

Twomey's stomach was riddled with nerves. He needed a drink to calm them down. Unconsciously, he headed for the nearest pub to the station. The Brandywell Inn. A watering hole for Catholics only.

His head was down and his eyes fixed on the pavement as his mind began to whir. *What the fuck have you done? What a mess! You should've known better, Eoin. Should he come clean to Steve Docherty and get the beating he deserved?* One thing was for sure, he would never work for the Proddie police. Never turn. That was inconceivable. Excuses started forming in Twomey's head. He'd popped around to help with some handyman stuff. Yes, that's what he was doing. Mrs Docherty had a problem with the plumbing. They'd buy that. Because everyone knew he used to be a plumber.

Twomey reached the wretched old pub and walked inside. The place was empty except for a couple of old codgers in the corner. The smell of mildew permeated the air. Twomey couldn't work out whether the reek came from the walls or the disintegrating old men with pints in their hands. 'A pint of the Black Stuff,' said Twomey to the barman, who casually grabbed a glass and placed it under the tap. 'And while that's pouring, I'll have a wee Bush.'

Twomey pulled up a stool at the bar. He needed to think. Something he wasn't very good at.

THIRTEEN

Thomson tested the water in the bathtub with his big toe. It was too hot. But that's how he liked it. He put one foot in, followed by the other. And slowly lowered himself into the water. His skin turned pink. This is what he needed after two days of travelling. The hot bath was heaven.

He splashed water on his face, rested his head against the side of the tub and closed his eyes. He emptied his mind. Breathed in deeply. And let himself relax.

Steam rose from the bathtub, misted up the mirror and left a thin film of water on the bathroom tiles. He felt calm.

But his state of bliss didn't last long. The sequence of events from a few hours earlier unfolded in his mind like a movie. The image of Granger pulling the rope, a stupid grin on his face. The shopping bag falling off the toilet seat onto the ground with a thud, followed by the sound of small grey stones bursting out and bouncing on the pavement. Granger shouting with triumph. 'I knew it. A hoax.'

Thomson was furious. And, in a rare moment, lost his composure. 'Are you out of your fucking mind?'

Granger twisted sharply, his face turning ketchup red. 'Who the fuck do you think you're talking to, Staff Sergeant Thomson?'

'If that was a bomb, we'd both be dead.'

'Sir,' insisted Granger through gritted teeth.

'If that was a bomb, we'd both be dead. Sir!'

'You think you know this place? You know nothing. I suggest you keep your mouth shut and keep your thoughts to yourself. If I need your opinion, I'll ask for it.'

Thomson opened his eyes, his teeth grinding against each other. He climbed out of the bath and wrapped a towel around his waist. The brief calm he had been enjoying was now a seething anger. That was a stupid move by the captain. If there were explosives in the bag and they'd gone off, the blast would have smashed through the wall and ripped both their bodies to shreds. The man was dangerous. Not just to himself but to others too. How had he survived the two months he'd been here? Surely the other ATs had noticed his erratic behaviour? Were they turning a blind eye?

His mind turned to Jean. He couldn't help but think that she could have been made a widow today. He could see her sobbing. His children crying. That made him angry.

But he knew there wasn't a damned thing he could do about the captain. He was the officer. The man in charge. He could always try and take it upstairs to CATO. Make a complaint. But that would just make him look like a whining snitch. And besides, nothing would happen. He'd seen others try to protest an injustice in the past only to have a black mark put against their name and see their career stifled.

No, all Thomson could do was make sure he was never put in a position like that again. *God*, he thought. *I hope I'm not riding with that bastard tomorrow. I might do something I might regret.*

* * *

The ops room was unnaturally quiet. Rip Kersey was sitting at the bar alone, enjoying the solitude. Immersing himself in the blissful silence after a day of din and commotion. It turned out to be a day without respite. The type of day that sucks the stamina out of your core.

Kersey swallowed the last inch of lager in his glass, relished the moment and leant over the bar to pour himself another pint.

The door of the ops room swung open. Kersey looked over his shoulder to see who was about to burst his bubble of tranquillity. It was Thomson. That was okay. He had time for the newcomer.

'Can I get you a beer?' asked Kersey.

'No, thanks,' replied Thomson as he pulled up a high stool and sat down.

'You okay?' asked Kersey noticing the worry etched into Thomson's face.

'Not really.'

'Ah, Granger,' said Kersey knowingly. 'What happened?'

'He did something stupid. Pulled the line right there, not three feet from the package.'

'He's a bloody idiot. Best stay clear of him.'

'He's done this before?'

'Yep.'

'He's going to kill himself,' said Thomson.

'Yes, he will.'

'What do we do?'

'What do you want to do, Dave? Report him?' Thomson ignored the question. 'Listen, the man's a nutcase. But he's a captain in the British Army. Which means there's not a bloody thing we can do about it. We can't report him. We can't stop him going on a job. And we certainly can't talk any sense into him. Which means we just have to get on with life. Do the job we've been sent out here to do.'

'We're just going to wait until he blows himself up?'

'He might not. He's survived so far.'

'Don't know how.'

'You know what they say in the Marines, Dave?' continued Kersey. 'Each man makes his own fate.' He took a swig of beer. 'Best leave Granger to his.'

Thomson pondered Kersey's philosophy, trying to dissect it. Find holes in it. But that one little phrase was indestructible. It made perfect sense.

'I'll have that beer,' said Thomson.

'Right you are.' Kersey leant over the bar, poured a pint of lager and placed the overflowing pint in front of Thomson. 'Welcome to Ireland, Dave. May you leave here with all your fingers.' Thomson picked up his drink and the two men clinked glasses before taking a gulp.

'I hope I'm not riding with that idiot tomorrow,' said Thomson.

'Ahhh,' grinned Kersey. 'That's where I have some good news for you my friend. I'm your mentor. So you'll be riding with me for a week or so.' Thomson laughed involuntarily. It was more relief than something he found funny. The tight knot he'd felt in his stomach had suddenly become a bit looser. First-timers to Ireland were assigned a mentor for their first week to help them settle in. Get a feel of the terrain before they went solo.

Kersey knocked down the last of his lager and slammed the glass on the bar. 'I'm off to bed,' he said as he wiped the foam off his moustache with the back of his hand. 'It's going to be another long day tomorrow.' Kersey slapped Thomson on the shoulder and headed out of the ops room.

Thomson had a sudden urge to call Jean. He walked over to the black-and-red phone sitting on the unused desk, picked up the receiver and called the operator. 'I want to make a call to England, please... Er, the number is 48…936…428…11.' The phone rang a few times before he heard Jean's voice.

'Hello.'

'Hi, it's me.'

She sounded happy to hear his voice. 'You arrived safely then?'

'Yeah, bit of a rough crossing.'

'So what's it like over there?'

'Not much different from England. Weather's bad. People are miserable. You know. A bit like Warrington.'

'Cheeky bugger.' Jean laughed. 'Have you…you know. Yet?'

'No, it's been quiet.' He didn't want her to worry. He certainly wouldn't tell her the truth. She'd be stressed enough as it was. 'How are the kids?'

'They're fine. They're missing their dad.'

The two of them chatted for half an hour. Chatting about ordinary things. Unimportant stuff. Thomson liked the small talk. He liked hearing her voice. Her northern accent. Her gossip. Her laugh.

His task in Ireland had just begun. And if the first day was anything to go by, it was going to be a slog. But at that moment, with Jean's words massaging his ears and soothing his soul, Thomson realised there was a more important mission. He needed to get back to her. At any cost. She was his life. The only thing that mattered.

FOURTEEN

The small flat was thick with cigarette smoke. Jimmy Brett, the IRA commander of the Derry brigade, was sitting in an old armchair by the curtain-covered window. Standing behind him silently was his bodyguard Barry Behan, a tall, sinewy Scotsman with two threads for lips. His ghoulish features were made worse by a Y-shaped scar on the right cheek. A memento from a drunken night in one of Glasgow's squalid pubs.

Jimmy Brett stubbed out his cigarette and immediately pulled another one out of its packet. Behan leant over and put a flame to its tip.

Brett nodded gratefully. Even though he was fifty years old, his line-wrinkled face, short grey hair and thick, black-framed glasses, made him look more like seventy. He wore a beige-and-brown plaid shirt underneath an old green cardigan, which covered the large paunch that was built on Guinness, chip butties and meat pies. He looked harmless enough. The kind of man that had retired and wiled away his days breeding pigeons or making toy boats in his workshop for a small grandson.

But Jimmy was nothing like a bored old man with meaningless hobbies. He was a ruthless killer. He was the man in charge of waging war against the British in Londonderry. There wasn't a bombing, kidnapping or killing that went ahead without his knowledge or consent.

He didn't do much dirty work himself. He couldn't. He was under constant surveillance by the security services. They knew who he was and the only reason he hadn't been brought to justice was because they couldn't mount enough evidence against him.

But once in a while, Jimmy managed to get his hands bloody. If someone was suspected of being an informant, they'd be brought to the commander. To a farmhouse out in the country. Or a house deep inside the Bogside, an IRA stronghold that had become a no-go zone for British soldiers and policemen. Jimmy would interrogate the suspect. Give them a chance to come clean. Most often they would deny their misdeed. Plead innocence. But it didn't matter. By the time you had been pulled up in front of Jimmy Brett, you'd been found guilty already.

Two volunteers would hold the suspect steady while Jimmy placed a polythene bag over the man's head. The commander would take joy in watching the traitorous bastard gasping for breath. Sucking for air that wasn't there. Fighting. Hoping he could somehow break free of the two men holding him in a vice-like grip. Hoping he could survive this ordeal. But he wouldn't. He would suffocate and his body would slump to the floor. Lifeless. The dead man would be wrapped in plastic, bundled into the boot of a car and driven across the border to be buried somewhere in a forest or in a ditch. Never to be seen again. One of the missing.

Jimmy took a long drag on his cigarette, sucked the fumes deep into his lungs and exhaled the thick smoke, fogging the room further.

Maureen Hogan, a seventy-nine-year-old widow, peeped her head out from the kitchen. 'Would you fellas like a cup of tea?'

'That would be lovely,' said Brett.

'Right you are,' replied Mrs Hogan as she disappeared back into the kitchen. It was her flat. But once in a while, the IRA would request its use for a meet-up. She was happy to oblige. The men in the living room were on the army's watch list. So they couldn't have a meet-up in the same place twice. They had to keep on moving from safe house to safe house to avoid the intrusive ears of Military Intelligence. Make sure the men in the shadows couldn't plant electronic bugs that liked to feed on plots and conspiracies.

Mrs Hogan never listened to the conversations. It was none of her business. And on top of that, if the army raided her place and interrogated her, she'd have nothing to give them. Ignorant of any words spoken. Of any plans. Of any intentions.

'Michael,' said Brett to a scrawny lad who was loitering in the far corner. 'Go help Mrs Hogan.' The lad disappeared into the kitchen and shut the door behind him.

Brett turned to the three men sitting opposite him. 'What happened?'

'They raided it this morning,' replied Steve Docherty.

'I fucking know that!' replied Brett, aggrieved at the inane response. Docherty was Brett's lieutenant. A hard, vicious man made of forged iron. But the brawn didn't make up for the lack of brain.

Jimmy Brett's eyes settled on Liam O'Mahoney. 'That's why we're fucking here. Talking about it. What I want to know, is how the fuck did they know it was there?'

'I don't know, Jimmy,' said O'Mahoney.

'You don't know. Well, I'll tell you what I know. We've got a fucking tout on the inside. A fucking tout. How many fucking people knew about it? How many?'

'Just a handful,' said Curly Coyle, the chief bomb-maker of the Derry brigade.

'A handful?'

'Aye.'

Jimmy Brett switched back to Docherty. 'Well, it should be easy to find the fucker then.'

An uncomfortable silence permeated the room.

'I'm fucking talking to you, Steve. You're supposed to be running the fucking shop.'

'Aye,' replied Docherty.

'Aye, fucking what?' Brett was losing his temper.

'I'll get the nutting squad on it,' said Docherty.

'Do that,' said Brett, the redness in his face dissipating as his blood pressure lowered. 'But I don't want those maniacs killing the fucker. I want him alive. Understand me?'

Steve Docherty nodded. There was nothing more to say. When Brett was in a foul mood, the less words the better. Docherty got up from his seat and walked out of the flat, a purpose in his stride. A traitor to find.

Brett lashed out at O'Mahoney. 'What the fuck are you hanging around for?'

'I'll be off then.' O'Mahoney got up awkwardly and nodded sheepishly at Behan, who returned the gesture of respect with a contorted grimace meant to be a smile. O'Mahoney put his head down and walked out of the flat.

'How much did we lose?' asked Brett.

Curly Coyle, who was fidgeting his fingers, shuffled to the edge of his seat. 'About two hundred pounds of explosives.'

The British Army had raided an IRA bomb factory the previous evening. The location of the factory was a secret. Only five IRA men, including Curly, knew its whereabouts. One of those five was a traitor. Who the fuck could it be?

'What are you so nervous about?' asked Brett. He liked Curly. Smart. Not like the other muttonheads he had to deal with.

'I'm not, Jimmy.' He *was* nervous. Jimmy had that effect on people. He was a volatile man. One minute he would be calm and the next he wanted to put a bullet in your eye.

'What about the other factories?' asked Jimmy Brett.

'I think we should move them,' replied Curly.

'I think that would be a fucking prudent thing to do.'

The scrawny lad walked out of the kitchen with five mugs of tea on a tin tray. 'Have the others gone?'

'What the fuck do you think?' said Jimmy.

'It's just that Mrs Hogan made five cups.'

'Well, we only need three now.'

'Right you are, Jimmy.' The scrawny lad handed one mug to the commander who grabbed the rim with the tips of his fingers.

Jimmy quickly placed the beaker on the table beside him, spilling some of the liquid onto the surface. 'Arrggh, that's fucking hot.'

'Sorry, Jimmy,' replied the lad, a hint of nervousness in his voice as he offered a mug to Behan.

'No thanks,' said the bodyguard dryly.

'As you please,' said Michael. 'Curly?'

'Ta, Michael,' said Curly Coyle, who grabbed the handle of the mug and took a sip of the hot milky brew.

'I'm running out of cigs,' grunted Brett, staring at the lad.

'I'll go get you some, Jimmy.'

'Player's No. 6.'

'Right you are,' said Michael as he rushed to the flat door and slipped out, closing it quietly behind him.

'Your brother's a bit dim,' said Brett.

'He's a good kid,' replied Curly.

'He's soft.'

Curly kept quiet. His brother Michael *was* a good kid. Nice. But nice wasn't a resounding credential for a wannabe soldier in the IRA. Nice is what grandmothers and mothers are. Or priests and kindergarten teachers. Party clowns and nurses. There was no room for nice in the IRA. Curly had tried to keep him out of the movement. But Michael was in. Brett, of all people, was the one who had opened the door.

'Maybe he needs to see some action,' said Brett.

'He's probably best working behind the scenes, Jimmy. He's better with his head than his fists.'

'Are you some kind of babysitter? Jesus, we're not running a kindergarten here. Your brother needs to get his hands dirty.'

'I can use him in the factory.'

Brett ignored the suggestion. Silence cloaked the room as the commander took a long drag on his cigarette. He turned his head away from Curly and toward the window, looking at the grey sky. Michael needed blooding. He needed to kill. Let the stench of murder infect his soul. And Brett was going to make sure it was done.

* * *

Michael gagged as he opened the front door of the little run-down corner shop. Stale tobacco, fused with the musty stench of mildew, hit his nose like an unexpected punch. The old man behind the counter had a grey leathery face and a large nicotine-tinged moustache. A rolled-up cigarette was hanging from the corner of his wrinkled mouth. 'What can I do for you?' said the man through a raspy voice.

'A packet of Player's No. 6.' *This man should be dead*, thought Michael as the shopkeeper erupted into a forty-a-day cough. 'You alright there?'

'Aye,' replied the man without making eye contact. 'Just a bit chesty.'

'You should cut down.' The old man lifted his head, his eyes locking onto Michael's. These were not happy eyes. They were filled with sadness, remorse and regret.

'None of your concern what I do and what I smoke.' The old man slammed the Player's onto the counter. Michael picked them up, shoved them in his pocket and left the shop.

The young IRA man inhaled deeply, clearing his nostrils of the stench from inside. The afternoon air was heavy and damp. As he exhaled, his breath turned into vapour. Just like it did on that fateful day. Over a year ago now but engraved in his memory for ever.

Fifteen thousand people had gathered at Bishop's Field in the Creggan Housing Estate. It was going to be the peace march that would change everything. A show of collective force from the Catholic minority. A demand for the end of internment. A demand for civil rights.

Michael had been persuaded to take part in the march by his best friend Jonathan Kelly. 'We're going to show those bastards. They can't push us around anymore. There's too many of us.'

'There's too many of them,' Michael had replied. 'They've got batons and water cannons. And a nasty fucking outlook on life.' Michael wasn't that bothered about the politics of Northern Ireland. It wouldn't change anything. Old women from the Bogside put it best. *Little new under either the sun or the Irish rain.*

Michael was happy collecting his dole and spending it on cheap beer and cigarettes. But Jonathan had a different view of the world. Unemployment among young Catholic men was high, but as far as he was concerned there was politics to fill the void.

'There's going to be journalists there. They wouldn't dare do anything stupid.'

'I'll come along for a laugh.'

Jonathan punched his friend on the arm. 'This is serious stuff, Michael. It's going to be a historic day.'

But by the time the crowd had reached Rossville Street it all went sour. The police were trying to herd the marchers away from their end point, the steps of Guildhall. A few teenagers, agitated by the blatant tactics, started throwing rocks.

It wasn't long before an armoured vehicle screeched to a halt in front of the crowd. A platoon of paratroopers jumped out of the back, jumped over the barriers, and rushed into the marchers snarling, spitting and screaming vulgarities.

Michael reeled in horror as a sergeant smashed his rifle butt into the head of a young woman. She fell to the ground unconscious, blood spurting from her scalp. Another para pointed a weapon at a middle-aged man who stood three feet away, arms linked with other protestors. The para let off a rubber bullet into the man's chest, knocking him to the ground and leaving him writhing in pain.

All around, paras were punching, kicking and smashing heads with batons. The ferocity of the attack was so vicious the officers commanding them rushed in to pull the soldiers back. They'd let trained killers off the leash and now they couldn't control them.

Jonathan was enraged. 'Come on, Michael. Let's sort these fuckers out.' Michael stood fixed in his tracks, paralysed by the havoc unfolding before his eyes. He watched on as Jonathan sprinted over to a barricade where a group of young men were picking up rocks and throwing them in the direction of the soldiers, the pathetic stones falling miserably short of their target.

And then it happened. The first shot rang out loud. The paras were shooting at innocent, unarmed people. Their SLRs capable of piercing a tree at one hundred yards and still having enough velocity to kill a man.

Michael spotted Jonathan running away from the barricade, eyes bulging with fear. Another loud crack and the sound of a bullet whizzing through the air. Jonathan's elbow shattered from the impact. A second bullet hit him in the chest as his body slumped to the ground. Michael managed to break his paralysis and dashed to where Jonathan lay. Blood was everywhere. He put a hand on his friend's wound. But the blood, like a fountain, pushed through his fingers. A relentless flow draining out of the dead boy's body.

Michael's mind snapped to the present.

He looked around the streets with fresh eyes and became aware of the dire changes that people had become accustomed to. Ugly incursions on life that were now accepted as normal.

Down one street, Michael could see a row of SLR nozzles sticking out of the alcoves of terraced houses, a platoon of soldiers hiding in them, making it as difficult as possible for snipers to shoot them. An old woman in her eighties opened her front door and gave the squaddie kneeling on her doormat an earful. He moved to the house next door. The risk of being shot was a better option than being assaulted by the vulgar words of an old witch.

Michael looked to his right. Wooden barriers had been set up at the top end of Limewood Street and cloaked in barbed wire. A gap had been made for pedestrians to pass through. Handbags, briefcases and satchels were searched by soldiers looking for hidden firearms, detonators and explosives. The women who passed through the gap chirpily chatted away with each other, some with babies in their arms, as grubby squaddie hands rummaged through their personal belongings.

To Michael's left, along Elmwood Road, a British paratrooper was splayed out on the ground, pointing his Bren gun around a corner looking for snipers in bedroom windows. A bunch of kids sauntered past him. One boy fearlessly prodded the soldier with a stick. 'Fuck off you little bastard,' mumbled the para. The kids laughed and continued on their way, skipping between the bricks that carpeted the road, the remnants of last night's riot.

That just isn't normal, thought Michael. *Nothing* about Londonderry was normal. Assassinations were rampant. Protestants shot Catholics on a regular basis. And Catholics shot Protestants in revenge. Tit for tat. Each side had always been suspicious of the other. Perhaps mildly antagonistic. But now they were outright hostile toward one another.

Then there was the rising incidence of kneecapping, a nasty punishment meted out by the IRA on people who, in their eyes, had committed a crime. Any crime. Large or small. It could be something major, like an unauthorised robbery, a burglary, or an assault on a volunteer. But it could also be a minor infringement. A girl could be hauled up in front of their kangaroo court for fraternising with a soldier. Or a woman for visiting the general hospital (which the IRA had ordered strictly off-limits). Or a drunken man could be nabbed for bad-mouthing the Republican cause in a public place.

If you were unlucky enough to go on trial and unfortunate to be found guilty, you'd be held up by two strong men, your trousers pulled down around your ankles. The nozzle of a pistol would be placed against the back of your knee, pressing against the soft skin and digging into the posterior cruciate ligament. And then the trigger would be pulled. The bullet would pass through your leg and shatter your kneecap, leaving a gaping, bleeding hole. The victim would be crippled for life.

No one, it seemed, *lived* in Derry. They simply *endured* it. Always on edge. Fearful for their kids, fearful for their homes and fearful for themselves. Michael used to be one of those people. Scared of his own shadow.

No longer. He was an IRA volunteer. He had a purpose in life. A reason for being. A soldier for the Irish Republican Army fighting for freedom.

Jimmy doesn't think I'm up to it, thought Michael. Doesn't think I can handle war. But I can. I've been on the battlefield. I've seen death. Smelt blood. Felt it on my hands.

Michael was suddenly aware of someone standing next to him. He looked up to catch Curly smiling at him. 'He gets testy if he hasn't got a fag in his hand.'

'I'm heading up now,' replied Michael as he brushed past the bomb-maker.

Curly shoved his hand in the crook of Michael's arm and pulled him back. 'What are you doing, Michael?'

'What do you mean?'

'You're not a killer.'

'I will be.'

'No. You won't.'

Michael was indignant at Curly's accusation. He loved his brother but despised his efforts at keeping him out of the fight. He wasn't a kid. He was a man. One who knew his own mind and was ready to fight for the cause. Michael reclaimed his arm with a brisk tug and headed toward the entrance of the flats. Curly watched him disappear inside. *What are you doing, Michael?* It had become a mantra in Curly's head.

Curly didn't like the idea of his brother doing bad things. The ugliness of the war should be left to ugly people. And Michael wasn't ugly. He was kind. If he'd been born anywhere else in the world, he'd be a teacher or a charity worker or a priest. Curly turned on his heel to head to the factory and caught his reflection in the shop window. *Yes,* he thought. *You're ugly enough.*

FIFTEEN

The bomb factory, one of several in the Bogside, was hidden in a lock-up in a small backstreet. It was a large garage with no windows and just two air vents near the ceiling. A heavy wooden workbench occupied the centre of the garage, with enough room for six bomb-makers to do their deadly work. This was the main factory. Bomb HQ. The one that supplied the smaller ones with equipment as and when they needed it.

The place was fully equipped. Vices, drills, hacksaws, screwdrivers and all the materials you needed to make bombs. The back of the garage was used as the storeroom. Stacks of explosives lined the back wall from ground to ceiling. ANFO (ammonium nitrate and fuel oil) and Semtex.

Three men had formed a mini production line. Terry McDermott, an apprentice bomb-maker with a face covered in volcanic acne, was first in the line. Eoin Twomey was second in line. And Seamus O'Grady, the bomb factory supervisor, took up the tail.

There was a knock on the lock-up door. Two raps followed by three. It was Curly. O'Grady opened the door and Curly Coyle bustled in, looking over his shoulder to make sure he wasn't being watched.

'How we doing?' asked Curly.

'Just finished a batch,' replied O'Grady.

'Twenty mortars ready to fly,' said McDermott as he plucked a mortar bomb from a canvas bag and held it in front of the chief bomb-maker's eyes. Curly took the device and looked it over. The mortar bomb was four inches long. Three small iron flights had been welded to one end, which made it look like a space rocket straight out of an American comic book. A hole, half an inch wide, had been drilled into the metal screw cap at the bottom of the mortar bomb. And a yellow J-cloth doused with sodium chlorate, a flammable substance, shoved into it. This was the fuse that would burn down and ignite the explosives inside the mortar bomb, shattering the metal and turning it into burning hot shrapnel that could cut through flesh and bone. Curly couldn't help but think the J-cloth looked a little bit silly. It somehow reminded him of a prop that a clown would use at a children's magic show. But it would do its deadly work despite its foolish appearance.

'Good job,' praised Curly, handing the mortar back. 'They found one of our factories.'

'I heard,' replied O'Grady. 'Fucking bastards.'

'Who the fuck tipped them off?' said Twomey. 'That's what I want to know.' McDermott had nothing else to offer. He was too junior to have an opinion.

O'Grady and Twomey, on the other hand, were two of the five who'd known the location. They were part of the circle of knowledge. Curly searched their faces for anything unusual. A sign of anxiety. Could it be O'Grady? Was he the tout? No. It couldn't be O'Grady. He was like a brother. They'd known each other for ten years. They'd been making bombs together for three. Holidays together. Christmas together. Drank themselves silly together more nights than he could remember. He'd shared all his fears, regrets and dreams with O'Grady. And O'Grady had shared his innermost secrets with Curly. No. It couldn't be him.

Twomey, on the other hand, had only been part of the team for a year. But he was known to be a Believer. A dyed-in-the-wool foot soldier who would sacrifice his life for the cause. The IRA was in his blood. It was hard to imagine that he could be the tout. But money was a wicked temptress. She could seduce the most committed of Republicans. Even one as loyal as Twomey.

Curly pushed the interrogative thoughts out of his head. He knew the final judgment was beyond his purview. Guilt or innocence would be determined by the nutting squad, the internal security unit of the IRA. A group of die-hard psychopaths whose job it was to investigate, interrogate and torture conceivable traitors. And if – after all the malarkey, the going back and forth, the double talk – their suspect was deemed to be guilty, a bullet in the skull would be administered. Or worse, a plastic bag over the head.

The nutting squad didn't always get it right. Many innocent men had been shot because of the squad's overzealous conclusions. But that didn't matter. *Better safe than sorry* was their motto.

'They're putting the nutting squad on this,' said Curly. 'And you two are going to be on the interview list.'

'I've got nothing to hide,' said Twomey.

'Nor have I,' said O'Grady.

'You should be worried,' said Curly.

'Fuck 'em,' said Twomey. 'I've done nothing wrong. And if I haven't done anything wrong, what the fuck should I be worried about?'

What a dense brain that man must have, thought Curly. Everyone knew Twomey wasn't the brightest spark, but his blasé attitude to the situation was verging on vegetative idiocy.

'We need to shut this place down,' said Curly.

'Shut it down?' replied O'Grady, a little taken aback. 'Tonight?'

'Is there a better time?' replied Curly.

The four men gathered up all the bomb-making ingredients and ferried them to the back of a Ford Transit van parked outside. There was at least a ton of explosives. *That would be one hell of a haul for the security services*, thought O'Grady. One hundred and fifty blocks of Semtex, twenty buckets of ANFO and twenty newly made mortar bombs. And then there were the accessories. Ten coils of wire, eighty detonators and twenty mercury tilts.

The four men had made quick work of it. The factory was shut down in less than an hour. Curly slapped a heavy padlock on the door of the lock-up and turned to his three associates. 'Seamus, you come with me. Eoin, Terry, you can fuck off to the pub.'

Twomey seemed a bit hurt by the exclusion. Didn't Curly trust him? Don't think about it. It's the bloody IRA. Everything's secret. Nothing's personal. 'We'll be off then,' said Twomey as he stuck his hands in his coat pockets. 'Come on, Terry, let's grab a pint at the Inn.'

'You'll have to pay,' said McDermott. 'I've got no money.'

'Don't worry. I'll buy you a pint.' The two marched up the hill and disappeared around a corner.

Curly sidled into the passenger seat of the van and gave O'Grady instructions. 'You're driving.'

O'Grady jumped behind the wheel. 'Where we off to?'

'Somewhere safe,' replied Curly.

* * *

The van glided along the smooth surface of the A6, its headlights illuminating the evenly spaced cat's eyes in the middle of the road. It was an inky-black night, a dark blanket occasionally broken by the pinprick of yellow light from farmhouse windows.

Curly stared out into the darkness, eyes heavy with tiredness. He closed them. It didn't take long for the past to invade his dreams. *How different life would have been*, he thought, *if events had taken a different course.*

As an eighteen-year-old, Curly was clever enough to get a scholarship at Saint Mary's College University where he studied Chemistry in between binges at the student union bar.

His mother was proud. No one from the Coyle clan had ever gone to university. They were a blue-collar family with dirty black jobs.

His father wasn't so approving. He wanted his son to follow in his footsteps and become a welder. But Curly was going to have none of that. He wanted to escape the dour life of a working-class Catholic. University was his tunnel to freedom.

Curly Coyle graduated with a master's degree in Chemistry. And worked at DuPont, an American chemicals conglomerate. The brash Americans that ran the Northern Ireland division didn't understand the Catholic–Protestant divide. Talent, in their mind, had no religion. You either had it or you didn't. And Curly Coyle had it. He was a young chemist who was going places.

Curly enjoyed his job at DuPont. It was the first time in his life he'd felt like an equal to his Protestant countrymen. It was the first time he'd felt hope for the future.

But all that changed on one fateful day. The day of the Apprentice Boys' parade. A march by Orangemen that commemorated a battle that was fought almost three hundred years earlier.

The march was symbolic. A reminder to the Catholics of a Protestant victory. A reminder of who was top dog in this ancient city. Of who had the power.

Rows of men dressed in antiquated uniforms marched stridently through Derry. Beating their drums, blowing their high-pitched flutes and carrying heavy linen Union Jacks. They wore medal-laden sashes over their chests and carried effigies of the 'traitor' Robert Lundy dangling from a hangman's noose.

Although the parade did not pass through the Bogside, it passed nearby. Along the junction of Waterloo Place and William Street. It was here the trouble broke out. Some loyalists had thrown pennies from the top of the city's walls at Catholics in the Bogside below. The Catholics retaliated by picking up their slingshots and firing marbles at their agitators. From those tiny sparks of anger emerged a blazing fire of hate and fury.

As the parade passed the perimeter of the Bogside, a large Catholic crowd started hurling stones at the marchers from behind makeshift barricades.

The police moved in. Not to bring peace, but to help the Apprentice Boys attack the Catholics. Their assault was halted in its tracks by a maelstrom of rocks.

In a bid to move forward, the police attempted to dismantle a barricade at Rossville Street. A gap was created. And a handful of Apprentice Boys slipped through.

News of the incursion quickly spread through the Bogside community, sparking fears that Catholic homes were going to be attacked and firebombed.

Curly Coyle was asleep in bed, recovering from a hangover, unaware of the escalating conflict taking place a mere forty yards away from his terraced house. His mother barged into his room and shook him awake. 'They're coming to destroy our home.'

'What?' said Curly through bleary eyes. He jumped out of bed, pulled on his jeans and a T-shirt, and rushed outside. It was chaos. 'Fuck me.'

A teenage boy, with long straggly hair, grabbed Curly by the arm. 'This way.'

Curly followed the boy into the Rossville flats. They climbed six flights of stairs to the roof. A group of young men and women were throwing stones at the Apprentice Boys who had ventured onto the wrong side of the barricade.

And then it happened. The first petrol bomb was thrown. It landed a few feet from the rogue Apprentice Boys and exploded. One of them started to burn. His comrades jumped to the rescue and put the fire out with a Union Jack. The men were shocked. Stones were one thing. But bombs. That was another. The Apprentice Boys turned on their heels and retreated to where they'd come from, joining the ranks of a growing police presence.

'We're not having that!' shouted a police commander as he urged his men to move forward.

It didn't take long for the whole Bogside community to rally behind the young heroes of Rossville flats. A continuous supply of petrol bombs was now being delivered to the roof. Ordinary men and women from ordinary homes filled every bottle they could find with petrol. The whole of the Bogside, it seemed, had become one big bomb-making factory.

Curly had taken charge on the roof and was directing the operation. 'Come on!' he shouted to the human chain filling the stairwell. 'Keep them coming. We're going to bomb these bastards to Hell.' As the police moved forward, a volley of petrol bombs landed on their heads. Men were on fire. Screams echoed through the air as human fire balls were being pulled out of the fray.

The battle raged for three days. At one point, the police resorted to flooding the area with tear gas. But that didn't quell the violence. Out of sheer frustration, the police called in the B-Specials, a Protestant militia that was armed to the teeth and ready to unleash their murderous firepower on the residents of the Bogside.

It was at that point the British Government decided enough was enough. They told the Northern Ireland security forces to stand down and sent in British forces to separate the sides and keep the peace.

At first, the Bogsiders welcomed the intervention. Old women handed out cups of tea and biscuits to grateful British soldiers. But Curly Coyle was sceptical. The British were not friends. They never had been. History made that very clear. The peace wouldn't last. The next day, he walked into DuPont and handed in his resignation.

Curly was jolted awake by the van bumping up and down. 'Fucking hell, Seamus,' said Coyle as his head hit the side of the van. O'Grady had pulled off the A6 and was driving along a small potholed road surrounded by tall pine trees.

'I can't help it, Curly. This road is fucked.'

'You know there's fucking explosives in the back?'

'Aye, I'm going as carefully as I can,' replied O'Grady, suddenly feeling a bit nervous at the thought of Semtex and ANFO bouncing up and down. 'Where now?'

'There's a small track on the left. About a mile up the road.'

O'Grady slowed down, keeping his eyes peeled for the turning.

'This is it!' shouted Curly. The car almost came to a stop as O'Grady traversed a tight bend that led onto a narrow muddy track.

Curly had scouted Loughermore Forest to the east of Londonderry a few weeks before. It was a large, wooded area with a spider web of small tracks running through it. No one came here. It was too thick, too creepy and too cold.

He'd found an ideal place to set up a stash. A small, abandoned lodge right in the middle of the forest. The slate roof had caved in. The red-brick walls had fallen over, leaving jagged four-feet-high ramparts.

And the whole place had become overgrown with vegetation and thorns.

'Here we are,' said Curly, pointing out a place for O'Grady to park. The two IRA men climbed out of the car, switched on their torches and looked around, picking out details of the building with circles of light. 'There's an old basement,' said Coyle as he walked to the back of the decrepit building. A large rusty iron door, fixed into a brick frame, lay on the ground. Coyle lifted it open. Its hinges squealed. Wooden steps led down into a subterranean cavern.

'What the fuck was this used for?' asked O'Grady as he scoured the eerie, dank basement with a beam of light, expecting to see a vampire's coffin somewhere in a corner.

'No idea,' replied Coyle. 'Let's get the stuff inside.'

The two got to work. They took the explosives out of the van and carefully stacked them at the far end of the basement. The accessories – detonators, tilts and coils of wire – were laid carefully on top. Finally, they covered the treasure trove with a large tarpaulin and pinned it down with loose bricks. That would keep the damp out. Keep the precious deadly cargo dry.

The two men covered the iron door with a pile of bricks, then a layer of old branches, and finally, a layer of thorn bushes. Their substantial arsenal was well and truly concealed.

'No one's going to find this,' said O'Grady.

'Aye. That's the point. And if they do, we'll know who to come after. Won't we?' Coyle slapped O'Grady on the shoulder and laughed. O'Grady laughed back. A tinge of nervousness reverberating at the back of his throat. Did Curly know?

SIXTEEN

The night was still, but the sleep was turbulent. Every time Seamus O'Grady nodded off, an uninvited phantom from his past would disturb his dreams. Surreal and menacing. By the time the alarm clock started to buzz, O'Grady's eyes were wide open. He silenced the alarm and sat up in bed. His mind turned to the rendezvous. Even though precautions were being taken, you never knew. There was always a chance of being spotted.

'Up so early?' grumbled his wife Janine, eyes still closed.

'Go back to sleep, love,' said O'Grady. If she found out what he was up to, she'd be horrified. *Wonder what she would think*, O'Grady thought. Would she stay loyal? Keep mum and fall in line? What else could she do? She couldn't turn him in. No wife would do that.

O'Grady pulled on his clothes, made his way to the ground floor and opened the small cupboard under the stairs. Inside was his fishing gear: tackle box, rod, reel, net, hat and a jar of worms that he'd dug up in the backyard the night before. O'Grady loved his fishing. He'd been hooked since he was a teenager. His old man would take him up to Lock Foyle and imbue him with the ways of the master fish catcher.

He slipped out of the house, quietly so as not to disturb the slumber of his wife and kids, and made his way to the bus stop around the corner. He'd take the Number 12 to Magheramason. Jump off at a bus stop a mile and a half before the village and make his way on foot toward a small track that would lead him to the River Foyle. He'd be lifted before he got there.

* * *

Even though it was early in the morning, a tractor, grumbling along at twenty miles per hour, was causing a build-up of traffic along the A5. Jonny McGuigan was tucked in behind the antiquated farm vehicle. He pulled the gear stick down to second and patiently cruised along, waiting for an ideal moment to overtake.

The tractor suddenly signalled right and peeled off into a field. The road was now open and McGuigan took advantage. He pressed his foot down on the accelerator, unleashing the liberating power of his German-made car.

As he approached Magheramason, the Special Branch man slowed down to fifty, keeping his eyes peeled for O'Grady. It wasn't long before he caught sight of the IRA man walking along the grass verge, carrying his fishing equipment in both hands. McGuigan sped past, looking around for anything out of the ordinary. A car driving too slowly. Men loitering where they shouldn't be. A motorcyclist parked up.

Nothing. No tails. McGuigan drove to Magheramason, made a U-turn and drove back toward O'Grady. This was how it was done. You'd ping the informant from behind, drive past, and then ping him again from the opposite direction. If it was all clear, it was safe to pick up the tout on the third pass.

The BMW stopped six feet ahead of O'Grady. The IRA man looked around nervously before throwing his equipment in the back and jumping in the front.

'Good morning for it,' said McGuigan cheerily.

O'Grady stayed tight-lipped, eyes focused on the road ahead. *He's a bit upset*, McGuigan thought. The Special Branch man ignored O'Grady's sulkiness and drove to Magheramason's Presbyterian church. Once there, he pulled into the little driveway that snaked its way to the back of the church and pulled up in the deserted carpark. It was an ideal place for a rendezvous with an IRA man. First, there wasn't a Catholic in sight. Magheramason was a staunchly Protestant village. Second, the tall trees that surrounded the carpark provided superb cover from the prying eyes of old women who had nothing better to do than spend the day peering out of their windows looking for gossip to spread.

'You need to get me the fuck out,' said O'Grady bluntly.

'Get you out? We're only getting started.'

'You couldn't fucking wait, could you?'

'You've lost me there.'

'The fucking factory.'

'Ah, that was out of my control, Seamus.'

'You gave me assurances.'

'I did. But the people above me…'

'Fuck the people above you. You broke your fucking promise. I'm a dead man.'

'Don't be so melodramatic, Seamus.'

'They're going to haul me up in front of the nutting squad.'

'The nutting squad?'

'There was only five people who knew about the factory. And I was one of them.'

'Hold your horses.'

'You need to get me out. Now.'

'It's not that easy. It takes time to make somebody disappear. Planning. Documents. Approvals.'

'You're fucking out of order, Jonny,' said O'Grady, spitting furiously through his words, his face twisted and pained. 'You're fucking killing me. You might as well put a knife in my heart and get it over with.'

'Calm down, my friend. No one's killing you.'

'You're not my friend.'

'I'm more of a friend than you think.' McGuigan pulled out a quart bottle of Jameson Whiskey, took a swig and handed the bottle to O'Grady. The nervy IRA man took the bottle and took a big gulp.

'Get me out,' said O'Grady, a quiet but desperate plea.

'I'll get you out, Seamus. But you need to give me a bit of time. I work for a big old bureaucracy. The cogs of the machine turn slowly. So sit tight while I work on it.'

'I'm dead.'

'Trust me,' reassured McGuigan. 'Someone else is going to take the fall.'

'What are you talking about?'

'You'll be okay.'

'You're setting someone up for something I did?'

'You'll be okay.'

O'Grady didn't push it further. He didn't want to know what McGuigan had been up to. Not that the Branch man would give him the details anyhow. 'How long's it going to take?'

'A couple of weeks.'

'I need to get back,' said O'Grady.

'Aren't you forgetting something?'

'I'm not giving you any more information until you get things sorted.'

'That's not the way it works, Seamus.'

'It is now.'

'You need to give me something. So my people know how valuable you are. So I can work on getting you out.'

O'Grady despised the blatant manipulation. But he was at the mercy of the Branch man. He would give him titbits. Nothing big. Nothing important. Just a crumb.

'There's a stash in Creggan. Next to the broken old garage. But don't make it obvious.'

'Thanks, Seamus.' McGuigan pulled a brown envelope from his coat and poked O'Grady's stomach with it. O'Grady took the envelope and peeked inside. He flicked the thick wad of five-pound notes with his thumb before slipping the envelope into his back pocket.

'If you get me out, I'll tell you where the big one is,' said O'Grady. That was the hook with a big juicy worm at the end of it.

'Big one?'

'Over a ton.'

McGuigan gave O'Grady a sly glance and started the engine. *The sneaky bastard*, he thought. *Holding out on me. That's okay. It's a game. Secrets on both sides. But a ton. That's a shitload of explosives.*

'Where?' asked McGuigan.

'Drop me off where you picked me up from,' replied O'Grady.

'I can drop you off at the bus stop.'

'Where you picked me up is fine. I've got some fishing to do.' O'Grady had a knot in the pit of his stomach. How did it come to this? How did he become a traitor to his own people? He knew the answer, of course. He'd overstepped the boundaries of his morality. He couldn't stomach the thought of killing any more innocent people. Every kill was rotting his soul. He was convinced he could smell the stench of his own sin.

McGuigan drove the car out of the church carpark and headed along the A5. He was disappointed that his relationship with O'Grady was coming to an end. He was a priceless asset. A spyhole into the inner circle of the IRA. McGuigan had learnt how to pull the strings of this sensitive, fragile puppet. He'd gained his trust. Made him feel he had a friend. An empathetic ear. A shoulder to lean on. But now there was hardly any blood left in the stone. Just one priceless drop, perhaps, to be squeezed out.

* * *

From the outside, the Strand Road police station looked new and modern. But inside it was tired and worn. In desperate need of new carpet and a lick of paint. It was also overcrowded. A direct consequence of The Troubles. As the violence escalated, the need for more police officers grew. But although more money was found for more people, someone at the top had failed to take into account the extra space required to house them all. So now everyone was climbing over each other in horrendously cramped working spaces.

McGuigan made his way to the Special Branch floor, walked past Detective Sergeant Drew McBride and, with his index finger, summoned him into his office.

'Hello, boss,' said McBride.

'I've got a job for you, Drew,' said McGuigan.

'I'm all ears.'

'There's an arms stash at Creggan. Near the old, abandoned garage.'

'A tip from your tout?'

'Aye.' McGuigan took the quart bottle of Jameson out of his coat pocket and took a swig.

He held it out to McBride.

'A bit early for me, boss.'

McGuigan took another swig and tucked it away. 'We've got to be careful with this one. I don't want to bust his cover.'

'What's the plan?'

'I want it found by a civilian.'

'You mean me.'

'Yes.'

* * *

The frayed streets of Creggan were relatively quiet. The area was staunchly Catholic and interminably poor. There wasn't much for the people in the area to do but stay inside and watch the telly, occasionally breaking their hypnosis to take the dog for a walk.

Drew McBride had dressed himself to resemble the middle-aged working-class man who inhabited these parts. He was wearing a pair of scuffed-up Clark's shoes, grey flannel trousers and an old brown anorak. His impersonation was topped off with a plaid flat cap pulled over his eyes. To foster the believability of his role, McBride had brought his dog along, a Jack Russell called Joey.

McBride walked along the street, one hand holding a dog leash and the other tucked in his anorak pocket. One old woman had pulled back the curtain to take a peek. Anyone walking around at this time of day in Creggan would be scrutinised. McBride waved at her, pretending they were on familiar terms. The old woman waved back. She didn't recognise him, but she must know him. Her eyes weren't as sharp as they used to be. It was probably the neighbour from number 32.

McBride came to a patch of wasteland and started throwing an old tennis ball for Joey to chase. He spied two men with their dogs on the other side. This is where everyone in the area takes their best friend for a walk. The place was covered in dog shit.

The decrepit garage was a hundred yards away. McBride threw the ball toward the garage. Joey chased it down with gusto and returned it with tepid enthusiasm. With every throw and return, McBride moved closer to his mark until eventually he was standing in a dense black shadow beneath the garage wall. As McBride moved along the wall, he brushed his foot across the ground, clearing away grit and stones, looking for signs of a stash. His search was interrupted by canine grunts. Joey was scratching the ground furiously with his front paws.

'What have you found, boy?' said McBride, walking to the spot that had aroused Joey's heightened senses. McBride stamped on the ground. It was spongey and hollow. This is it. The stash. 'Well done, Joey.' McBride knelt down and searched for an edge. He found it. The fingers of his left hand curled under a large pane of hardboard and lifted it five inches to reveal a hole. He pulled a small torch from his anorak pocket and shone a beam of light into the stash. A block of Semtex was caught in the glare.

McBride let go of the hardboard, which sprang back into place, concealing the deadly explosives below. He stood up, attached a leash to Joey's collar and dropped the green tennis ball on top of his find. The X that marked the spot. 'Come on, boy. Let's go home and put the kettle on.'

* * *

Sergeant Dooley, a fifty-something copper with a fat head and belly to match, was on duty at the Strand Road police station. He didn't feel much like a copper these days. He felt more like an operator at a telephone exchange. Call after call, day after day. It was relentless. There's a bomb on Glenshane Road. There's a suspect package on the steps of St Eugene's Cathedral. There's a milk churn by the side of the road at

Bogay. Dooley didn't get excited by any of this. The unusual had become the normal. More than that, it had become a chore.

The phone started ringing. He gave it a few seconds. Then picked up. And said what he always said. 'Strand Road police station. How can I help you?'

'There's some explosives at Creggan,' said the caller with a muffled voice. Was he speaking through his hand? Is he trying to disguise his voice? Whatever.

'Have you seen these explosives, Sir?' asked Dooley.

'Yes. My dog sniffed it out.'

'Clever dog.'

'It's next to the old garage. You know, the abandoned one. There's a green tennis ball right on top of it.'

'A green tennis ball? Would this be your green tennis ball, Sir?'

'No. But the explosives are under it.'

'Okay. Can you give me your name please?' The line went dead. It always did.

Dooley did what he had done a thousand times before. He called the Police Liaison office, relayed the information and then hung up.

The fat copper lit up a cigarette and kept his eyes fixed on the telephone in front of him. It would only be a matter of minutes before another call came in. 'Just a fucking order taker,' he said to himself under his breath.

SEVENTEEN

It was Granger's day off. But he did what he always did on his day off. He loitered in the ops room, waiting for news, wishing the tedium of the day would end, hoping he could get out there, back into the action.

It was 6 p.m., and a lonesome quiet shrouded the room. The other ATs had been called out on jobs. Granger pulled up a stool at the bar and climbed onto it. He contemplated pouring himself a beer but decided against the idea. Instead, he reached into his trouser pocket and pulled out a small, overused King James Bible. He kept the holy book on his person at all times. It was his trusted companion. The thing he drew strength from.

He flicked through the thin pages until he came to one with its top corner folded, an earmark to help him find his favourite passage. Deuteronomy 31:6. He had read the ancient words many times. He read them again now, inside his head. *Be strong and of good courage, do not fear nor be afraid of them; for the LORD your God, He is the One who goes with you. He will not leave you nor forsake you.* The words made him fearless. It was as if they'd been written specifically for him. He was meant to be in Ireland. The Lord would protect him. Show him the way.

As Granger closed his Bible, the ops room phone started ringing. A rush of adrenalin rushed through Granger's body as he picked up the receiver. 'Captain Granger here.'

'Evening, Sir,' replied a young soldier calling from the command centre. 'Got a call from the police. Found something at Creggan. Is Duty-One back yet?'

'No, Private. Everyone's out.'

'I'll call them on the radio, Sir.'

'What have they found?' asked the captain.

'A massive haul, Sir,' replied the soldier. 'They reckon it's a weapons stash.' This was the sort of job that got you into the news. Got you noticed by the powers-that-be. Earned you a medal. Granger decided there and then he would take the job himself. He would be breaking CATO's standing orders. But the old man wouldn't find out. Granger could keep it under wraps.

'Don't bother calling Duty-One,' ordered Granger. 'I'll take the job.'

* * *

A police car was parked at the edge of wasteland. The evening sun was being blocked out by dark, wet clouds, throwing the area into dusky darkness. The police switched on their headlights and kept them pointed at the abandoned garage.

The Saracen rumbled along the vacant road and came to a halt next to the police car. Granger's Land Rover pulled up behind it.

Ninety-Nine and his men had already climbed out of the armoured car and were scouring the area. There wasn't a soul in sight. Even the dog walkers had slipped back inside to avoid the oncoming downpour.

Granger climbed out of his vehicle and moseyed over to the two police officers slouching by their car.

'What do we have?' asked Granger.

'A hole by the wall,' replied a tall, lanky constable. 'Filled with weapons and explosives, apparently.'

'Apparently?' asked Granger.

'A man was walking his dog and the dog sniffed it out.'

'Where is this man?'

'He phoned it in. Didn't give us his details.'

'Have you had a look?'

'No. The bugger might go off?'

'The infantry?'

'Got held up, Sir,' chipped in a small, chubby policeman with a jacket that seemed to be one size too small for him. 'But they'll be here soon.'

'Let's have a look, shall we?' said Granger with a grin on his face.

'Shouldn't we wait, Sir?' asked the lanky police officer.

'No, it's fine,' said Granger. 'Pretty routine.' The captain turned toward Henderson. 'Torch, number two.'

Henderson rummaged around in the back of the Land Rover and pulled out a large silver flashlight. He flicked the switch on and off several times to make sure the batteries were working. Satisfied that they were, he handed the torch to Granger. 'Shall I get the wheelbarrow out, Sir?'

'No need,' replied the captain as he switched the torch on, pointed it at the ground and followed the beam over the potholed wasteland toward the old garage. As he neared the dilapidated wall of the building, the torch beam picked out a square slab of hardboard still half covered with dirt. A limp green tennis ball, punctured by canine teeth, was sitting on top.

Granger kicked the ball away and knelt down on one knee. He grabbed the board with one hand and lifted it up by six inches. He shone his torch though the gap where he could make out plastic bags and the handle of a pistol. Granger's heart was now racing. Not from fear but from excitement. This was a big one. And it was his. He slipped both hands under the hardboard and lifted the slab upward until it rested against the red brick wall, exposing the treasure trove of weapons and explosives.

'Brilliant,' he muttered to himself as he counted the items inside: around twenty polythene bags filled with plastic explosives, five old rifles, ten pistols and six homemade mortars.

He could see the newspaper headlines in his mind announcing the stash. Hear the voice of a newsreader proclaiming the ingenuity of the AT who had found it. Feel the slap on his back from MacIntyre as he muttered something about a George medal.

Granger placed the torch on the ground. He reached into the hole and picked up a homemade mortar bomb. In his haste, he was oblivious to the fishing line tied around the tail. Unaware that the other end of that line was attached to an explosive device that had been rigged to a mercury tilt. Unconscious of the fact that the mercury was running from one end of the glass tube to the other, enveloping two exposed metal nodes. Clueless that his action was closing the electrical circuit that would give the explosive the spark it needed to unleash its spiteful power.

The noise of the explosion was deafening. The bright flash of light illuminated the wasteland, momentarily burning out the dull grey of day.

* * *

It was one of those rare days in the highlands of Scotland when the sky was blue and the low-hanging sun flung its beams of light across the meandering hills. MacIntyre stood on top of a knoll. The wind blew against his face as the thick scent of heather filled his lungs.

A stag casually walked out from a pine forest to the right of him and gave the brigadier a blink of its paintbrush-lashed eyes. MacIntyre smiled to himself. This was bliss. Mountains, sky and nature. Nothing could make you feel more at one with the world.

The serenity was interrupted by a phone ringing. MacIntyre turned his head toward the source of the sound. A bright-red telephone box had been placed on top of a small peak, just ten feet away. How strange. Why on earth would anyone put a phone box in the middle of nowhere? He walked toward the red booth. And as he did, the ringing got louder. He put his hand on the door and opened it.

MacIntyre woke up. He was back in Ebrington Barracks, Londonderry. The black phone on his bedside table was ringing loudly. The brigadier reached over, took the receiver off the hook and placed it against his ear. 'Yes?' he asked in an irritable tone.

'Control room, Sir,' replied a private from the command centre.

'Yes?' asked MacIntyre again, his patience wearing thin.

'Captain Granger has been killed, Sir.'

MacIntyre sat up in bed. He could feel the blood draining from his own face. 'What happened?'

'We don't know, Sir.'

MacIntyre's stomach was churning. He thought about Granger's mother and father. His friends. His wife. Thank God he wouldn't have to break the news to her. That burden would be piled on some other poor sod. A young lieutenant, perhaps. From Granger's own corps. No one likes the task of telling a woman she's lost her husband. She'll ask to see the body. But there won't be a body to see. Just parts. Burnt and blackened.

'Sir?' asked the Private.

'Who's on duty?'

'WO2 Kersey and Staff Sergeant Thomson, Sir.'

EIGHTEEN

Thomson had shadowed Rip Kersey for five days. They'd been called out to more than twenty jobs in that time. Most of them hoaxes.

It was early evening and, since there had been a lull, Kersey decided to show Thomson the grimy underbelly of Northern Ireland.

Strabane was a poor Catholic slum to the east of the city. The area was decrepit. Crumbling roads were mottled with holes. Streets were strewn with plastic bags, broken glass bottles and old newspapers. The kids were dressed in worn-out woolly jumpers and trousers with holes in their knees.

A stream of tired old men walked through the doors of a tired old pub with rusty iron bars over the windows. The suspicious eyes of the locals fixed on their Land Rover as it slowly rumbled by. Adults threw insults, while kids as young as five threw stones.

Thomson caught the eyes of a toddler. The snotty-nosed urchin unleashed a rock from his tiny hand. The missile didn't get very far. Four feet. But the hatred in the infant's eyes was real. The tiny lips twisted as vulgarities flowed out of the cherub mouth. Fuck this and fuck that. How could someone so young, so innocent, have so much hatred building up inside? He knew the answer, of course. The mind of a child is malleable. It can be moulded. Indoctrinated. Made to believe a lie.

'This is what we're fighting,' muttered Kersey. 'They fucking hate us.'

'Feels like a foreign country,' replied Thomson.

'It is,' said Kersey glumly. 'Look at them. They don't want to be here. And the Proddies don't want them to be here either.'

'Even the kids hate us.'

'Which is why it'll never end. As soon as one of them pops out of his mother's womb, he's taught how to make a Molotov cocktail and say, "Fuck off, you British bastard".'

Thomson laughed. 'When did you become so cynical?'

'About a day after I arrived.'

'Tragic,' said Thomson.

'What? Me or this mess?'

'This mess,' replied Thomson as he eyed the squalor and sensed the hopelessness.

'Just don't get caught out here by yourself. They'll lynch you.'

'Don't worry. I won't be coming back here any time soon.' As they turned a corner, Thomson watched on, a little perplexed, as children of all ages along the street picked up stones and threw them at the vehicle. 'Little bastards,' said Kersey as a rock landed on the Land Rover's bonnet.

'Don't the little buggers go to bed?' asked Thomson.

'Obviously not,' replied Colby as he took his foot off the accelerator, the Land Rover slowing down as it pulled up at a T junction. A glint of metal caught the corner of Thomson's eye. He craned his neck to the left.

'Fuck me.'

'What?' asked Kersey, a little startled by the outburst.

'That woman,' replied Thomson as he opened the door and jumped out onto the street.

'Holy mother of God,' said Colby as he spied what Thomson had spied. A young woman had been shackled to a lamppost with heavy chains around her hands and feet. Her hair had been shorn and her head daubed with blue indelible ink. A cardboard sign, which read SOLDIER DOLL, had been hung around her neck.

'What the fuck are you doing?' shouted Kersey. 'You'll get yourself bloody shot.'

Thomson rushed over to the girl and knelt down beside her. 'Are you okay?' Her body was shaking uncontrollably, tributaries of tears running down her face. A runner of snot hung pendulously from her nose. 'Christ,' said Thomson as he put an arm around her shoulder in a futile attempt to console her. But she couldn't be calmed. She couldn't have been more than sixteen years old. What kind of animal does this to a kid? Thomson and the girl were soon encircled by the Saracen's infantry escort, their rifles scanning the area for any potential threat. This wasn't a good place to stop. Word would be spreading through the area like a flu epidemic. Soon everybody would hear about a bunch of squaddies lurking around their patch. Isolated. Exposed.

Kersey was by Thomson's side, kneeling down. An arm across his shoulder. 'We can't hang around here, Dave.'

'We can't leave her like this,' said Thomson.

'We've called in the police. They'll be here soon.'

'Let's wait,' said Thomson.

A group of older women, scarves on their heads and aprons around their waists, came swarming toward them from what seemed like every direction. One of the women broke ranks and ran toward the girl chained to the lamppost. It was the girl's mother. 'Rosy. Rosy. What have they done to you?'

'Back off,' shouted an infantryman pointing his rifle at the women. 'Fuck off, you British bastard.'

Thomson stood up and put his hand on the soldier's weapon, pushing the nozzle downward. 'She's harmless.'

The group of women, ten strong, surrounded the girl. One put a blanket across her shoulder while another eased her hands out of the chains. A few of them turned toward the soldiers and started screaming insults and spitting phlegm.

'Come on, Dave,' said Kersey. 'We're not wanted here.'

An object whizzed past Thomson's ear. Followed a fraction of a second later by the sound of a rifle firing. The bullet missed its target and pinged against the metal of the armoured vehicle.

'They're shooting at us,' shouted a lance corporal as he pointed at a house across the road. 'There.' All four men in the escort lifted their SLRs, pointed them at the upstairs window of a terraced house and started firing. The glass shattered under a barrage of fire and the brick around the window frame was peppered with holes. The women crouched down on the pavement and huddled together in a protective circle.

The sniper had either been shot or had made his escape. Either way, it was time for the troop to get out of there.

'Let's go,' shouted the lance corporal corralling the two ATs back to the Land Rover.

Thomson and Kersey jumped into their vehicle. A second later, Colby slammed his foot on the accelerator. The Saracen followed behind, providing cover from any further fire. Thomson's hands were shaking. He breathed deeply in an attempt to calm his nerves. That was too close. If the bullet's trajectory was an inch to the right, Thomson's brains would have been splattered all over the pavement.

'That's why we don't get out, Dave,' said Kersey curtly.

'Sorry,' replied Thomson. 'Just trying to do the right thing.'

'Doing the right thing gets you killed.'

Thomson's thoughts turned to the girl. How could anyone do that to a kid? He thought of his own daughter. If anybody did that to Karen, he would track them down and cut their balls off. The image of the angry women muddied his mind. He was just trying to help the girl. Do some good. But there was no appreciation from the mothers and aunts. Just a mouthful of spite. He wondered if they'd serve up the same vitriol to the men that had savaged the girl. Or would they turn a blind eye in the name of the cause?

'Why did they do that to the girl?' asked Thomson.

'It's what the IRA does to girls they think are sleeping around with British soldiers,' said Kersey.

'Bastards.'

'Yeah.'

Thomson took one last look over his shoulder at the group of women in the distance, the girl now on her feet, still sobbing uncontrollably.

As they left the decaying neighbourhood behind, a voice crackled over the radio. 'Duty-One, there's been an explosion in Creggan. Can you check it out?'

NINETEEN

Corporal Henderson, hands shaking, pulled a pack of Benson & Hedges from his pocket. He opened the top and tried to pull one out. But his trembling fingers couldn't grab hold of the orange filter.

Thomson took the pack from him, took out a cigarette and held it toward Henderson's mouth. The corporal grabbed it between parted lips. Thomson took one too, grabbed the lighter from his pocket and lit both. 'I can't believe he's gone,' said Henderson.

'What happened, Jock?' asked Thomson. It wasn't a question he needed to ask. He knew the answer. The captain would have been gung-ho. Nonchalant. Blasé. He would have marched into the scene confidently and rummaged around without any concern for the possible danger. He would have been careless at the very moment when he should have shown caution.

'He went to check out the stash and it went up,' said Henderson as tears swelled up in his eyes until they overflowed and trickled down his cheeks. Thomson didn't know what to say. It wasn't often you saw a grown man cry in the army. He wanted to give the corporal a hug, but instead put a hand on his shoulder. No words. No condolences. They weren't necessary.

Thomson looked up and scanned the scene around him. It was almost 11 p.m. and the army had flooded the area with light from two large spotlights. The blast had ripped the old garage apart. In its place was a twenty-foot crater, six feet deep. The surrounding area was littered with red brick, splinters of charred wood and twisted iron.

The infantry had turned up moments after the explosion and set up a cordon a hundred yards around the blast site. The local residents, shaken by the ear-splitting noise, had streamed out of their houses to see what was going on.

Men from the Green Howards had formed a human barricade to keep the growing crowd at bay. The word had started to spread that a British soldier had died in the blast. Not long after, the crowd, buoyed by the news, started taunting the soldiers with Republican chants. *Another soldier dead. Another soldier dead. Go back home, another soldier dead.*

Thomson watched the twisted face of a weathered old woman, rollers in her grey hair, shouting insults at a young soldier two feet in front of her. The poor lad avoided eye contact as the foul stench of stale cigarettes from the woman's breath hit his nostrils.

A waving hand caught the corner of Thomson's eye. It belonged to Kersey. The ex-marine was having a powwow with a major from the Green Howards and wanted Thomson to join them.

'Stay here, Jock,' said Thomson to the distraught corporal. 'I'll be right back.' He patted Henderson on the shoulder and walked briskly toward Kersey and the major.

'Staff Sergeant Thomson,' said Kersey as Dave approached. 'This is Major Williams.'

'Pleased to meet you, Sir,' said Thomson as he saluted the officer.

Major Williams returned a one-fingered salute. 'Good evening, Staff,' he said with a posh accent, a hint of Welsh lurking within it.

Williams was what they called a late bloomer. He joined the army as an officer at twenty-three with high hopes of flying to the top. He was now fifty and had hit a ceiling at the rank of major. The men he'd trained with at Sandhurst had left him behind. They were now brigadiers and generals, men with positions of power and influence.

Major Williams groomed the tips of his thick grey moustache with his thumb and finger.

'We have a bit of a problem,' continued Kersey. 'There's no light and it's about to piss it down.'

'We need to get the job done,' said Thomson.

'I suggest you gentlemen get a couple of hours of sleep,' advised the major. 'We'll stay here and protect the area. When it's light, you can come back and do your stuff.'

The crowd was starting to enjoy itself. The hundred or so Catholics who'd gathered around the scene continued with their singing. They'd had enough of the old chant and started a new anthem. *You can't find his body, he's blown to bits. You can't find his body, he's blown to bits...*

'Is there no respect?' asked Thomson as the chant got louder.

'Not in these parts,' replied Kersey.

'If I had my way, I'd shoot the whole lot of them,' said the major. 'I'd line them against a wall and mow them down.'

Thomson was taken aback by the comment. But he wasn't surprised. This was an officer with a colonial outlook. He was born sixty years too late. He would have thrived in the First World War. Arrogant. Entitled. Incompetent. 'I think they'd call that murder, Sir.'

The major was indignant at Thomson's retort. 'It was a joke, Staff Sergeant Thomson.'

'Of course, Sir.'

The major flashed a sneer, turned on his heels and walked off to order some idle infantrymen around.

'What a stuck-up arse.' Kersey chuckled.

'Too many of them in this army.'

'Tell me about it.' Heavy droplets of rain started dropping from the sky.

'Shall we get back to camp?' asked Thomson.

'Best idea you've had all day.'

Thomson and Kersey strolled back toward the Land Rover. To their surprise, Henderson was walking toward them with a shotgun in his hands, tears streaming down his face.

'What the...' blurted out Thomson.

'He's got a bloody shotgun.'

Thomson rushed over to Henderson and blocked his path. 'Where you going, Jock?'

'They killed the captain,' replied Henderson, looking over Thomson's shoulder toward the crowd. 'And now they're disrespecting him.'

Thomson put his hands on the corporal's shoulders and stared into his eyes. Kersey stayed back. He'd seen this before. Good men who'd reached breaking point. Overwhelmed by anger and fear. Thomson seemed to have the situation under control, a situation that needed the soft touch.

'I can't let you go over there, Jock,' said Thomson. The chants from the crowd were getting louder as more and more people poured out of their houses and joined the swelling crowd.

'Listen to them,' replied Jock as his throat trembled with anger. The Scotsman had locked eyes with the weathered old woman in curlers who seemed to be spewing vulgarities directly at him. 'Look at that old cow. She deserves what's coming to her.'

Thomson glanced over at the distorted face. Ugly and twisted. He turned back to Henderson. 'It's not worth it, Jock. They'll lock you up and throw away the key.'

'But Sir, the captain.' A fresh batch of tears sprouted from Henderson's red eyes as his shoulders slumped and his head bowed.

Thomson released his grip on Henderson's shoulders. 'I'll take that,' he said to the sobbing corporal as he gently pulled the shotgun from trembling hands. Thomson sighed with relief as he held the weapon out behind him with a straight arm. Kersey shifted forward and grabbed it.

'Come on,' said Thomson as he put an arm around Henderson and led him toward the Saracen where Ninety-Nine and his squad were keeping an eye on the crowd. 'Let's get you a hot mug of tea.'

'He's gone.'

'I know, Jock. There's nothing we can do about it.' A loud crack of thunder clattered over their heads drowning out his words. The thick blanket of clouds above released their heavy load.

Thomson looked over his shoulder at the spite-filled face of the old woman in curlers. She would never know how close she had come to a face full of shot.

* * *

Bill MacIntyre was sitting patiently behind his desk in his office. He'd made himself a hot mug of black instant coffee. He needed it to keep himself alert. Get his mind sharp. Focused. Ready for all the commotion that always followed the death of a soldier in Northern Ireland. There'd be investigations. Reports. Post-mortems. Paperwork.

He looked at the framed photograph of his own wife and kids who took pride of place to the right of his leather-bound writing pad. He wondered how they would react if he was the one who had died. If a stranger turned up to their door and broke the news, said sorry, and then walked away, leaving them with the cruel burden of loss.

The brigadier's thoughts were broken by a sharp knock on the door. 'Come in,' he shouted. Kersey and Thomson entered the room. The two men saluted. 'What a bloody mess.'

'Yes, Sir,' replied Kersey solemnly.

'Did you find his body?'

'No, Sir,' said Thomson. 'From what Jock told us…'

'Jock?'

'Corporal Henderson, Sir.'

'Ah.'

'Captain Granger was right over the stash when it went up.'

'What about the dead dog?'

Kersey and Thomson looked at each other as if one or the other might know what MacIntyre was talking about. 'Dog, Sir?' asked Kersey.

'The infantry found a dead dog. Was it one of ours?'

The two ATs were struggling with the question. 'I'm not sure what you're talking about, Sir,' replied Thomson.

'Was there a dog handler at the scene?' asked MacIntyre, losing his patience.

'Not as far as we know,' said Kersey as a flurry of water, driven by the wind, pelted the window. 'We'll go back once this storm calms down.'

'No matter. I want you to find what's left of Granger.'

'We'll check it out first thing, Sir,' continued Kersey.

'Right you are,' said MacIntyre glumly. 'You boys must be tired. Get some rest. We'll discuss this tomorrow when we know more.'

'I'm sorry,' said Thomson.

'What?' asked MacIntyre.

'I'm sorry about Captain Granger.'

The brigadier relaxed in his chair and let out a sigh. Granger's face popped into his mind. It was hard to imagine the young captain was gone. 'Yes. It's a damned shame. He was twenty-nine, you know. Damned good AT.'

Thomson wanted to tell MacIntyre the truth. Granger was a lousy AT. Incompetent. Dangerous. Irresponsible. But the man was dead. And any slight on his name would be seen as disrespectful, vulgar and unbecoming of a soldier in Her Majesty's Armed Forces. It was best to let the delusions endure.

MacIntyre put a cigarette in his mouth. 'Go on, get some shut-eye.'

The two men walked out of the office and closed the door gently behind them. 'I bet you had to bite your tongue,' whispered Kersey.

'I wanted to tell him.'

'He's dead. We're all safer for it. Let people believe what they want to believe.'

* * *

It was dawn and the sun was low in the sky, casting long shadows with every object it touched. The rain had stopped, leaving shiny roads dotted with pothole puddles. Kersey and Thomson had managed to get two hours of sleep. And now they were back in the Land Rover following the Saracen back to Creggan, their eyes heavy and their heads cloudy.

Colby had prepared a flask of hot milky tea. Kersey did the honours. He unscrewed the top, poured the light-brown liquid into a metal cup and handed it to Thomson. 'That'll wake you up.'

Thomson took a sip just before his face scrunched up. 'Bloody hell, Brian. How many sugars did you put in this?'

'About thirty teaspoons,' replied Colby.

'I'll lose all my teeth if I drink this,' said Thomson.

'Stop moaning,' said Kersey. 'It'll make you as bright as a button.' Kersey poured a cup for Colby and one for himself. Both men took a sip. And both men scrunched up their faces but didn't complain. 'This place is quite nice this time of the morning.'

'Peaceful,' replied Thomson. The streets were soothingly quiet as Londonderry was starting to wake up. Bedside lamps illuminated bedroom windows. Mothers were getting up to make breakfast. Fathers were getting dressed for work and children were making excuses to stay in bed. A milk float quietly whined along the street. A ten-year-old paper boy, with a large canvas bag slung across his shoulder, pounded the pavement, stopping occasionally to squeeze a daily tabloid through a letterbox.

'This could be home,' said Colby as he steered the Land Rover along the dim streets.

'Aye,' chipped in Kersey. 'Except for the bit where a whole load of maniacs are trying to kill you.'

The Land Rover followed the Saracen round a corner and onto the wasteland where the old garage had once stood.

'We're here,' announced Colby. The chanting crowd of Catholics had disappeared. They'd had their fun. Shouted their taunts. And now they were back inside their homes warming themselves against a coal fire. Soldiers from the Green Howards loitered around the cordon. They were relaxed. Smoking. Drinking tea from metal mugs. No longer having to put up with the ferocity of old women spitting malice in their faces.

Major Williams spotted Thomson and Kersey and marched over toward them. The two ATs saluted as he approached. 'Morning, gentlemen,' he said in a sprightly manner. 'Manage to get some kip?'

'Yes, Sir,' replied Thomson.

'We hear a dog got killed,' said Kersey.

'Yes. Over here by the cordon,' replied the major as he led Thomson and Kersey to the spot. 'We called it in last night. Thought maybe it belonged to your lot.' The major loomed over a blackened headless body with four stumpy legs.

'Not one of ours, Sir,' said Kersey. 'We don't use them out here.'

Thomson crouched to take a closer look. It must have been a big dog. A Rottweiler or German Shepherd. And then it hit him. 'That's not a dog. That's a human torso.'

'Granger,' muttered Kersey involuntarily.

'Oh dear God,' added the major as he put his hand over his mouth, as if somehow that would contain his queasiness.

'Well, we'd better get to work,' said Kersey coolly. He'd seen many dead men and, like all seasoned veterans of war, had become desensitised to the sight of blood, flesh and bones.

Thomson, on the other hand, was feeling nauseous. He'd never been so close to the visceral reality of a blown-up man. The smell of roasted human meat was sticking inside his nostrils. He pinched them.

'Are the medics here?' asked Kersey.

'Yes,' replied the major. 'They've been waiting for you to return. Didn't want to enter the area until you'd done your investigation.'

'Not much to investigate,' said Kersey. 'Where are they?'

'By the ambulance.'

'Of course.'

The major raised his hand and summoned the medics. The two young soldiers, with medical kits slung across their shoulders, jogged across to the officer, stood to attention and saluted.

'This is WO2 Kersey and Staff Sergeant Thomson.'

'Morning, Sir,' said a tall, skinny kid, no older than eighteen. The other medic was short and wiry and obviously took his lead from his lanky mate.

'This belongs to our captain,' said Kersey.

'We were told it was a dead dog,' replied the tall skinny soldier.

'No, Private. It's a body.'

'I can see that now,' said the private, bending down to get a closer look.

'We need to pack it. And then look for more parts.' The medic stood up, opened his medical bag and pulled out several pairs of disposable latex gloves. He handed a pair to the ATs.

'You'll need these.'

Thomson and Kersey took the gloves and pulled them on. The young medic offered up a pair to the major.

'Are you serious?' said the major. 'I've got a squad to lead.'

'Sorry, Sir,' replied the medic. The major grunted and walked back to his command post.

'Wanker,' muttered Kersey. The two young medics giggled but soon stopped when they caught Kersey's disdainful stare. 'Are we done?'

'Yes, Sir,' replied the lanky soldier, who quickly turned to his companion. 'Have you got bags, Jo Jo?' The short medic dug into his satchel, pulled out a stack of plastic bags and handed them out.

'You get this one wrapped up,' instructed Kersey, nodding toward the torso, 'and we'll start scouring the area for the rest.'

Kersey and Thomson lifted their feet over the cordon and walked toward the epicentre of the explosion. The wasteland was scattered with bricks, iron pipes and wooden splinters. They reached the edge of the crater and looked inside. The bottom was filled with water from the previous night's downpour.

'That was a big explosion,' said Thomson.

'I'm surprised there's anything left of him.'

'I'll do this side.'

'Happy hunting.'

Thomson laughed. 'Do you take anything seriously?'

'Yes. My life.'

Thomson scoured the right side of the wasteland, while Kersey searched the left side. It didn't take long for Thomson to make his first find. A blackened hand with two fingers and a thumb. He picked it up and put it in a bag. He was feeling nauseous again. He looked across at Kersey. He'd found something too and was leaning down on one knee to bag it.

The two medics, who had wrapped the torso in plastic sheeting and placed it in the back of the ambulance, joined the ATs in search for more body parts. The pieces were small. Bits of legs and arms. Along with fragments of charred skin attached to scraps of khaki clothing. After thirty minutes, they were done. The men combed the area one last time to make sure every piece had been found.

'I think that's it!' shouted Kersey.

Thomson suddenly had a realisation. There was one piece of the body they hadn't accounted for. 'What about the head?'

TWENTY

Angry talk and the stench of cheap booze saturated the living room. Dorothy Campbell walked in with a bowl of Planters roasted peanuts and placed it in front of her husband. No manners. No thanks. Just a dismissive glance.

'I'm off to the bingo tonight,' said Dorothy quietly. Robert Campbell ignored her and continued talking to the other three alcohol-tanned men in the room, elders of the Ulster Volunteer Force, the Protestant equivalent of the IRA.

The UVF was smaller, less potent and less organised than its Catholic rival. But it had one thing going for it that IRA didn't. It was supported by corrupt men in power. Senior police officers, British Army generals and radical elements from within the Northern Ireland Parliament. None of it official, of course. Couldn't be. The official line in Whitehall was that no terrorist group was acceptable. Every terrorist, no matter Catholic or Protestant, would be prosecuted under the full weight of the law.

Campbell was the head of the Londonderry chapter of the UVF. The figurehead in the fight against the Catholics. He took his position seriously. This is where the war began. This is where the minority

Protestant community was outnumbered by four to one. This is where the Ulster way of life was most under threat.

By day, Campbell worked for the Derry Council in the Department of Housing and was actively involved in keeping poor Catholics out of the system. He conspired with powerful men in government, Paisley's men, to fix waiting lists and ensure the Catholics stayed in their slums. Under the Orange thumb.

'Jonny's late,' said Campbell, putting his hand in the bowl of nuts. 'Shall we wait? Or shall we get started?'

'I've got to be off in an hour,' said Doug Carlson, a burly man with a mastiff neck, the owner of a large property development business that monopolised government contracts in Derry.

'Let's get started then,' said Campbell. 'What's top of the agenda?'

'Eliminations,' said Stephen Adams, a slim man with eyes the colour of weak tea. The emotionless face was that of an ex-British soldier who had served with the Royal Irish Fusiliers. A rogue insurgent who had been involved in unauthorised raids against the South. Until a bullet ripped away half of his left calf. He retired from the Old Fogs in 1968 with an army pension and, acutely agitated by the rise of the Catholics in Derry, joined Campbell and his band of corrupt city councillors.

'Eliminations?' asked Campbell 'There hasn't been any.' Eliminations was just another word for assassinations in the UVF. They preferred to use the word because it sounded less sinister. More apposite. More legal sounding.

'No,' replied Adams. 'We can't get close to any of the leaders. They're well-hidden and well protected.'

'Maybe we need to lower our sights,' said Carlson. 'Pick off the ones at the bottom.'

'And why would that work?' asked Campbell. 'Kill one foot soldier and another one takes his place.'

'But at least it sends a message,' said Carlson. 'Better to kill a runt than kill nobody at all.'

Campbell turned to Adams. 'Who we looking at?'

The wily old soldier didn't answer. Instead, he shifted his gaze toward Dorothy who was lingering by the door. This wasn't a conversation for women. Their mouths were too loose.

Campbell turned to Dorothy and snapped at her. 'Didn't you say you were going to bingo or something?'

'Yes,' replied Dorothy. 'I'll see you later.' Dorothy left the room, put on her coat and opened the front door just as Jonny McGuigan, with his unmistakeable flash of orange hair, was walking up the front garden path toward her.

'Evening, Dorothy,' said McGuigan. 'Where you off to?'

'Bingo,' replied Dorothy.

'Bingo?'

'Better than hanging around in there.' Out of all the men that came to her house, Jonny was the only one that treated her with respect. He was polite. A gentleman. Or as close to a gentleman you could find in Derry. But although she felt an affinity with McGuigan, there was something unsettling about him. As there was with any policeman. Too many skeletons locked away in the cupboard. Dirty laundry left unwashed.

'They're worse than gossiping women,' said McGuigan.

'So why do you bother turning up?' asked Dorothy. McGuigan's intense blue eyes seemed to penetrate Dorothy's mind. Attempt to uncover her secrets.

'Someone's got to keep them in line.'

'Better you than me.' Dorothy slipped by McGuigan and headed down the road.

McGuigan's eyes were glued to the curvaceous figure until it disappeared around a corner. He had sympathy for Dorothy. Her husband had the manners of a toothless pig. She deserved better.

The detective inspector slipped into the living room and stood in the corner with his arms crossed.

'Good of you to join us,' said Campbell.

'What have I missed?' asked McGuigan.

'We need to up our kill rate,' said Adams.

'Is that right?' asked McGuigan.

'We're going to bring up Lenny Murphy from Belfast,' said Carlson.

'Over my dead body,' asserted McGuigan as he straightened himself up. Lenny Murphy headed up the Shankhill Butchers, a gang of ultra-extreme loyalists operating in and around Belfast. Even though he was just twenty years old, it was reckoned Lenny Murphy had murdered more than twenty Catholics. The majority of them innocent, law-abiding citizens.

Murphy, whose family was resolutely Protestant, was ashamed of his surname. It was a Catholic moniker. And as such, a personal embarrassment for a Protestant loyalist. As a teenager, his schoolmates would poke fun at him. Goading him. Calling him Catholic scum. He would argue back the only way he knew how: with his fists. And as he got older, a hammer, his psychosis rising to the surface with every slight.

Murphy wanted to change his surname at one point but thought it would be seen as an act of weakness. Recognition of an inferiority complex. So he decided to live with it.

When The Troubles escalated, Murphy decided to join the UVF. He took it upon himself to strike at the Catholics any way he could. The sadistic psychopath and his fellow maniacs would drive around The Falls district, a staunchly Catholic area. If they spotted an individual roaming the streets, they would pounce. Clobber the pedestrian on the head with a club. Drag them to the car and throw them in the boot. His kidnappings were indiscriminate. It didn't matter if it was man, woman or child. The only criterion was religious belief. The only good Catholic was a dead Catholic.

Murphy would drive his victims to an old farm on the edge of the city. Tie them to a chair and torture them for hours on end. Burn them with a cigarette on the hands, the arms and the face. Cut them with his knife. A slice here and a stab there. Punch them in the face. Break the nose and crack the teeth. Break a finger with a pair of pliers. Smash a foot with a hammer.

The brutality was relentless. Once the battered quarry had been reduced to a blithering mess of jelly, Murphy would finish them off with a butcher's knife etched deeply into the victim's throat, blood squirting from the jugular and spraying the floor red.

'He's exactly what we need,' said Adams with steel in his words.

'If he turns up here, I'll shoot him in the head myself. I'm not having a maniac like that roaming the streets of Londonderry.'

'But we've got to take the war to the Catholics.'

'We've got to take the war to the terrorists. We don't target innocents.'

The group of men remained quiet, like children scolded by a head-master. This is why McGuigan came to these meetings. To make sure stupid decisions were averted.

* * *

Dorothy was happy to get out of the house. She couldn't stand the men her husband kept company with. Worse, she couldn't stand her husband. He was a very different person to the young man she'd fallen in love with at school. Back then he was gentle and loving.

And then he got a job with the council. As he rose through the ranks, his hatred toward the Catholics grew. He became more bigoted. More intolerant. And with it more intolerable. Why had she married him? Stinking misogynist animal.

As she became increasingly unhappy in her marriage, Dorothy started to go out more. Mostly bingo, but sometimes to the pub with her girlfriends. It was during one of those nights out she met O'Mahoney. She bumped into him at the bar and struck up a conversation. Allowed herself to be charmed, to get involved. A stupid mistake that only a pubescent teenager would make.

Dorothy walked slowly down the street. She looked at her watch and realised she was running late. So she picked up the pace, her high heels clicking and clacking loudly on the pavement. As she turned the corner, she spotted O'Mahoney's blue Vauxhall Victor parked at the back of the Angel Pub. She walked over to the passenger side of the car, looked around to see if anyone was watching and climbed in.

'You're late,' said O'Mahoney with a snarl.

'Sorry,' replied Dorothy. She despised this man. She was also frightened of him. One day he was going to kill her. She was sure of it. But there was nothing she could do. She was trapped.

'Tell me what your fat, stinking husband's up to.'

TWENTY-ONE

It had been two weeks since the death of Granger. And today was the commemoration of his life. Thomson walked alongside Kersey, step for step, as they made their way to the small red-brick building located at the far end of Ebrington Barracks. A storehouse that had been converted into a chapel. A lick of fresh paint had recently been slapped onto the wooden window frames to make it appear more youthful. Thomson could smell the pungent paint. An odour that lingered days after the paint had dried. It was a smell he liked. One which conjured up fond memories of home. The time when Jean was pregnant with their first child and he had painted the baby's bedroom a powder blue as she brought endless cups of tea and gave him endless instructions. The memory was fleeting as he approached the entrance of the chapel. An usher stood outside handing out leaflets containing the hymns to be sung at the service.

'You first,' said Kersey. Thomson took a leaflet and walked in. Kersey followed closely behind him. The chapel was full. Even though 321 EOD was a small unit, it was highly regarded and senior-ranking officers from the regiments had come to pay their respects to Captain Granger.

Keith Cooper had planted himself at the front on the left-hand side of the chapel. The two seats next to him were vacant. Thomson and

Kersey walked to the front and claimed them. Bill MacIntyre was sitting at the front on the right-hand side, reading a sheet of paper and making comments in the margins with a pen. Thomson wanted to say hello but thought better of it. The man was obviously preoccupied, studiously writing Granger's eulogy. Instead, Thomson turned to Cooper. 'Where's Alan?' he asked in a quiet voice.

'Got called out,' replied Cooper.

'Well, the captain's got a good turnout,' whispered Kersey.

Thomson looked over his shoulder and quickly scanned the room. Soldiers in their combats sat dour faced. Murmurs and small chat filled the chapel as people waited impatiently for the service to begin. This wasn't the official funeral. That would take place back on the mainland. The captain's remains were flown back in the hull of a Hercules. It would be a closed coffin funeral. Not least because the corpse was headless.

After Thomson and Kersey had collected the scattered pieces of Granger's body, they spent another hour looking for the head. They climbed into nearby gardens to see if it had landed on a lawn, in a flowerbed, or under a hedge. But to no avail.

The pathologist in charge of the autopsy theorised the head had been vaporised by the blast. 'He must have had his face right in there for that to happen,' mused Kersey at the time.

The corps would give the captain a traditional send-off. Soldiers dressed in their ceremonial uniforms carrying their rifles upside down. Boots, spit-polished and glinting in the sun. A coffin draped in the Union Jack. A bugler playing the 'Last Post' as an army chaplain speaks words of tribute. Eulogies from senior officers. A three-volley salute.

'Here he comes,' said Kersey as the army chaplain, dressed in a long black robe over his green uniform and clutching his large red bible, walked through the door.

The sombre priest made his way to the front of the chapel where a three-foot-long pine wooden cross had been attached to the wall. To one side was a makeshift pulpit, behind which the chaplain settled and looked up to scrutinise his audience. 'We are here today to say farewell to Captain Leyton Granger and commit him into the hands of God. Let us sing the first hymn.'

The congregation rustled to their feet, shuffled around for a moment and peered down at their leaflets. The organist in the corner, who'd been silently hiding behind his sheet music, hit the keys with his fingers, unleashing the notes to 'Jerusalem'. The chaplain led the singing. Out of tune but strident.

And did those feet in ancient time, walk upon England's mountains green?

As soon as the singing echoed through the chamber, Brian Colby sheepishly entered the chapel and tip-toed to the front. He reached over and tapped Kersey on the shoulder. Kersey turned his head. No words were needed. He was Standby-Two. And a job had been called in. The IRA didn't stop for any man's funeral. And nor did the unit. Kersey put his leaflet down on the chair and followed Colby out of the small building. The singing continued.

And was the holy Lamb of God on England's pleasant pastures seen? And did the Countenance Divine shine forth upon our clouded hills?

Thomson liked this hymn. It had a catchy melody. He sang loudly. Brashly. He wasn't a particularly good singer, but what he lacked in talent he made up for in passion.

Bring me my bow of burning gold! Bring me my arrows of desire! Bring me my spear! O clouds, unfold! Bring me my chariot of fire! I will not cease from mental fight, nor shall my sword sleep in my hand, till we have built Jerusalem in England's green and pleasant land.

The hymn came to an end and the congregation settled back into their seats. The chaplain shuffled through some notes, gathered his thoughts and spoke. 'We have lost a brave soldier. Captain Granger was taken from us while performing his duty. A duty to God, country and the people of Londonderry. His work was not to kill, but to save lives. And, while in the pursuit of doing that job, his own life was forsaken. He was proud of his place in 321 EOD. It was a job he loved. A job he lived for. Captain Granger epitomised the professionalism, the courage, and the selfless duty befitting of an officer and the timeless traditions of the British Army...'

Thomson's mind started to drift. If only they knew the truth. The man was an amateur. His arrogance was being misrepresented as courage. And his selfless duty was a thinly disguised cover for the self-serving publicity he craved.

The chaplain's voice had become a monotone of meaningless white noise. Thomson was thinking about the next job. Thinking about death. His own potential demise. Imagining his own service with a chapel filled with mostly strangers, looking at their watches, impatient to get on with the busy schedule of the day. Too busy for tears. Too anxious to linger on the memory of the recently departed.

His thoughts were interrupted by a tap on the shoulder. It was Ninety-Nine. 'We've been called out, Staff,' the Welshman whispered. Thomson looked across to MacIntyre. The brigadier gave a nod. It was a signal that said he understood. Soldier first, mourner second. Thomson nodded back, rose up out of his seat and followed Ninety-Nine out of the chapel. As the door closed behind him, he could hear the congregation break into the second hymn – 'Amazing Grace'. *I like that song,* he thought to himself as he walked to the Land Rover that was waiting for him outside.

Jock Henderson was sitting behind the steering wheel, knuckles white as he clung on tightly. Thomson climbed into the front passenger seat. 'You didn't make the service.'

'I couldn't do it, boss,' replied the wiry Scotsman with a tremble in his throat. 'I would've broken down.'

Thomson put a hand on his shoulder. This was a man who cared. A man who wasn't entirely in control of his emotions. But a loyal man nonetheless. 'I'm glad you're my Number-Two, Jock.'

'Thank you, boss.'

Thomson, by default of Granger's death, had been handed the captain's escort and driver. It was a strange feeling. They had been loyal to Granger, a man Thomson deeply disliked. He hoped he could earn that degree of loyalty for himself.

The Saracen in front roared forward. Henderson put the Land Rover into first gear, put his foot on the accelerator and chased after it.

As the distance between the Land Rover and the chapel grew greater, Thomson looked over his shoulder, spying the old storehouse through the open back of the canvas-covered vehicle. He couldn't help but feel sorry for Granger. For all the glory he craved, he would just be another statistic in the dusty files of the Ministry of Defence. He peeled his eyes away and focused them on the road ahead.

TWENTY-TWO

On the day of Granger's service, the IRA got busy. Really busy. It was as if they knew that they'd be piling disrespect on the man they'd inadvertently killed. Not a single AT from 321 EOD saw the captain's sacrament all the way through. All of them had been called out while the service was in progress.

Thomson had been summoned to five back-to-back jobs. The first was to a terraced house on the Waterside. A plastic Co-op bag had been left on the seat of an outside dunny. It was like déjà vu. Was God playing a prank on him? Remember this? Ha, ha, ha. The irony wasn't lost on Thomson. On the day of Granger's service, he was being reminded of the captain's reckless ways. The foolhardy behaviour which would eventually lead to his death. This surely was a message. What it meant, he had no clue. But it put him on edge and made him extra cautious.

Just like the first time, it was a hoax. The bag was filled with grey stones. It was likely planted by the same people who had deposited the first one. Some low-ranking mugs whose job it was to plant fake bombs in stinking dunnies.

The second job had been on a small country road near Limavady, a small town seventeen miles from Londonderry. A suspicious milk churn had been placed against a telegraph pole and called in by a local policeman.

By the time Thomson turned up to the scene, there was no need to let it soak. The bomb had been placed there at least three hours earlier. He stuck a couple of pounds of plastic to the side of the churn and blew it up. Then something unexpected happened. The telegraph pole next to the churn was uprooted from the ground by the sheer force of the explosion and was flung into the air. The churn must have been packed full of explosives. Much more than Thomson had anticipated. The eyes of every soldier followed the trajectory of the projectile as it travelled one hundred yards toward a field of grazing cattle.

An eruption of cheers went up as the pole came down on the grass with a thud. Thomson was just glad it didn't hit a cow.

This was the best entertainment the men from the Duke of Wellington Regiment had seen in the past two months. The major in charge turned to Thomson and shook his hand vigorously. 'Brilliant, Felix. Brilliant.'

From Limavady, Thomson made his way to the law courts. A briefcase had been left in the middle of the road. Dark clouds had gathered overhead, blocking out the light from the sun. The Royal Hampshire Regiment had cordoned off the area and set up a large spotlight that picked out the suspect device. Thomson felt as if he was on stage. The centre of attraction. Like a lead actor waiting for roses to be thrown at his feet.

The soldiers behind the cordon, miserable and cold, looked on as Thomson pointed his shotgun at the brown leather box. He pulled the trigger. The shot tore a hole in the briefcase the size of a fist. Thomson put three more rounds into his target, the pellets ripping the briefcase apart. Tiny pieces of paper started floating in the air, like confetti at a wedding. It was a hoax.

After the law courts, Thomson had been called to Foyle Street in the centre of town. A car had been parked in the middle of the road with a piece of cardboard wedged into the windscreen. The word BOMB written with a felt tip.

Thomson let it soak, watching the car from the safety of the Land Rover and smoking a cigarette. And then it happened. The car exploded, taking everybody by surprise. 'Fuck me,' said Henderson as he almost choked on a cheese sandwich. The force of the blast blew out all the windows in the surrounding buildings. The orange flames billowed upward, emitting black smoke into the sky. *It was one hell of a spectacle*, thought Thomson, mesmerised by the glowing ball of fire that quickly gutted the car.

The last job was called in from the Diamond, Londonderry's main shopping centre. A suspicious shopping bag had been left at the side of a clothes shop. It was a Co-op bag. *Those little bastards again*, thought Thomson. *They've been busy today.*

Thomson aimed his shotgun at the bag and pulled the trigger. It only took one shot to establish that the suspicious item was a hoax. The signature grey stones scattered across the concrete pavement.

By the time Thomson arrived back at camp, it was two in the morning. He'd put in a fifteen-hour shift. Granger's service seemed an age ago, already becoming a distant memory.

Thomson was struggling to keep his eyes open and headed straight for bed. It had been a long week. He'd hardly had an hour's sleep. An endless stream of jobs made sure of that. But he was going to get some kip-eye tonight. He was now off duty. A whole day off.

As his head hit the pillow, he fell into a deep slumber. But that didn't stop an onslaught of images invading his dreams. Granger's burnt, pungent torso. Jock Henderson, tears streaming down his face, marching toward the crowd with a shotgun in his hands. The telegraph pole flying through the air. The delight on the face of the major from the Duke of Wellington regiment. The scenes were on a loop, playing in his mind over and over again. Relentless, disturbing and vexing.

Granger appeared out of the mind's mist to give Thomson some advice. 'You're too careful, Staff. They're amateurs. They can't make bombs. It's all a big hoax.' The captain laughed, picked up a shopping bag from the middle of the road and threw it toward Thomson. 'Catch!' shouted the captain. The bag turned into a bright light. No explosion. No noise. Just warmth.

*　*　*

It was late morning and the sun's rays forced themselves through the crack of the curtains onto Thomson's face like a spotlight. He slowly opened his eyes, leaving behind the irksome dreams. An object lay on his pillow. As his eyes came into focus, Thomson found himself nose to nose with a grey mouse.

'Arrggghh!' he screamed and jumped out of bed at the same time. He grabbed a boot and whacked the rodent three times. The mouse didn't move. Something wasn't right. Thomson bent over to take a closer look. 'What the...' he said to himself as he picked the thing up by its tail for closer inspection. It wasn't a mouse. It was a toy. A very realistic toy. 'Bastards,' murmured Thomson as he dropped the mouse on his bed and picked up the clock on his bedside table. It was 9 a.m. He'd slept for seven hours straight. A record.

He walked drowsily over to the sink in his bedroom, looked in the mirror and briefly inspected the dark bags under his eyes. He looked dreadful. He switched on the tap and splashed icy-cold water on his face. That woke him up. He shaved, brushed his teeth and combed his hair. He climbed into his combats and wondered what he would do with the free time on his hands. Maybe watch a film. Or read a book. Or take a long stroll around the camp.

* * *

After a hearty breakfast, followed by a dessert of three cigarettes, Thomson, with nothing better to do, made his way to the ops room. As he reached the door, he could hear chatter and laughter. Was someone throwing a party? It was good to hear high spirits in a usually glum environment. Thomson swung open the door and entered the room. The three ATs were squabbling over a game of Gin Rummy.

Sutton had just placed a triumphant three nines on the table. '*Vide et credere.*'

'What the bloody hell does that mean?' asked Cooper.

'See and believe,' replied Sutton as he collected the winnings with a sweeping hand from the centre of the table.

'Have you been fixing the deck?' asked Cooper.

'I'm not a magician, dear boy,' replied Sutton.

'You're just having a run of bad luck, Keith,' said Kersey.

'No one has a run that bad. You two are stuffing me up,' replied Cooper.

Kersey laughed. 'You're just not a very good player. Admit it.'

Thomson walked over to the table and pulled up a chair. 'Morning, Dave,' said Cooper. 'Watch yourself. We've got a couple of thieves in the den today.'

'Socrates once said, when the debate is lost, slander becomes the tool of the loser,' retorted Sutton smugly.

'Sod Socrates.'

'How's sleeping beauty?' Kersey asked Thomson. 'Have a good kip?'

'Not bad. Until I woke up to find this little bugger sharing my bed,' replied Thomson, holding up the toy mouse by its tail.

'Ah, you've met Lucy.' Kersey laughed. Thomson flung the toy over to the Royal Marine, who caught it with one hand.

'Bastard.'

'You're not the only one,' said Cooper. 'He hands them out like candy. We've all got one.'

'It's a lucky charm, Dave,' said Kersey as he threw the mouse back. 'And now you've got to know her, that little mouse will save your life one day.'

'Save my life? Nearly gave me a heart attack,' replied Thomson.

'Like to see him play that trick on MacIntyre,' said Cooper. 'He'd have him running around the camp all night with a log over his head.'

'Your face, Keith,' said Kersey through a chuckle, remembering the day he'd played the same trick on Cooper. 'All uppity he was.'

'Bollocks,' said Cooper. 'Are we going to play this game or not? Before that damned phone starts ringing.'

'No calls yet?' asked Thomson, surprised the ops room had a full complement of ATs.

'Saturday morning, dear boy,' replied Sutton. 'Always slow at the beginning of the weekend.'

'The Paddies get smashed on Fridays,' said Cooper. 'They love their ale that lot. Still in bed most of them with a cracking hangover, no doubt.'

'Which is why we have rummy Saturdays,' said Kersey. 'Wanna chuck your hand in?'

'Don't mind if I do.'

Kersey dealt the hand, flicking the cards out like a pro. Thomson picked his cards up, held them close to his chest and took a peek. He couldn't believe his luck. Three kings. His face was emotionless. He feigned a subtle expression of disappointment.

The phone filled the room with its high-pitch ring. 'That'll be for me.' Kersey strolled over to the phone and picked up the receiver. 'Duty-One…got it.' He hung up. 'The Paddies are awake. See you later, boys.' With that he headed out the door.

'Just the three of us then,' said Cooper.

'Let's get on with it,' said Sutton.

The phone started again. It was Cooper's turn to answer. 'Standby-Two…thank you.' A moment later he was gone.

'I don't think this game is going to happen, is it?' said Thomson. The phone, as if set on a timer, came to life again.

'No. Afraid not,' replied Sutton, as he stood up ready to receive his orders. 'Standby-Three here…thank you.' He replaced the receiver on its hook, put his hands together as if in prayer and tilted his head toward the ceiling. '*Deus, gratias ago tibi.*'

'Someone's happy,' said Thomson.

'The SPAR Supermarket,' said Sutton. 'Always Saturday. Always in the morning. Always a breeze.'

'Lucky you,' said Thomson.

'Absolutely, dear boy. Like winning the pools. I'll be back before you know it.'

Within seconds, Sutton was out of the door, a joyful bounce in his stride.

Thomson threw his three kings onto the table. The only witness to his winning hand was the mouse. Thomson picked the furry toy up and held it a foot from his face. 'Want to watch some telly?'

TWENTY-THREE

The nutting squad had picked Twomey up from his home at a mutually agreed time and had driven him to a farmhouse near a small country town called Newtownstewart. The man that owned the farm was a staunch IRA supporter and would vacate the premises for a day or two whenever the nutting squad would require its use.

It had been a pleasant enough journey with friendly banter between the men in the car. Twomey was escorted into the house and forced to sit on a wooden chair facing a blank white wall. Three members of the nutting squad were standing behind him. He only knew one of them by name. Darragh Quinn, the commander of the squad. A man with a terrible reputation. A maniac, it was said, who revelled in torture and death.

But Twomey wasn't worried. He'd been here before. This very building. It was routine. The interview was just part of the process of elimination. O'Grady had been hauled all the way out here the day before. *Nothing untoward had fallen upon him*, thought Twomey. *So there was no reason why anything should happen to me. Let's get this over and done with. And then we can get back to Derry before closing time.*

'Are you the tout?' said Quinn.

'No, I'm not,' replied Twomey with a smirk. Perhaps with a touch too much arrogance.

'Why didn't you tell us you'd been lifted?'

'I did.'

'You didn't tell us.'

'I told Seamus.'

'That was two days after it happened. Why did you wait so long?'

'I forgot. Those Branch men did my head in. I wasn't thinking straight.'

'You know the drill. You're supposed to call us as soon as you get out. You didn't.'

'It was an honest mistake.'

'Honest mistake?'

'Yes. I…you know. I…I went for a drink. People can vouch for me.'

'Are you working?'

'No I'm fucking not.'

'I'm going to ask you again? Are you working?'

'No. Never.' Quinn pulled a rounder's bat from the inside of his coat and whacked Twomey across the head with it, knocking him off the chair. 'This is going too far,' sputtered Twomey, blood gushing out of a deep gash. 'Please.'

'Have you been shagging?' asked Quinn.

'No.'

'That's a lie. We have it on good authority you've been shagging.'

'Yes. But…you know. Just a bit of play. No harm meant.'

'You're a fucking lying little toad, aren't you, Twomey?'

'No. I wouldn't do anything against the cause. I'm yer man.'

'Did you tell them where the bomb factory was?'

'No. I wouldn't do that.'

'How much did they pay you?'

'You've got it all wrong,' squealed Twomey. How could this be happening to him? He was innocent. The two junior members of the nutting squad pulled Twomey up and planted him on the wooden chair.

'I'm going to ask you one more time. How did they make contact?'

'Please. Please. This is wrong. There's been a mistake.'

'Hold him,' said Quinn.

Blood was seeping into Twomey's eyes. But that didn't stop him seeing a shadowy figure walking through the door. As the man approached, Twomey recognised the face. Horror shivered through his body.

'You don't think I know what you've been up to?' said Steve Docherty as he pulled a pistol from his coat pocket.

TWENTY-FOUR

Thomson picked up a book and tried reading for a while. *The Day of the Jackal* by Frederick Forsyth. But he couldn't focus. Too much stuff was shooting through his mind. He found himself reading a couple of pages and then realising he hadn't absorbed a single word or sentence. So he put the book down and picked up a writing pad. He wrote Jean a letter. It was full of banalities about the food, the sparse living conditions and the miserable weather. He asked how the kids were doing and told her how much he missed her. How much he loved her. That had taken about half an hour.

Now he was sitting in front of the TV with a cup of tea and a digestive biscuit watching *The French Connection* starring Gene Hackman. He was halfway through the movie when Alan Sutton walked in. 'Put the kettle on,' said Sutton as he shrugged off his jacket and laid it over a wooden chair. Thomson put his movie on pause, pulled himself up from the settee and walked over to the kettle. He touched the outside with his hand. It was still hot. He filled it up anyway and plugged it in.

'How was the Co-op?' asked Thomson.

'Same, same,' replied Sutton as he plonked a teabag into a mug. 'The IRA, as usual, put their bomb in the shop. And as soon as they buggered off, the owner put it in the street.'

'Very nice of him,' said Thomson. 'I'm surprised the IRA let him get away with it.'

'So am I. He's been doing it for months.'

The kettle came to a boil and Thomson poured the steaming water into Sutton's mug, drowning the teabag and releasing its bitter brown flavours. 'Milk?'

'Just a squirt.' Thomson grabbed a half-empty milk bottle, poured in a dash of white creaminess and handed the warm brew to Sutton, who grabbed the ceramic mug with two cold and grateful hands. Just as Sutton was about to take a sip, the ops room phone started ringing. '*Deodamnatus.*'

'No rest for the wicked.'

Sutton rushed over to the phone and picked it up. 'Sutton...on my way.'

'Anywhere nice?'

'The country.' Sutton rushed back to his mug of tea, sipped as much as he could without burning his gullet and rushed out the door. Thomson returned to the settee to watch the rest of his film. He was feeling guilty about his rest day. While he was lounging around twiddling his thumbs, the rest of the unit was rushing from one call to the other. Overstretched and undermanned.

There was a knock on the door. MacIntyre walked into the room with a tall, slim captain by his side. Thomson stood to attention.

'Morning, Staff Sergeant Thomson,' said MacIntyre. 'Everybody out?'

'Yes, Sir.'

'This is Captain Jardine, your new OC.'

'Good to meet you, Sir,' said Thomson as he stepped forward and offered up his hand. Jardine took it. 'Staff Sergeant Thomson.'

'Nice to meet you, Staff,' said Jardine with a New Zealand accent that had been tempered by a decade in the British Army.

'I'm going to leave him with you, Staff, if that's alright,' said MacIntyre.

'No problem, Sir,' replied Thomson. MacIntyre, his baby-sitting duties over, turned on his heels and headed back to his lair.

'How's it been?' asked Jardine.

Thomson could smell the rank and file in Jardine's DNA. Ex-rankers were down to earth. Better connected to the men under their command. Warmer than the officers baked into an elitist mould at Sandhurst.

'Nonstop,' replied Thomson. 'You don't get much sleep around here.'

'I heard it was busy.'

'Busy is an understatement. Frantic would be a better way of putting it. The jobs come in thick and fast.'

'Any advice?'

'Be patient.'

'That's what MacIntyre said.'

'He says it to everyone,' said Thomson. 'Best advice you'll hear.'

'I was sorry to hear about Captain Granger.' Thomson kept quiet. Jardine hung on for a riposte but soon realised he wasn't going to get one. 'Is there something I should know?'

'No, Sir.'

'Was Captain Granger patient?'

Thomson was caught off guard. That was a clever question. 'No, he wasn't, Sir.'

'Well, Staff. I'm as patient as they come. I can watch paint dry for a week and not get agitated.'

'That's good to hear, Sir.'

'We have a mentorship programme, I understand.'

'Just the first week, Sir.'

'I've been assigned to WO2 Kersey.'

'My ears must be burning,' said Rip Kersey, closing the ops room door behind him. 'Did I hear my name?'

TWENTY-FIVE

The front doors of the Bogside Inn were bolted and locked. Outside, the pavements were empty and the roads eerily quiet, with only the occasional army patrol disrupting the still, sleepy air.

Jimmy Brett was inside sitting at the stainless-steel counter in the back kitchen, with Behan standing guard by the back door. Byrne was the only other person in the building and was busy at work in the corner knocking up a couple of ham sandwiches. An early morning snack for his guests.

The commander, who was smoking a cigarette and sipping a cup of tea, was noticeably irritable. He looked at his watch. It was 6.12 in the morning. Docherty was twelve minutes late.

There was a knock at the back entrance. Behan peeked through the spyhole and unlocked the door. Docherty's head popped into view. Red and sweaty. Brett looked at his watch again. It was now 6.13.

'One of the bookies was behind on his payments,' said Docherty. 'I had to sort him out.'

Brett stared at Docherty contemptuously, letting him know his intolerance for tardiness. 'My time's precious.'

Docherty stood in the middle of the kitchen feeling awkward. 'Sorry Jimmy. He didn't want to give up the money. So I had to crack a couple of fingers.'

'I don't give a shit. When you've got a slot with me, you fucking stick to it.'

Docherty wanted to push back against the old man but thought better of it. *Keep your mouth shut Steve. He's in one of his fucking moods.*

'Pull up a stool.' Docherty obeyed the order and positioned himself across from the commander. 'We've got orders from Belfast.'

'I'm all ears.'

'They want us to blow up a pub full of squaddies.'

'Which one?'

'The Droppin' Well.'

'Sounds familiar.'

'It's a nightclub in Ballykelly. Next to Shackleton Barracks.'

'I think I know it. Popped in for a pint a couple of years ago. It's a shithole. Full of Proddie whores.'

'All the better.' Brett stubbed out his cigarette and leant forward with enthusiastic eyes. 'Cleaners go in there around 4 p.m. One of them is working for us. She'll be there early. Go by the back door. She'll open it for you.'

'Who do you want me to bounce?' It was IRA protocol to give extremely short notice for a job. As soon as there was a knock on the door (the bounce), the volunteer on the other side was activated instantly. Sucked into the operation without notification. It was an effective way to stop a potential mole from leaking the details of the mission. The tout, if there was one, had no wiggle room. No time. They just had to go along with the flow. Be a fellow conspirator.

'McDermott. He's your bomb-maker,' said Brett.

'And the back-up?'

'Take Michael with you.'

'Michael?'

'Aye.'

'He's a bit green for a job like this.'

'I want him in.' Brett dangled a set of car keys in front of Docherty's face. 'There's a car parked up around the corner on Meenan Drive. Brown Austin Allegro, HOF712L.' Docherty grabbed the keys and shoved them in his trouser pocket. The Austin was a stolen car from the city centre. No one in the IRA ever used their own car. To do so would be tempting a prison sentence. Any vehicle used on a mission like this would be a forensic scientist's dream. Aside from potential witnesses, there would be traces of explosive and fingerprints to go with it.

'Curly's got the package.'

'I'll be off then,' said Docherty making his way to the back entrance. Behan unlocked the door and opened it. Docherty slipped past the bodyguard and rumbled into the backyard where crates were stacked high and rubbish bins were overflowing with waste. The door locked behind him. Docherty looked at his watch. He had plenty of time to collect the package, bounce the crew, drive up to Ballykelly and plant the bomb.

* * *

Curly put the device in a large canvas bag. It was a forty pounder. Made with Semtex. He wrapped the mercury tilt in cotton wool, put it in a brown paper bag and placed it on top. Mercury tilts were tricky. Deadly if mishandled. And were always put in place at the scene.

There was a rap on his front door. Curly rushed to open it. Docherty's large frame filled the entrance, his beady eyes darting nervously left and right. 'Come in,' said Curly.

Docherty shuffled inside. 'Is it ready?'

'Right here.' Curly picked up the canvas bag and handed it over.

Docherty grabbed the handle. 'That's heavy.'

'It's a big bomb.'

'How big?'

'Forty pounds.'

'That's going to make a bit of mess.'

'The mercury tilt is in the brown paper bag on top. Terry knows what to do.'

'I shouldn't be telling you this,' said Docherty. 'But we're bouncing Michael.'

'He'll do a good job.'

Docherty laughed and walked out of the house without saying as much as a goodbye.

* * *

Even though it was the afternoon, Michael Coyle was caught in a deep sleep. Motionless, like a mannequin in pyjamas. Empty beer cans were scattered on the floor around him. He hadn't been able to go down the pub for the past three days. He'd run out of dole money. So he did the next best thing. He scrounged a few quid and bought a case of Tennent's Super. A nasty beer that had the double advantage of being very cheap and very strong.

He drank himself silly while watching corny sitcoms and silly soap operas on TV.

But now all the beer was gone and all he could do was sleep it off.

The doorbell rang. Michael was unperturbed. It was just a sound in his dreams. Then it rang again. And again. And again. Michael opened his eyes and looked at the luminous clock on his bedside table. It was

2 p.m. Who the fuck is that? Michael wasn't expecting company. He jumped out of bed and moved cautiously to the front door. He shouted, 'Who's there?'

'Steve. Open up,' replied Docherty. Michael opened the door.

'Alright, Steve. What's up?'

Steve smirked at the scrawny figure in his baggy pyjamas. 'Get dressed.'

'Where we going?'

'You've been bounced.'

'A job?'

'Get dressed,' said Docherty impatiently.

Michael rushed inside the flat and emerged moments later dressed in jeans, T-shirt and coat. At last, he was going to see some real action. He was dizzy with excitement.

Docherty walked to the Austin and climbed behind the steering wheel. Michael jumped into the back where McDermott was sitting patiently. 'Alright, Terry?'

'Aye.'

Docherty started the engine and pulled away.

Half an hour into the drive and the two young volunteers were jabbering away about mundane things. About that girl and this girl. About the price of a pint in this club versus that club. About Georgie Best and why Man United didn't deserve him.

Docherty was getting irritated. Ballykelly was an hour away and he'd had enough of the small talk. He switched on the radio. 'Summer Holiday' by Cliff Richard blurted through the crackly speaker.

'I love this song,' bleated Terry. Docherty ignored him. He hated the song. But if it kept the young idiots quiet, he could suffer it.

* * *

The traffic on the road was heavier than normal. Which meant they were running late. It was almost 4.15 p.m. The carpark was empty except for a couple of vehicles that had been left overnight because their owners were too drunk to drive them home. Docherty pulled the Austin into a parking space at the back of the Droppin' Well, a ramshackle place that was painted a dirty matt black. Some hoodlums had sprayed red paint over the heavy wooden door – cocksucker. A primitive shape of a penis to reinforce the point. *The place looked grim in the hard light of day*, thought Docherty. *It was probably a lot more alluring at night with its splendid neon lights masking its dingy façade.* 'Okay lads, let's get to work.'

The three men climbed out of the car and slammed the doors behind them. Terry walked round to the boot, opened it up and pulled out the canvas bag containing the device. He handed it to Michael, whose eyes were wide and alert. Filled with a mixture of excitement and anxiety. 'You okay there, Michael?' asked Terry.

'Aye,' replied Michael.

Docherty watched on as the young volunteers got themselves ready for the mission. He couldn't help but notice Michael's shaking hands. 'Are you okay?'

'I'm fine,' replied Michael, trying to get a grip on his nerves.

'Calm down. Everything will be alright. You'll be in and out of there in fifteen minutes. Take a deep breath and stay focused.'

'He'll be okay,' interjected Terry.

Docherty gave Terry a *who the fuck asked you* type of stare. 'You'd better get on with it,' said Docherty as he climbed behind the steering wheel of the car.

Terry led the way, with Michael following a couple of feet behind, his eyes darting around looking for trouble that wasn't there. He put his hand on the revolver he'd stuck in the front of his jeans, patting it gently as if it were some old canine companion. The two men came to the side wall of the Droppin' Well.

Terry rapped on the metal door three times. A moment later it opened. Tammy Matchett, a thirty-something woman, poked her head through the gap. 'You were supposed to be here at three-thirty,' she snarled. 'Come in. Before someone sees you.'

The two men hurried inside, the door closing shut behind them with a heavy clack. Tammy was nervous. Her face was sallow and joyless, the mouth of a melancholic clown. The corners were drooping downward, unable to smile even if she wanted to. Her hair was greasy and her overalls dirty. She was a shabby woman. Michael felt an involuntary loathing for the dishevelled female.

Sweat was starting to sprout on Tammy's furrowed forehead. She put a cigarette between her lips and held up a lighter to the end. Her hands shaking. 'You okay there, woman?' asked Terry.

'I'm fine,' replied Tammy. 'Let's get this over and done with.'

'Show us the way.'

Tammy shoved her way past the two men, making small but quick steps along the sticky carpet that covered the corridor. Terry and Michael followed her. They entered the main room of the disco. Two other cleaners were busy clearing up glasses and wiping down tables. They didn't seem to notice the two men walking toward the toilets. 'Who are they?' whispered Terry into Tammy's ear.

'Nobody. Just old biddies doing their job. Nothing to worry about.' But Terry *was* worried. He thought they'd be alone in the disco. He didn't like the idea of strangers hanging around while they did their business. 'This is it,' said Tammy. 'Make it quick.'

The two men hurried into the toilet. There were three cubicles to the left. Terry opened the door of the middle one. He gagged, almost throwing up. Some dirty bastard had puked all over the place. In and out of the bowl. The stench was foul. 'Not this one,' said Terry as he closed the door shut. 'Let's try the first trap.'

Michael pushed the door open. Three used johnnies had been flung on the floor. He wondered whether it had been one randy bastard or three different men. And who was the woman who had let herself be shagged in the cubicle of a public toilet. Some Protestant slag.

Terry hurried in after Michael. He placed the canvas bag on the floor and unzipped it. He pulled out the mercury tilt first, unwrapped it from its cotton wool cocoon and handed it to Michael. 'Hold this.'

Michael did as he was told. Terry pulled out the explosive device, covered in a plastic sheet.

'Are you ready to make your first bomb?' asked Terry.

'Yes,' said Michael.

'Good. We'll make a bomb-maker out of you yet.' Terry took the mercury tilt off Michael and held it up. 'This fucker is a little bastard. And if you don't treat it with respect, it will kill you.'

Michael inched his face closer to the glass tube, inspecting it in detail. It was a hermetically sealed glass cylinder with two exposed wires, a couple of millimetres apart, fixed inside. Also inside the cylinder was a blob of mercury. When the glass cylinder was tilted, the mercury blob would move freely down the glass tube and envelop the two exposed wires, essentially connecting them. It was that connection which would close the circuit and set off the bomb.

'Watch how I put it together,' said Terry as he went to work with deft fingers. He hooked the wires up between the battery, the detonator and the mercury tilt. As Terry lifted the device off the ground with two steady hands, Michael noticed the detonator hanging over the side.

'Are you going to stick the detonator into the explosive?' asked Michael.

'No, not yet. We leave that to last. The mercury tilt is too sensitive.'

The mercury tilt was the IRA bomb-maker's favourite little toy. A bomb rigged up to a tilt was extremely difficult to dismantle. As the British Army, to their dismay, had discovered. Bombs hooked up to these tricky devices were the leading cause of death among ATs in Northern Ireland.

But they caused problems for the IRA, too. In the past five months, three bomb-makers had blown themselves up while planting their bombs. The men were either too impatient, too careless, or too arrogant.

Whatever the cause of their demise, Terry would not end up the same way as those foolhardy men. He treated his mercury tilts with care. He always remained intensely focused when handling one and always took his own sweet time.

'We're going to put it up there,' said Terry, nodding to the toilet cistern which was high on the wall. The old-fashioned type, a string dangling down with a mock ivory handle at the end of it. 'I need you to take the top off the cistern.'

Michael stepped onto the toilet seat, removed the ceramic lid and stepped back down onto the floor. Terry gently picked up the device and stepped onto the toilet seat. He slowly lifted his arms and placed the device inside the cistern, making sure that one end of the bomb was resting on the mechanical flushing system. Once the device was wedged firmly in place, Terry placed the mercury tilt at an angle so the silvery liquid metal was separated from the two exposed wires inside the tube. He looked the device over with eagle eyes, checking for anything that might be out of place. Once he was convinced everything was in order, he held the detonator between thumb and forefinger and gently pushed the metal rod into the plastic explosive.

He pulled his hand away slowly and released the air he'd been holding in his lungs. 'Phew.'

Michael was still holding the ceramic lid. 'What do I do with this?'

'Give it to me.' Michael handed over the lid and Terry placed it back where it belonged, ever so carefully.

'What now?' asked Michael.

'We wait for someone to come in for a piss. And when they flush, the tilt will move and then…boom.'

* * *

Mrs B was sixty-five years old and fifty pounds heavier than she should be, her waist fattened by cream cakes. The old woman's knees were bad, burdened by the years of excess weight. They didn't like going up and down the stairs anymore. Too painful. How wonderful it would be to be nineteen again. Dancing and frolicking. A youthful body and agile limbs. How the young men had loved her back then.

But although Mrs B was rickety on the outside, she had a sharp mind on the inside. She'd caught the two men sneaking in with Tammy out of the corner of her eye. That whore was up to no good again. She was sure of it.

There was no love lost between Mrs B and Tammy. The old woman was a staunch Protestant. And she held a deep mistrust of anybody of the Roman faith. Like Tammy. Who in the mind of Mrs B was a light-fingered, filthy, lying Fenian. They'd had fights in the past. Only last week, money had disappeared from Mrs B's purse. She'd accused Tammy of having something to do with it. That set the younger woman off. She'd hurled abuse at Mrs B, calling her a nosey cow. A wrinkly old bitch. The two of them had to be pulled apart by the barman, clumps of hair in each other's fist.

There's something fishy about this, thought Mrs B. The disco was popular among young soldiers. Maybe she should call her nephew. He was serving in the RUC. Yes. She'd do that. Just in case. Because you never knew with these Catholic degenerates. For all Mrs B knew, they could be IRA men planting a bomb.

TWENTY-SIX

The RUC police car pulled up outside the Droppin' Well. Docherty watched in dread as the four coppers stepped out onto the road, placed their hats neatly on their heads and walked up to the main entrance. A short chubby policeman, with a ruddy complexion, led the way. He tapped his knuckles on the heavy wooden entrance. A moment later, the door was opened by Mrs B. The officers casually walked inside.

The men had only been out of sight for a minute when gunfire pierced the still air. Three shots in quick succession. Fuck. This isn't happening. Get out of there, boys. Four more rounds were fired before three policemen bundled out of the disco, dragging a fourth comrade along the ground. He'd been shot in the chest.

The short chubby officer shouted into his walkie-talkie. Docherty couldn't quite make out what was being said. But he knew it was time to get out of there. It wouldn't be long before back-up would arrive from the army. They'd start scouring the area for accomplices.

He switched on the engine of his motor, quietly slipped out of the carpark and pulled onto the main road. He looked in his rear-view mirror to see if he'd been spotted. The policemen hadn't noticed him. They were too busy ripping the clothes off their bleeding comrade. *He's dead*, thought Docherty as he watched blood drain from the listless body onto the pavement.

* * *

Michael was breathing heavily, scouring the room for a way out. He noticed a small narrow window at the top of the far wall. But he wouldn't be able to fit through that. Besides, the police had probably surrounded the building by now.

He looked down at Terry. He was dead. Glazed eyes staring without seeing. A bullet had caught him in the side of his face. Blood was seeping out of the wound, leaving a large red puddle around his head. Strangely, it reminded Michael of church. Of the stained-glass windows that featured saints with a circular nimbus around their heads. But Terry was no saint. That was for sure.

The younger Coyle checked his pistol. He was out of ammunition.

'Come out with your hands up,' a man with an English accent shouted from outside. The army had arrived. There was no way out. Better surrender to the Brits than the RUC. Less likely to get shot.

Michael opened the toilet door and threw his pistol out into the corridor. 'I'm coming out. Don't shoot me.' The IRA man edged out of the toilet with his hands in the air. A young private aimed his SLR at Michael's face while another rushed in, grabbed his arms and threw him to the ground.

'Don't fucking move, you Irish bastard, or you'll get a bullet.'

* * *

At 5 p.m., the Sergeants' Mess was bustling. Mostly with men who had returned from the day shift. Sergeants, staff sergeants and warrant officers – from four different regiments – were walking up and down a long counter piling their plates with heart-clogging food.

Large stainless-steel containers served up pork sausages, fried chicken, beef burgers, chips, baked beans and some mushy green stuff that was supposed to pass as vegetables. There was a separate station manned by a chef in a white tunic, a tall catering hat atop his head. Shiny corporal stripes, forged from the same stainless steel as the food containers, were pinned to the sides of his sleeves. If a soldier wanted a fried egg, poached egg or an omelette, he would cook it up.

Two huge stainless-steel urns, one filled with tea, the other with coffee, were placed on a separate table with mugs and cups stacked three-feet high by the side.

The army had a tight budget on many things: equipment, transport, apparel. But food wasn't one of them. Napoleon Bonaparte, more than one hundred and fifty years earlier, had said, *An army marches on its stomach*. That was an ideology the British Army had stolen from the French during the Napoleonic wars and had lived by the maxim ever since. A hungry soldier resents the fight. A satiated soldier relishes it. Thomson pushed open the swinging doors at the entrance to the mess and walked in with Kersey and Cooper. It was unusual for them to have dinner in the mess. They were normally out on a job – and condemned to an egg mayonnaise or ham and cheese sandwich dinner. But today there was a respite and the opportunity to get some decent grub in their stomachs.

Thomson went for his usual. Chicken, chips and green stuff. His two compatriots piled their plates higher, food falling off their plates as they made a beeline for the table that Thomson had managed to secure.

'You can get seconds,' said Thomson.

'I know,' said Kersey. 'Got to finish this first.'

Cooper laughed. 'This is better than the rubbish they serve out in the field. So better stuff ourselves in here than starve out there.'

'I'm with you,' said Thomson.

Jock Henderson walked into the mess, stood near the entrance and looked around.

'Your number two's here, Dave,' said Kersey.

'Better finish this off quick.' Thomson scoffed what was left on his plate, washed it down with some hot milky tea and stood up. 'See you later.' Cooper and Kersey, their mouths full, nodded a goodbye. Thomson walked stridently toward Jock.

'We've been called out to Ballykelly,' said Jock. 'The IRA have planted a bomb in a disco.'

'That's not nice.'

'They've caught one of the bombers.'

TWENTY-SEVEN

Before Thomson could climb out of the Land Rover, the officer was upon him with white tombstone teeth framed within a smile. 'Good to see you again, Felix,' said Major Scunthorpe.

Thomson saluted as he planted his feet on the tarmac. Who the hell is this? He'd seen so many officers from so many different regiments he couldn't distinguish one from the other anymore.

'Blown up any telegraph poles recently?'

Ah, that's who he was. The cheery officer from Limavady. 'Afternoon, Sir. Good to see you again.'

'The lads still talk about that day.'

'I'm sure they do,' replied Thomson with a nervous grin. 'What's going on here?'

'They planted a bomb in the toilets. Got caught red-handed by the RUC. One of the policemen was shot. He died on the way to hospital. The RUC killed one of theirs. The other one held out for a while. Surrendered when we showed up.'

'Smart thing to do.'

'Wouldn't be alive now if he'd surrendered to the RUC. They're mad as hell. They were pissed off when we turned up.'

'What do we know about the bomb?' asked Thomson, cutting to the chase.

'Not a lot. We believe they planted it in the men's toilet.'

'How long ago?'

'Well, we've had in him cuffs for three hours.'

No need for a soak, thought Thomson.

'One more thing,' said the major. 'Two men from Special Branch showed up just before you did.' The major motioned toward a Saracen with his head. Two men in plain clothes were standing outside it. One slim and tall with fiery ginger hair. The other medium in height and a larger than average waistline. He was like every other plain clothes copper Thomson had met. Too much time spent behind the wheel during the day and too much time spent behind the bar at night.

'What do they want?' asked Thomson.

'Their pound's worth,' replied the major. 'Shall we have a chat?'

Scunthorpe walked the AT over to the Saracen where Thomson introduced himself. 'Staff Sergeant Thomson. EOD.'

The man with the orange hair stuck his hand out. Thomson took it. 'Detective Inspector McGuigan – Special Branch.' The overweight copper nodded but stayed back like a stray dog that had been kicked once too often.

'Have you interviewed the suspect?'

'Not yet.' McGuigan tilted his head toward the Droppin' Well. 'There's still a bomb in there. Thought you might want to interview him first.'

'Thanks for the courtesy,' said Thomson.

'Think nothing of it.'

Thomson opened the door of the Saracen and peered inside. It was dark and took a while for his eyes to adjust. Sitting on the left was the IRA prisoner, wedged in between two soldiers. On the right was an

RUC sergeant glaring at the IRA man with intense hatred. Thomson climbed in and took a seat next to the RUC sergeant. Major Scunthorpe climbed in by his side and McGuigan squeezed in next to him. The air was thick and stuffy. And the new contingent of people, crammed in shoulder to shoulder, made it worse.

'What's your name?' Michael remained silent. 'Did you plant the bomb? Tell me about it.'

At that moment, a switch was flipped inside the IRA man's head. Michael was no longer Michael. The normally kind and polite young man had taken on the persona of an obdurate victim. A freedom fighter. Political prisoner. A wronged native of a land unjustly confiscated. 'It's going to blow you all the way to fucking Hell.' It was the kind of fiery rage that would be expected of an IRA captive. Conduct, in the face of the enemy, that would be applauded by Jimmy Brett and his brother Curly.

The RUC sergeant next to Thomson sprung to his feet, baton in hand, and unleashed a vicious blow to the side of the IRA man's head. A sickening thud echoed throughout the small chamber. 'You'll be the one going to Hell, you bastard.' Blood gushed out of a deep gash in Michael's head and streamed, like the delta of a river, down the side of his face. The pain was excruciating. Michael wanted to scream. But he was too proud to let these bastards know they'd hurt him.

The soldiers in the Saracen, although somewhat shocked, didn't protest at the sergeant's assault. Deep inside, they were glad he did it. The policeman turned to Thomson. 'Ask him again.'

'What type of bomb is it?' asked Thomson.

'Plastic.'

'Booby trap?'

'Aye. A nasty little fucker.'

'A tilt?'

'Could be.' Michael laughed. Taunting Thomson. Sewing doubt in the bomb man's mind.

'Where is it?'

'I'm not going to fucking tell you that,' said Michael, a smile breaking across his face. He stared into the RUC sergeant's eyes. 'Go on, hit me again.'

* * *

Thomson kept his eyes fixed on the closed-circuit TV as Jock Henderson handled the control box and navigated the wheelbarrow through the corridors of the night club. 'That's where they were caught,' said Thomson as the toilets came into view. The double swinging doors had been wedged open to allow the wheelbarrow to drive through.

The wheelbarrow was a primitive robot that had been brought into service a year earlier after a spate of ATs had been killed in a period of just two months. The inventor of the contraption, a colonel who had a passion for tinkering with electronics and making mechanical toys, had been tasked with finding a way to help ATs dispose of bombs remotely. An idea had jumped into the colonel's mind while mowing his lawn. He'd excitedly rushed off to a local garden centre with the intention of buying a gutted lawnmower. The sales manager of the place had struck up a conversation with the colonel and, after learning the purpose of the lawnmower, suggested that the chassis of an electrically powered wheelbarrow might be more suitable. The colonel thought it was ideal and bought one on the spot. The name wheelbarrow stuck, but it was anything but a wheelbarrow. The robot had the proportions of a giant cigarette packet. Five-feet long, three-feet wide and six inches deep. It had three wheels on each side set within mini tracks, which gave it the appearance of a miniature tank without a turret. A six-foot-long aluminium arm was attached on top. The arm had a joint halfway up, which meant it could bend and be pointed in almost any direction. The ATs attached cameras, shotguns and all sorts of other devices to the arm. Anything that would help them get the job done.

But the wheelbarrow had its limitations. The houses in Derry, especially in the old town which the IRA targeted regularly, were old. The doorways were too narrow and the wheelbarrow was too wide to get through them.

Luckily, the Droppin' Well was different. It was a modern, one-story building, which had been purpose-built as a place of entertainment. The front door was wide. The corridors were wide and the doors to the toilet were wide – which was good for business. Soldiers could rush in, have a piss and get back to buying and gulping beer.

Jock drove the wheelbarrow into the middle of the room, bumping into Terry's listless body. 'Watch it, Jock,' said Thomson.

'He's dead, boss,' replied Jock.

'I know. But nevertheless.' Jock pivoted the wheelbarrow until the camera landed on the row of cubicles. Muddy footprints were concentrated around the first one, a tell-tale sign that this is where the IRA men had done their work. 'Can you see it, Jock?'

'Doesn't seem to be anything on the floor.'

'Crane the camera up.' Jock tilted the camera up toward the cistern. The ceramic lid was slightly lopsided. Something inside was stopping it from being closed tightly. 'That's it,' said Thomson.

'That's not good, boss,' said Jock. The Scotsman didn't have to explain. Thomson knew the problem. He couldn't use a shotgun. The shot wouldn't penetrate the ceramic. And the only way to use a pigstick, or a hook and line, would be to remove the ceramic lid. That was dangerous. It could be booby-trapped.

A knot tied itself in Thomson's stomach. He was used to being in control. But this was one of those rare times when he wasn't. Fate was the puppet master here. The decider between life and death. Could this be the one that gets him? Jean flashed into his mind. He didn't want to leave her just yet.

'Let's have another chat with the prisoner.'

* * *

Thomson was sitting across from Michael in the small confines of the Saracen. It was the same cast. Thomson felt a sense of déjà vu. 'Tell me about the bomb.'

'I'm not telling you a thing,' replied the IRA man. 'I'm a political prisoner and I have the right to remain silent.'

'Is the lid booby-trapped?'

'I'm not telling you a thing.'

'Is there a mercury tilt?'

'I'm not telling you a thing.'

The RUC sergeant sitting next to Thomson was getting impatient. He'd had enough of the IRA man's bullshit. 'Why don't you get him to do it?'

Thomson laughed. Michael laughed too. The idea was ridiculous.

After a long, uncomfortable pause, McGuigan leant into Thomson. 'Can I have a word with you and the major outside?' The three men shuffled out of the Saracen and formed a huddle twenty yards from the armoured vehicle.

'What's this about?' asked Scunthorpe.

'I think that copper's got a point,' replied McGuigan. 'I'd get the little bastard to do it.'

'Do what?' asked Scunthorpe.

'Dispose the bomb,' said McGuigan.

'You can't be serious,' said Thomson.

'I'm deadly serious,' said McGuigan. 'Put some explosive around his neck and send him in. And don't let the bastard out until he's done the job. If he gets blown up, we'll cover for you.'

Thomson looked at Major Scunthorpe. He was the superior. The man with authority. He wouldn't go along with it, surely.

'How dangerous is the situation, Felix?' asked Scunthorpe.

'Complicated,' replied Thomson. 'We can't use the equipment, so I have to go in and use my hands.'

'Can you neutralise it with your hands?' asked Scunthorpe.

'If it's a mercury tilt, it will be difficult.'

The major felt for Thomson. It was an impossible situation. The AT had no choice but go in and do the job the army expected of him. Even if that meant his life was on the line. Scunthorpe had a choice to make. Did he play it by the book? Or did he rip out a couple pages and toss them in the wind?

'Do what you need to do, Felix?'

Thomson wasn't expecting those words to come out of the major's mouth. Was an officer of the British Army giving him the green light to do something illegal? Something that could get them all locked up in the stockade? And even though Thomson had been given permission to commit a crime, why would he do it? He had lived by the book all his life. Abiding by the rules was in his DNA. Ingrained in his psyche. Breaking them was inconceivable.

'I can't put a detonating cord around a man's neck.'

'What choice have you got?' said McGuigan.

'We don't do stuff like that in the British Army.'

McGuigan laughed. 'You should spend a week with Military Intelligence.'

The Special Branch man edged closer to Scunthorpe and murmured in his ear. 'Can you give us a moment, Sir?'

Scunthorpe searched Thomson's face for a green light to leave. Thomson gave it with a nod. 'I'll be over by the Saracen,' said the major as he casually walked back to the armoured vehicle.

'Are you religious?' asked McGuigan.

'No. I'm not,' replied Thomson.

'Do you believe in an afterlife?'

'Once you're gone, you're gone.'

'That's where you and me are different. I'm religious. I believe in God and I believe in Heaven. So I don't worry too much about dying. I know I'll be going to a better place. But if I was a nonbeliever, I'd be thinking to myself, shit, it might be all over.'

'I don't think about it that way.'

'But here's the thing, Dave. If I was handed a break like you're being handed now, I'd take it as a sign. As an intervention from the big man himself. But even if you don't believe in that kind of thing, you'd be a fucking idiot to pass up the opportunity to save your own skin.'

McGuigan stared into Thomson's eyes like a hypnotist. Willing the army man to bend to his way of thinking. And it was working. The seed had been planted in the bomb man's head. And it was sprouting.

Jean's face filled Thomson's mind. He had a choice to make. Do right by the rules or do right by her. If he played it by the book, he might never see her again. It was an unpleasant thought and, at that moment, Thomson's heart was weighed down by dread. No. It wasn't an option. He was going to get back to his wife and kids. That was his mission. And a little runt with a contempt for life wasn't going to get in the way of it. Thomson needed to step up. Be dominant. Call the shots. Break the rules.

Putting a detonating cord around a terrorist's neck was a good idea, thought Thomson. What harm could come of it? It wasn't as if he'd actually blow the guy's head off. It was just a bluff. And anyhow, what was the alternative? Death? Anything would be better than that. A few years in prison trumped an eternity six feet under.

'Okay,' said Thomson. 'Let's do it.'

* * *

The RUC sergeant spied the detonating cord in Thomson's hand. An indebted grin blossomed across his face. It was like winning a raffle. 'Let's fucking do it.'

'You can't fucking scare me,' said Michael.

'Hold him down,' ordered Scunthorpe. The two soldiers on either side of Michael grabbed his arms as Thomson placed the detonating cord around his neck.

'Fuck off, you bastards!' screamed Michael as he struggled to break free.

'I wouldn't struggle like that if I were you,' said Thomson. 'If that detonating cord goes off, you'll lose your head.'

'You can't do this.'

Thomson held up the trigger in his right hand, his thumb on the switch. 'I think you'll find I can.'

* * *

Michael stood on the toilet seat, lifted the ceramic lid off the cistern and threw it carelessly to the floor. The lid shattered, the sound reverberating throughout the nightclub.

'What's going on in there?' shouted Thomson from the corridor.

Michael didn't reply. He slowly reached for the detonator and gently pulled it out of the plastic explosives, neutering the bomb. He then placed both his hands inside the cistern, gently pulled out the plastic-covered device, stepped slowly off the toilet seat and placed the device on the ground. The detonating cord around his neck was irritating his skin. He gave his neck a good scratch. 'Fucking bastards,' he mumbled to himself as he pulled a cutter from his top pocket and went to work on the wires. He was done in less than a minute, the mercury tilt ripped from the heart of the would-be mass murderer. 'I'm done.'

Thomson peered into the room and, seeing the mercury tilt on the floor, slinked inside. 'Well done. If you weren't a terrorist, you'd make a good AT.'

'Fuck you,' replied Michael.

Thomson pulled the detonating cord from Michael's neck and disarmed it. 'You can leave.'

Michael stood up and walked past Thomson into the corridor. Ninety-Nine and his men, rifles pointed, were waiting to take him into custody.

Thomson smiled to himself. He was experiencing one of those rare moments in life of utter joy. Making an IRA man dispose his own bomb had been deeply gratifying. This was the first time Thomson had been able to put a face to a bomb. Which had made it seem less harmful for some reason. It was a ridiculous thought and Thomson pushed it out of his mind.

The staff sergeant picked the mercury tilt off the floor and studied the glass cylinder. It looked harmless between his fingers. But Thomson knew how lethal this little piece of glass could be. This was the culprit of many a death.

He shifted his eyes to the bomb. The IRA man had done a good job. But he wasn't taking any chances. He stood up, aimed a pigstick at the device and let it off. The high-powered jet of water smashed into the package, tearing it to pieces, decapitating the device into a useless mess.

* * *

Thomson sucked hard on his cigarette and watched as Jock packed up the last of the kit, placing it neatly it in the back of the Land Rover.

The operation was winding down. The RUC had already left with their IRA prisoner and the last remaining soldiers from the Duke of Wellington regiment were climbing into the back of their troop carrier.

A flash of orange hair caught Thomson's eye. The Special Branch man was making a beeline toward him. 'Detective Inspector McGuigan,' said Thomson.

'Call me Jonny,' said the Branch man.

'Jonny! I'm Dave.'

'It's been a good day, Dave.'

'A good day is sitting on a beach in Spain eating an ice cream.'

'Yes, that would be a good day too.' Thomson pulled out a packet of cigarettes from his pocket and offered one to McGuigan. 'No, thanks. They'll kill you. More dangerous than the IRA those things.'

Thomson laughed. 'Not sure I agree with that.'

'You got family, Dave?'

'Yes. A boy and a girl.'

McGuigan pulled out his wallet and flipped it open. Inside was a photograph of his wife and two girls. 'Five and three.'

'Beautiful,' Thomson pulled out his wallet and showed McGuigan a picture of Jean and the kids. 'Nine and five.'

'Good-looking family, Dave.'

'Thank you.'

'You're doing a great service for us all over here. Every bomb you dismantle saves lives.' McGuigan held up his wallet so Thomson could see the photograph clearly. 'Lives like these. Wives, sons and daughters.'

'Just doing my job, Jonny.'

'This is a country of contradictions, Dave. We're all united by our Irish heritage. But we're divided by our religious differences. Brothers and enemies all at once.'

'Tell you the truth, Jonny. I don't get it. This thing between the Catholics and the Protestants.'

'Sometimes, I don't either. All I can tell you is religion is taken a lot more seriously over here than on the mainland. We don't like the Catholics and they don't like us. Maybe that's wrong, Dave. But the hatred is fed to us from when we're wee babies. On both sides. By the time you're ten years old, you have no choice but to hate. Your brain's wired that way.'

'Sad.'

'It is what it is. But until we can find a way to live together, we've got to keep the terrorist bastards on a leash.'

'On a leash? There's an old saying my old man used to tell me. The underdog bites at the testicles.'

'Yeah. Until you clobber it on the head with a big fucking stick.'

'Seems to me, they've got a big stick too.'

'We'll see.' McGuigan stood up and held out his hand. Thomson took it. 'You did a good job today.'

'Let's just hope it doesn't come back to bite us on the bum.'

'He'll tell his lawyer.'

'Should I expect a call?'

'I've seen worse things buried, Dave. Don't worry. We'll take care of it. It's the word of one man from the wrong side of the tracks against many from the right side.'

'I hope you're right.'

'You know, Dave. You're a lucky man. I can see it in your face.'

'I'm not superstitious.'

The detective inspector slapped Thomson on the arm. 'And you don't believe in God. But maybe God believes in you.'

TWENTY-EIGHT

What a fuck-up. And on his watch. Who would believe it? Docherty couldn't contain the flood of emotions streaming through his veins: frustration, anger and disappointment bubbling up into a toxic stew.

The IRA man was driving nervously along Altaghaderry Road. His hands shaking. He put a stop to that by tightening his grip on the steering wheel. Just before Creggan, he turned left onto a muddy track and drove onto half an acre of wasteland surrounded by sad trees and scruffy scrub.

Liam O'Mahoney was sitting patiently behind the steering wheel of his Vauxhall Victor, his sharp eyes following Docherty's car as it meandered around the empty plot. Where are the other two? Something's not right.

Docherty pulled up ten yards away, jumped out of the driver's seat and opened the boot of his car. A canister of petrol was tucked away in the corner. Docherty grabbed it and poured the flammable liquid over the front and back seats. The thick fumes from the petrol quickly clogged the air, seeping into Docherty's throat and biting it. The IRA man coughed violently before ripping off his clothes, including his shoes and socks, rendering himself naked. He shovelled the pile of clothes up with both arms and threw them into the back of the car. A shiver shot down Docherty's spine as a sudden gust of icy wind flayed his naked body.

O'Mahoney honked his horn. That annoyed Docherty. There was no need. He was working quickly and didn't appreciate the impatience. The impudence. The IRA strongman walked casually over to the Vauxhall, bare feet sploshing in the mud, and opened the front door on the passenger side. A Woolworth's carrier bag, filled with spare clothes, was plonked upright on the seat. Docherty quickly dressed himself, jumped in the car and slammed the door shut. 'Let's get out of here.'

O'Mahoney started the engine and pulled forward slowly until he was parallel with the petrol-doused Austin Allegro. He wound down his window, lit a match and flicked it at the car. A ball of flames enveloped the interior, the leather seats crackling under the intense heat. Within ten minutes, any evidence of bomb-making, bomb-ferrying and bomb-handling would be burnt to a crisp. Every fingerprint melted and vanquished. Nothing for the army forensics team to work with. No one to be fingered.

'Where are the others?' asked O'Mahoney.

'They got caught,' replied Docherty bluntly.

O'Mahoney clenched his jaw and shook his head. Jimmy Brett wasn't going to be happy.

* * *

Liam O'Mahoney parked the car in front of the designated safe house. A small farm next to the Irish border. Docherty was the first to get out of the car, his face tight with anxiety. He knocked twice on the front door. Heavy bolts from within banged and clanged. A moment later, the door opened as far as the thick safety chain would let it and Barry Behan eyed the two men up and down.

'Are they here?' asked Docherty.

Behan uncoupled the chain and let the two men in. Jimmy Brett and Curly Coyle were sitting at a heavy wooden dining table. A pot of tea was resting in the centre, steam rising out of its spout.

'It's all over the fucking news,' said Brett leaning forward, elbows on the table and hands clasped together as if he were in prayer. Docherty and O'Mahoney planted themselves on wooden chairs opposite the two-man inquisition.

'We were taken by surprise. Four coppers came out of nowhere,' said Docherty.

Brett lit up a cigarette. 'I've got to tell you, Steve, it's made us look like fools.'

'It was just bad luck,' said Docherty defiantly. The catastrophe reflected poorly on the strongman. But Docherty wasn't going to apologise. It wasn't the first time a fuck-up had happened and it wouldn't be the last. That was the nature of the game.

Brett stubbed out his cigarette. Slowly. Calmly. As if the world was on pause just for him. 'They killed Terry.'

Docherty was taken by surprise. After a lengthy pause he said, 'That's shit.'

O'Mahoney was smiling inside. It wasn't often you saw Steve Docherty cowering like a perpetually beaten dog.

'What about Michael?' asked Docherty.

'They bagged him,' said Curly.

'It gets worse,' said Brett. 'Our lawyers have been to see him. One hell of a story he told them.'

'And what would that be?'

'A bomb man, a British fucking soldier, put a detonating cord around his neck and threatened to blow his head off.'

Docherty folded his arms and remained tight-lipped.

'They stepped over the line,' continued Brett. 'And it doesn't sit well with me. What they did to Michael. That's below the belt in any war, let alone this one. They might as well have taken a shit on my mother's grave.'

'We're not happy,' said Curly, a flash of anger sweeping over his face just for a fraction of a second. It was an unusual lapse for the chief bomb-maker. He was normally composed. Emotionless and still. But this was different. It was personal. It was his brother who had been disrespected. His family's honour that had been polluted.

The room remained silent. Brett stubbed out a half-smoked cigarette and immediately lit up another one. His mind was distracted. The commander got up from his chair and paced the room.

'What do you want us to do?' asked O'Mahoney, breaking his silence for the first time.

'I want you to find the man and I want him killed,' said Brett.

TWENTY-NINE

The pain in her head came in pulsating waves as if set to a metronome. Dorothy dropped three aspirin into a glass of water, let them fizz for a while and threw the concoction down her neck.

Her husband had gone out to the pub with his cronies the night before. So she had spent the night at home watching TV and drinking cheap whiskey, wallowing in her loneliness and self-pity.

Dorothy glanced at her watch. She was running late for work.

She slipped out the door and rushed toward the bus stop. But before she could get there, a blue Vauxhall Victor pulled up beside her. She recognised the car. What the fuck was he doing here? Dorothy was angry. Why the fuck was this man harassing her so early in the morning? She was tempted to ignore the vehicle and walk the other way. But that wouldn't be a wise thing to do. He'd beat her up for that. Badly. Dorothy looked around nervously to see if anyone she knew was looking. Nobody. She opened the door and climbed in.

O'Mahoney put his foot on the accelerator and the car glided along the half-empty road. He looked across at a very agitated Dorothy. 'How you doing?'

'I was doing fine until you turned up,' replied Dorothy with an unusual calmness, her eyes firmly fixed on the road. But the rage inside her couldn't be kept at bay. She swung her head to face O'Mahoney. 'What were you thinking? Someone could have spotted me.'

'You worry too much, Dorothy.'

'You're going to fuck my life up.'

'I'm doing no such thing. You fucked your own life up the day you decided to cheat on your husband.' O'Mahoney took great pleasure in reminding Dorothy of her infidelity. She had been an easy target. Just one of a thousand pubic scalps hanging from his belt. A woman looking for love in the arms of a tall, handsome stranger.

The mission was originally focused on Robert Campbell. The IRA had been keeping tabs on him for a while. Waiting for the right moment to ambush him. Put a bullet in his head. Rid the Catholic community of one more Protestant agitator. But it didn't take long for them to realise his wife Dorothy worked at Ebrington Barracks. For a brigadier of all people. The mission changed. Dorothy became the target. And Liam O'Mahoney was given the task of roping her in.

It was almost a year ago since they'd met in a trendy pub near the Diamond. Dorothy was enjoying herself at a table with a bunch of rowdy female friends. O'Mahoney stood at the bar trying to make eye contact with her whenever he could.

Dorothy had noticed him. He was a good-looking man. Brown hair, high cheekbones, full lips and turquoise-blue eyes.

The girls at the table had run out of alcohol and Dorothy volunteered to get the next round. She made her way to the end of the bar where O'Mahoney stood, pretended not to see him and ordered five vodka cranberries.

It was easy for O'Mahoney to strike up a conversation. 'Looks like you're having a good time.'

'What's it got to do with you?' replied Dorothy.

'Oh, I'm sorry. I don't mean to stick my nose in.'

'Haven't seen you here before.'

'No, I've been away for a while.'

'Oh, aye.'

'London.'

'And what did you do there?'

'A very boring job.'

'How boring?'

'I'm an accountant.'

Dorothy was impressed. Most of the men in the bar were labourers with weathered faces and calloused hands. 'What brings you to Londonderry?'

'My ma is getting old. You know, want to be here for her.'

'Have you brought the wife with you too?'

O'Mahoney laughed and held up his ring-less wedding finger. 'Still looking for Mrs Right.'

'And you think you can find her in this dump?'

'Definitely,' said O'Mahoney with bright, lustful eyes.

Dorothy smiled. 'I'm married.'

'I don't care. You're the most beautiful woman I've ever seen.' Dorothy's pulse started to race. Just the presence of this man made her wet. She wanted to wrap her arms around him there and then. Devour his lips with hers.

'Why don't we get out of here?' said O'Mahoney.

'I'm with friends.'

'Tell them you're not feeling well. I'll wait outside.'

Don't do anything stupid, Dorothy said to herself. But it was no use. Her heart was overpowering her head. Primal passion swelling up inside her. Dorothy couldn't contain the urge. Emotion, passion and excitement overwhelmed her rational inclinations. A switch inside her flipped. Her sexual instinct had won. 'Give me fifteen minutes.' Dorothy carried the drinks back to the table while O'Mahoney slipped outside.

Half of an hour later, Dorothy was walking through the front door of O'Mahoney's flat. Kissing, groping, pulling off clothes. 'Slow down,' said O'Mahoney. 'Let's have a drink first.' He poured Dorothy a vodka spiked with Flurazepam, watched her sink it in one and led her into the bedroom. A moment later they were both naked and on the bed.

O'Mahoney slipped inside her. Dorothy groaned as he started to thrust. Slowly at first but gradually faster and harder. Dorothy's back arched as she reached a climax. But her orgasm was interrupted by a series of blinding flashes. What the fuck is that? Is someone else in the room? Are they taking photographs?

There was nothing she could do. She lost control of her mind and her body – and a moment later, passed out.

O'Mahoney had used those photographs as leverage ever since. And Dorothy, out of fear of her husband seeing them, conformed to every request that was made of her.

'What do you want?' muttered Dorothy.

'I've got an important job for you.'

'And what would that be?'

'I need you to find someone for me. One of those bomb disposal men. Tall. Good-looking. Blue eyes.'

She knew immediately who he was talking about.

* * *

Dorothy stood at the camp gate with a large handbag slung over her shoulder. She flashed her ID and handed her bag over to the guard for inspection. The young private flashed a grin. 'Morning,' he said as he stole a quick glance at Dorothy's large bosom.

'Morning,' replied Dorothy, who had noticed his roving eyes. Even though she was past her prime, she was still attractive. And she knew it. 'How are you today?' she said with a teasing smile.

'Good. And you?'

'Fine. Just wish we had nicer weather.'

'Tell me about it,' replied the soldier. He rummaged through the handbag casually as he did every day. He was well aware that she was the brigadier's secretary. *Lucky bastard,* he thought to himself. Wonder if he's poking her on the side. The private handed the bag back to Dorothy. 'Here you go.'

Dorothy walked through the camp gates and strolled to the main building. By the time she had clambered to the top floor, she was out of breath. Tiny beads of perspiration had formed on her forehead. Her hand reached into her bag and pulled out a handkerchief. She gently tapped her brow with the soft cotton and headed for her desk.

Dorothy usually arrived half an hour earlier than her boss. This gave her time to get the place organised. First, she placed a copy of the *Belfast Telegraph* on the brigadier's desk. Then she sorted the mail and memoranda and placed anything addressed to MacIntyre in his in-tray. After that she put the kettle on and popped three teabags in the teapot. MacIntyre liked to get his cuppa as soon as he walked through the door. Finally, she arranged her tasks in order of importance. The urgent reports took priority, followed by the administrative chores.

The curvaceous secretary enjoyed her job and she liked working for MacIntyre. He was a gentleman. A rare thing in the hardened city of Londonderry where misogyny and chauvinism were accepted as a normal way for a man to behave.

Dorothy slipped a sheet of paper into the typewriter and hit the keys with the tips of her fingers. It was the first report of the day. There would be many more before she packed up and headed home.

MacIntyre walked through the door. 'Morning, Dorothy.'

'Morning, Sir,' replied Dorothy as she got out of her seat, picked up the kettle and poured hot water into the teapot. MacIntyre planted himself behind his desk and sifted through his mail, ripping open envelopes with his paper knife. Dorothy handed him a cup of tea on its saucer, sugar already added. 'Here you go, Sir.'

'Thank you, Dorothy.'

The phone on MacIntyre's desk came alive. The brigadier picked up the receiver. 'Hello.' Dorothy could hear the faint garble of someone on the other end speaking. Lisburn was a word she picked out amid the incessant jumble. 'I can be there in an hour.' MacIntyre replaced the receiver, picked up his cup of tea and took a sip.

'Shall I call your driver, Sir?' asked Dorothy.

'Yes, please. Tell him to be downstairs in ten minutes. I want to enjoy this lovely cup of tea you've made me.'

'Would you like some biscuits to go with that?'

'Now you're spoiling me.'

Dorothy smiled, walked back to her desk and picked up the receiver of her phone. 'The brigadier needs his driver. Ten minutes.' A moment later, she returned with two digestive biscuits on a small plate.

'Thank you, Dorothy,' said the brigadier as he picked up that morning's copy of the *Belfast Telegraph* and studied the front page.

Dorothy made her way back to her desk and continued typing up the report. She'd only gotten halfway through the first page when MacIntyre wandered out of his office and into her room. 'I'll be back in the afternoon, Dorothy.'

'Okay, Sir. Have a good trip.' Dorothy watched the brigadier walk out onto the stairwell and listened to him scampering down the four flights of stairs. Once the sound of his footsteps became inaudible, she made her way to the window. She witnessed the brigadier climb into the passenger seat of a Land Rover that, moments later, roared to life and drove off, a Saracen following closely behind.

Dorothy reached into her handbag and pulled out a packet of cigarettes. Her hand was shaking as she lit up. The cigarette calmed her nerves. Now or never. She placed her cigarette in an ashtray and poked her head out into the stairwell. She looked left and right. The fourth floor was quiet. Just the faint sound of keys clanging as secretaries typed up report after report inside their tiny, battery-style offices.

Dorothy sidled back into her room and closed the door behind her. She picked up her handbag, emptied its contents onto her desk and reached inside, yanking out a false bottom. A Yashica TL Electro camera was hiding underneath. She grabbed it and walked into MacIntyre's office. She opened the top drawer of his filing cabinet and flicked through the brown files. Quickly. Skilfully.

The flicking stopped. There it was. The file she was looking for. She plucked it out and placed it on MacIntyre's heavy desk. Staff Sergeant Thomson's photograph stared up at her. Dorothy pointed her camera at the file, pulled the lens into focus and pressed the button that released the shutter. Her hands were trembling ever so slightly. So she took two more shots just to be sure she'd captured a sharp picture.

The secretary closed the file and put it back in its place in the filing cabinet. I can't believe I'm doing this. I must be mad. She rushed back into her room, put the Yashica in her bag and covered it with the false bottom. Her heart was racing as she placed all the contents back on top.

Done. Dorothy let out a huge sigh of relief. She picked up her smouldering cigarette from the ashtray. Her fingers were trembling more vigorously now. She took a long drag and slid back into her seat. She wasn't very good at this.

A young secretary from the adjutant's office walked in and placed a sheet of paper into Dorothy's in-tray. 'Morning, Dorothy.'

'Morning, Josephine,' replied Dorothy. She eyed the single sheet of paper. It was titled: 321 EOD duty roster.

THIRTY

Byrne put a pint of Guinness on the table in front of O'Mahoney. 'Thank you, landlord,' said O'Mahoney as he put the dark liquid to his lips and downed half a glass in one go. It was eight in the morning and he was in a good mood. The blonde bitch had come through. He didn't think she had it in her. But here it was. Tucked away inside his jacket. The photographs. The priceless intelligence.

There was a knock on the back door of the Bogside Inn. Byrne galloped over and peeped through the spyhole. It was Brett and Coyle with Behan lingering at the back.

The landlord opened the door and let them in. 'He's over there,' said Byrne with a look and a nod. The three men navigated their way through the maze of tables and joined O'Mahoney in a corner booth.

'Breakfast?' asked Curly as O'Mahoney took another large swig of the black stuff.

'You want one?' asked O'Mahoney.

'Too early for me.'

'Let's get on with it,' said Brett impatiently.

O'Mahoney pulled a folder of photographs out of his pocket, placed it on the wooden table and grinned.

Brett opened up the folder and fingered his way through each photograph. He stopped halfway through. Thomson's face was staring up at him. The eyes were piercing and, although the image was black and white, he could tell they were icy blue. So this was the man. The bastard who put a detonating cord around Michael's neck. Was he a coward? No, he was smart. Calculating. An adversary worth taking stock of. 'Your woman did good,' said Brett as he flicked through the rest of the photographs.

'Aye, she's worth her weight in gold that one,' replied O'Mahoney as he reached over and tapped his finger on one of the photographs.

'What's that?' asked Curly.

'It's the duty roster,' said O'Mahoney as he picked it up and held it in the air for both men to see.

'And?' said Brett.

'Our man. He's Duty-One on Tuesday,' said O'Mahoney.

'What the fuck does that mean?' asked Brett.

'He's the first one to get called out.'

'Which means we can control the time and the place,' said Curly.

THIRTY-ONE

Even though the bedroom was cold, sweat was dripping off his face forming a small puddle on the floor below his chin. Forty-seven, forty-eight, forty-nine, fifty. The final push-up was a struggle as the last ounce of strength drained from Jardine's arms. In his rugby-playing days, he'd have had no trouble completing fifty push-ups. And then some more. But he was older now and, as an ATO, had lurched into a more sedentary lifestyle. More time in the office and less time on the field. Nevertheless, he stuck to his morning exercise regimen. Just half an hour. Push-ups, sit-ups, squats, jumping jacks and a bit of shadow boxing. It kept him sane. Got him prepared mentally for the day ahead.

Jardine looked over at the clock on his bedside table. It was 4.30 a.m. He had half an hour to wash and shave and get to the shed where he'd called an early morning meeting with the entire unit. It was the only time he could get the whole crew together in the same room. ATs were either coming back from a job or being called out to one. Passing each other like ships in the night.

* * *

Jardine arrived at the shed ten minutes early. But to his surprise, the rest of the unit were already gathered in a huddle, waiting impatiently for him.

'Morning, fellas,' said Jardine. 'Hope it's not too early for you.'

'Who needs sleep?' shouted Kersey, raising a lazy chuckle from the others.

The shed was an oversized workshop where all the unit's bomb disposal equipment was stored. Strong neon strips hanging from the ceiling flooded the place with shadowless light. Land Rovers were parked at the front with all the maintenance tools needed to fix and keep them running. Wheelbarrows, closed-circuit TVs, batteries and coils of electrical cord were stored to the left. Shotguns, cartridges, pigsticks and detonators were stored at the far end. And miscellaneous equipment such as torchlights, screwdrivers and wire-cutters were stored to the right.

Captain Jardine took his place at the centre of the shed, a young corporal from the Signals Corps standing sheepishly next to him. Behind them stood a lonely table with a large white sheet draped over it.

'Shall we get on with it,' said Jardine.

'All ears, Sir,' said Kersey.

'This is Corporal Stevens. He's going to show us a new bit of kit today. Something the scientists from RARDE have cooked up for us. That's nice of them, isn't it?'

'Let's see what it is first,' blurted Kersey.

'They call it electronic counter measures,' continued Jardine. 'Is that right, Corporal?'

'Yes, that's right, Sir.'

'Well, the stage is all yours.' The captain moved to one side, giving the corporal plenty of room to speak.

'Er, thank you, Sir,' said Stevens, turning to face his audience. 'Nice to meet you. I've heard a lot about 321 EOD. And I just wanted to say how, you know, happy I am to be working with you all.' The young corporal was nervous, eager to make a good first impression. The ATs stared back at him with tired, stony faces.

'Nice to meet you too,' said Kersey with a blank face. 'It's going to get busy soon. Shall we put the foot on the pedal?'

'Yes. Of course.' The young signaller grabbed the white sheet covering the table behind him and pulled it off with the flair of a Vegas magician. Beneath the shroud was a box with dials and knobs on the front and a foldable aerial on top.

'What is it?' asked Cooper.

'A frequency jammer.'

'What does it do?' asked Kersey.

'It jams frequencies.'

'I think what we're trying to find out,' said Thomson, 'is how that's going to help us in the field.'

'Ah, right you are,' said Stevens.

Henderson cupped his hand and whispered in Thomson's ear. 'This boy's as green as my piss, boss. Shouldn't he be in school?'

Thomson forced a smile as he continued to listen to the young signaller.

'The IRA have been using more and more radio-controlled devices,' said Stevens. 'These types of bombs rely on a radio frequency. Without the right, you know, frequency, the bomb…'

Kersey couldn't contain himself. 'You're preaching to the converted, son. What I want to know, Corporal…sorry, what's your name?'

'Corporal Stevens.'

'Your first name?'

'Er…' Stevens looked at Captain Jardine for guidance.

'Don't worry, Corporal. He doesn't bite,' said Captain Jardine.

'It's Gus.'

'Gus, we know how radio-controlled devices work,' said Kersey. 'What we don't know is how *that* thing works.'

'I'll show you.' The squad huddled around the corporal and the little grey box, inquisitive but cynical. 'There are two main parts to it.' Stevens pointed to a dial on the left. 'The equipment scans for frequencies in the area. This dial here tells us when it's found one.'

'What if it's the BBC?' asked Cooper.

'Then we'd know. Because it would read 99 FM. And we'd know it was a radio station. What we'd be looking for is unique frequencies.'

'And then what?' asked Thomson.

'Then we use this dial here.' Stevens pointed to a dial on the right of the box. The corporal tweaked the knob with his index finger and thumb. 'Once we've homed in on a frequency, we use the same frequency to jam it.'

'Same frequency?' asked Cooper.

'Yes, Sir. If the signal of our frequency is stronger than theirs, then it basically replaces it. Making their frequency redundant.'

'Pretty clever,' said Kersey. 'Has it been tested?'

'I think so.'

'You think so?'

'I believe they've done tests. Yes.'

'Have they done tests in the field?' asked Thomson.

'Not that I believe,' replied Stevens.

Silence fell on the shed. The ATs stood and stared at the box as if waiting for it to do a magic trick. Jardine realised the show was over.

'Thanks, Gus,' said Captain Jardine. 'You can go.'

'Well done,' said Kersey as he patted Gus on the shoulder. 'Sure it will come in handy.'

Stevens, a little disheartened, pulled the white sheet over the box as the ATs dispersed and made their way out of the shed.

Alan Sutton, who had been watching from the back of the huddle, like a father watches a son from the sidelines playing football, walked over and tapped his pipe on top of the equipment. '*Condemnant quo non intellegunt*,' said Sutton.

'Beg your pardon?' said Stevens.

'You have something useful there, dear boy,' said Sutton. 'Don't let their denigration of you get you down. I'm sure your innovation will be a triumph.'

'Thank you, Sir,' said Stevens flatly, a feeling of dejection knotting his stomach.

* * *

From the shed, Thomson made a beeline for the Sergeants' Mess. No gossip. No breakfast. Not even a cigarette. Every part of his body was heavy, as if it was filled with wet sand.

He'd been called out the previous night to Strabane, a small town fourteen miles from Londonderry. The infantry had cordoned off a section of the road on top of a hill overlooking a Catholic housing estate.

Thomson had climbed out of his Land Rover into the worst weather he'd seen in the two months he'd spent in Londonderry. Most days, the gods dispersed their water across the city with a sprinkler. But that evening, they had decided to fill up their buckets and tip their load, unleashing a deluge on Strabane. To make matters worse, the wind was whipping in sideways, slapping faces with barrages of stinging rain.

The Green Jackets hadn't been able to find the device the IRA had called in. So within an hour, the whole operation was wrapped up and Thomson made his way back to camp. As soon as he made himself a hot cup of tea, the phone started ringing. The IRA called in again. And so Thomson made his way to Strabane for a second time. The weather had deteriorated further and the Green Jackets, who had scoured every nook and cranny along the road with search lights, still couldn't find the device.

They're taking the piss, thought Thomson as Jock drove him back to base.

Thomson placed his drenched combat jacket over the radiator in the ops room. It was like tempting fate. The phone started ringing one more time. 'They've called again, Sir,' said a young private on the other end of the line. 'They've shown us where it is.'

So for the third time, Thomson made his way back to water-drenched Strabane. The IRA, frustrated the army couldn't find their device, had painted the word BOMB on the road in large white letters. Above the word was an arrow pointing toward a pile of thick brush by the side of the road. Rivers of white were streaming along the black tarmac as the rain attempted to wash away the IRA fresco.

Thomson grabbed a hook and line and ventured toward the sign. He was cold and wet, the rain attacking him from all sides.

It took five hours for Thomson to clear away the brush, find the device – a red fire extinguisher – and attach a couple of pounds of plastic to the side. By the time he was ready to flick the switch on the trigger, Thomson's fingers were numb, his clothes were drenched, and every time he took a few steps, his flooded boots squelched.

Thomson flipped the silver switch on the trigger. The explosives boomed like the thunder above. A large orange fireball went up into the air, the flames quickly doused by the unnaturally heavy rain. All done.

By the time Thomson had got back to camp, he was shivering. He wiped himself down with a towel, changed into dry clothes and made his way to the shed for the early morning meeting with Jardine and the corporal from the Signals. That had lasted just half an hour. Now it was time to make for the Sergeants' Mess and to the bed that would swallow him up in a swaddle of sleep for the next few hours. Much-needed kip-eye before the next shift.

As Thomson walked up the stairs toward his room, he felt a scratch at the back of his throat. He raised his fist and coughed into it, trying to clear the phlegm that was building up on his chest.

THIRTY-TWO

The new bomb factory had been set up in a third-floor flat along Colmcille Street, a Catholic district a mere five-minute walk from the Bogside. The army made raids in the area from time to time. But not as often as they did in the Bogside. Colmcille Street was more middle class. More white collar. Less troublesome.

'Not a bad setup, is it?' said Curly with a wry smile.

'Bit small,' replied O'Grady.

'That's because you're a fat fucker. If you lost two stone, you'd fit just nicely.'

O'Grady didn't see the humour. The flat was run-down and squalid. The wooden table, fundamental to the work of bomb-making, occupied most of the living room. It was a tight fit, with just a couple of feet to manoeuvre on either side.

There was a coded knock on the front door. Two slow raps followed by three fast ones. Curly looked through the spyhole and, satisfied it was the man he was expecting, opened the heavy door. A young volunteer walked in with a box of tools.

'Meet your new apprentice,' said Curly as he closed the door and secured it with the deadbolt.

'Nice to meet you,' said Donal McFaddon extending an eager hand.

O'Grady took it and gave it a brisk shake. *Here we go again*, he thought. Another sheep. An idealistic idiot ready to be moulded into a mindless, clockwork thug. 'What do you know about making bombs?'

'Nothing.'

O'Grady glanced over to Curly and communicated his displeasure through disdainful eyes. 'Can we have a chat?'

'Sure,' said Curly as the two men went into the bedroom, leaving McFaddon to unpack his box of tools.

'I need people who know what they're doing,' grumbled O'Grady.

'We're short-handed at the moment, Seamus,' said Curly. 'Michael got fifteen.'

'Aye, I heard. Sorry.'

'He knew what he was getting into when he joined up.'

'To get caught on your first job though. That's bad luck.'

Curly changed the topic. 'That little fucker in the next room. He's got potential.'

'What about Twomey? Where's he fucked off to?'

'Twomey's gone.'

'Gone where?'

'Heaven or Hell. One of the two.'

O'Grady felt a pinch in his stomach. So Twomey was the fall guy. The victim of McGuigan's little game of chess. How did the Branch man do it? What sleight of hand was at play?

'Now I've got a very important job for you Seamus.' Curly pulled out a photograph and held it up to O'Grady's eyes. 'This man put a detonating cord around Michael's neck. And we can't let that go.'

'What do you want me to do?'

'I want you to make something special.'

THIRTY-THREE

The alarm clock came to life and broke Thomson's sleep with a high-pitched ding-a-ling sound that would drive you insane if you were exposed to it for more than a few seconds. Thomson's hand reached out and slammed the clock quiet. He opened his eyes to a bright room. It was 8 a.m.

'Oh fuck. I feel like shit,' he grumbled. Thomson pulled himself up straight and let his legs hang over the side of the bed. His nose was blocked. His head was throbbing. And his whole body felt as if someone had been thumping him with a clenched fist all night.

It was Tuesday and Thomson was Duty-One. He had to get up and get ready to go. The calls would be coming in soon. If he was a civilian, he'd probably go back to bed. Snuggle up with a Lemsip and a paracetamol. A day off wouldn't make much difference in a bureaucratic world where the biggest danger to your person was a papercut. But he wasn't a civilian. He was a soldier. People's lives depended on how well you did your job. A mere head flu wasn't an excuse to shirk your responsibilities.

The staff sergeant dragged himself out of bed, washed his face with cold water, shaved off a day of stubble and pulled on his combats.

Then he turned to his bed. He pulled off the sheets and set about making it from scratch. In the five minutes it took to finish, it was flawless. Perfectly symmetrical, the sheets pulled tight and square, tucked in without leaving a crease. No drill sergeant in the world would have found fault with it.

No matter how tired Thomson was, making the bed was a ritual he followed every day. It was a task that prepared him for the bigger challenges ahead. A psychological trick. An act of positivity that shaped his outlook from morning to night.

And if it was a really bad day, if the shit hit the fan, his mood decimated by cruel events, at least he had a nice bed to come back to. Those cool, crisp sheets could make all the difference in the world to an otherwise horrible day.

Thomson took a few deep breaths before heading out of the door. He wasn't hungry. So he'd skip the mess and head straight to the ops room. Maybe a cup of tea would make him feel better.

* * *

Keith Cooper lounged back on the settee and opened up the *Telegraph*. It was the usual nonsense. The miners were threatening to go on strike again, the Cod Wars were still raging and the pound still falling. There was little coverage of Northern Ireland. *Typical*, thought Cooper.

The door of the ops room swung open and Thomson staggered in. Cooper looked up from his newspaper. 'Are you okay, Dave? You look like death.'

'I'm feeling like shit,' replied Thomson as he made his way to the settee and slumped down by Cooper.

'You need a hot cup of tea,' said Cooper. 'I'll make you one.'

'Thanks, Keith.' Thomson's body bent up double as a sneeze erupted from his nose. Cooper jumped up and headed for the kitchenette, returning a moment later with a hot brew. Thomson took a sip. He couldn't taste a thing. The flu had assaulted his taste buds and shut them down.

'Lie down, Dave. Get some rest.'

'Forty winks might do it.' Thomson laid his head on the arm of the settee and closed his eyes. Images entered his mind as he began to drift off into dreamland. Rats, worms and snakes racing around in dark, slimy holes. Rain pelting down and exploding on his head. This was a flu dream. Hallucinogenic. Dark. Unpleasant.

* * *

It was noon and the Londonderry Arms was already filled to the rafters. Donal McFaddon slipped in the front door, a briefcase clutched under his arm, and squeezed past fat bellies with pots of ale resting on them. 'Excuse me. Excuse me. Excuse me,' he said every time he had to wedge himself through a tight spot. He finally reached the bar and caught the eye of the bartender. 'What can I do for you?' asked the puller of pints.

'A pint of the black stuff, please,' replied McFaddon. The barman grabbed a glass, placed it under a tap and pulled the handle. The man watched as the white, creamy liquid streamed slowly into the glass. It was the closest experience to watching paint dry. Guinness wasn't like lager. It wasn't a fast drink. It took time to pour. Slow and easy. The liquid finally reached its mark at the top of the glass, white bubbles swirling, taking their time to settle down.

'Here you go,' said the barman as he gently placed the glass on the bar in front of his customer.

'Grand,' said McFaddon. 'Where's the toilets?'

'Up the stairs and to the left,' said the barman as he hopped to the next thirsty bar dweller.

'Can you make sure no one takes that?' said McFaddon, pointing to his Guinness with his eyes.

'It won't be walking anywhere.'

McFaddon left the pint on the bar and pressed his way to the stairwell. He made his way up the creaky stairs and surveyed the area. To the left was the loo. Ruddy-faced men were rushing in and out, squeezing past him to get down the stairs. He couldn't leave the briefcase in there. It would be spotted too quickly.

To the right there was a private room with a large wooden table occupying the centre. That was a better place. Empty. No one nosing around.

McFaddon slipped in, threw the briefcase under the table and slipped out again. That was easy. He went back down the stairs and headed straight out of the front door onto the street. He looked over his shoulder at the mob of drunken, pot-bellied Proddies. How he would love to see the bomb go off and blow them to bits. But not today. Some other time. This bomb was aimed at one person and one person only.

McFaddon walked round the corner and inserted himself into a red telephone box. He lifted the receiver from its hook and dialled.

'Strand Road police station,' said the voice at the other end of the line. 'How can I help you?'

'You need to get your fat arses down to the Londonderry Arms. There's a bomb waiting to go off.'

* * *

Thomson could hear laughter. Bloody racket. What the hell's going on? He opened his eyes and pulled himself up to a sitting position. The whole unit was lounging around the ops room. Sutton was reading a book, Cooper was writing a letter, Kersey was watching a film and Jardine was twiddling his thumbs.

Kersey was the first to spot that Thomson was awake. 'He's alive.'

'Are you alright, Dave?' asked Jardine.

'I feel terrible,' replied Thomson.

'You've been sleeping like Hypnos,' said Sutton.

'What time is it?' asked Thomson.

'Nearly 2 p.m.,' replied Kersey.

'What's going on? Shouldn't we be out?'

'There hasn't been a single call all day,' said Jardine.

'Odd as hell,' said Cooper. 'Never seen it this quiet.'

'Don't tempt the gods,' said Sutton, tapping Cooper on the shoulder with his pipe. The ops room phone came alive. 'You really must learn, dear boy.'

'Looks like they've woken up,' said Cooper. 'Must have been on the piss last night. Maybe someone had a wedding.'

Thomson got up creakily from the settee, walked to the phone and lifted the receiver to his ear. 'Thomson…okay, got it.' His head started to spin as he replaced the receiver on its hook. A moment later, he fell backwards, his body losing all sense of balance, and landed with a thud on the floor. Kersey was the first to reach him.

'I've got you.' Kersey grabbed Thomson from behind and lifted him to his feet. 'Are you okay?'

'Yeah. Better get going.'

'You're not going anywhere,' said Jardine as he peered into Thomson's bleary eyes. 'You need to go and see the doc.'

'I'm Duty-One,' insisted Thomson.

'Not today,' said Kersey. 'Keith is Standby-Two. He'll take it.'

* * *

'Here you go,' said the army doctor, handing over a little plastic bag filled with antibiotics. 'Two in the morning. Two at night.'

'Thanks, Doc,' said Thomson as he popped a couple of the yellow capsules in his mouth and swallowed them. 'How long will they take to work?'

'They're the strongest we've got. So you should be feeling better in two or three days. Until then, get to bed and drink lots of water. Flush the bugger out.'

* * *

Peter Stormont, the landlord of the Londonderry Arms, was standing behind the cordon biting his nails. Here we go again, he thought. His place had been targeted before and he'd become increasingly nervy over the past two years. Owning a pub had been a dream of his. But now it was taking a toll on his health. The worry. The stress. Always on the lookout for suspicious-looking customers. Suspicious-looking shopping bags. Suspicious-looking anything.

The Royal Anglian regiment had cleared out the boozy, griping residents and cordoned off the area. Half of them would have remained in their seats drinking given the chance.

Cooper let the suspect package soak for two hours. This was the worst sort of job. The type that needed you to get your nose up close. The wheelbarrow was useless. It wouldn't fit through the old, narrow door. And even if you could squeeze it through, it wouldn't be able to get up the stairs.

Cooper grabbed his grappling hook and slowly walked the hundred yards to the pub. He stopped at the entrance and looked over his shoulder at the stony-faced crowd looking on silently with a shared anxiety. He was anxious too. He walked through the old wooden doorway into a dark stairwell. The place stank of stale beer. It was a run-down old building with peeling wallpaper and sticky carpets. It was a real tip.

Cooper made his way to the second floor where the suspect package had been spotted. He entered a small room that was reserved for private functions. A heavy wooden table in the middle of the room had eight wooden chairs tucked under it. Cooper could imagine clandestine meetings taking place in this dank space, Orangemen plotting their misdeeds against the Catholics they so hated. He put his hands on both knees and bent down to get a better look under the wooden top. Was that a briefcase he could see? Light from the sun, low in the sky, was flooding through the window and blinding Cooper's view. The AT moved round to the other side of the table so his back was against the sun, blocking its rays. He knelt down again to get a better view of the package sitting innocuously in its hiding place.

A flash of fiery light blinded him. The force of the explosion ripped out the side of the second floor. A punch of energy pushed Cooper off the floor, flinging him viciously through the window and onto the pavement below.

'Shit,' shouted a major from the Royal Anglians as he watched plumes of black smoke pour out of the pub. The infantrymen looked on, mouths agape, not quite believing what they were seeing. 'Get the medics.'

Cooper looked up at the sky. It was blue for a change. *That's nice,* he thought to himself before trying to figure out where he was. His ears were filled with a high-pitched sound and his head was numb. Plumes of black smoke interrupted the pristine view. His mind snapped back to reality. Shit, did that fucking thing go off? Am I dead? Is this Heaven?

The face of a medic peered over him. The mouth of the man was shouting but no words or sounds came out of it.

'What the fuck are you saying?' shouted Cooper. He couldn't hear himself. The medic shouted again, but still no sound. 'Mate, I can't hear you. I've been blown up. You'll have to speak louder.' The medic's face disappeared and Cooper felt his body rising off the floor. 'What the fuck are you doing? Where the fuck are you taking me? Can you hear me? Stupid sod.'

The slam of the ambulance door reverberated through his body, awakening the pain that had been suppressed by his unconscious mind. The agony burnt in his arms, legs and chest. It was as if a sledgehammer had pounded every inch of his body over and over a thousand times. A sudden jolt in the vehicle raised a headache that was ten times crueller than his worst hangover, made worse by the piercing squeal in his ears.

This is Hell. Please, God. Let me die.

* * *

O'Mahoney mingled among the throbbing crowd and watched the proceedings from behind the cordon. Debris and bricks were strewn all over the road, smoke rising from the punctured roof of the pub.

The medics put the injured bomb disposal man on a gurney and ferried him to the back of an ambulance. O'Mahoney was agitated at the show unfolding before his eyes. How the fuck did that man survive that blast? It's a fucking miracle. But more importantly, why isn't it Thomson on that stretcher?

The IRA man watched the ambulance drive away. He pulled his collar around his ears and walked the other way, muttering curses under his breath.

Had Dorothy got it wrong? Or was she playing him? He was going to have a word and she'd better have a good excuse. Or else there would be hell to pay.

THIRTY-FOUR

Thomson was beginning to feel like his old self. The three days lying in bed had done him the world of good. The flu bug was all but dead. No match for the potency of the little yellow pills he'd been throwing down his neck. He was back on the job, refreshed and ready to do his bit.

'I'll just be a moment, Jock,' said Thomson as he jumped out of the Land Rover with a WH Smith's white, brown and orange bag in his right hand.

'Take as long as you need, boss. Send my regards.' Thomson marched over to the entrance of the British military hospital, pushed through the front doors and walked up to the reception. It was quiet.

A rotund middle-aged nurse was busy organising medical records. She felt Thomson's presence but ignored him for a while, continuing with the menial task she'd set herself. She closed a brown folder and looked up, her face deadpan. Miserable. Like most people in this town. 'Can I help you?'

'I'm looking for Keith Cooper.'

The nurse scanned her eyes across a plan of the ward. 'Room 23,' she replied as she nodded lazily in the direction of the room.

'Down here?' asked Thomson, pointing a finger.

'Yes, yes. Just up the hall there,' said the nurse testily.

'Thank you.' Thomson walked along the corridor, passing nurses and doctors who were strolling around, looking at their watches and inspecting clipboards.

Thomson reached room 23. He knocked on the door and walked in. A doctor, captain by rank, was leaning over Cooper pressing a stethoscope against his chest. 'That's bloody freezing,' shouted Cooper.

'You're shouting again,' replied the captain.

'What?' boomed Cooper. 'Can't hear you.' Cooper caught sight of Thomson. 'Dave.'

'Keith, how are you feeling?'

'What?'

'He can't hear you,' interrupted the captain.

'Can't hear you,' added Cooper. Thomson pulled a pile of magazines out of the carrier bag and plonked them on Cooper's bed.

'Thanks, Dave,' shouted Cooper appreciatively. 'I've been bored shitless in here.'

'You're in pretty good shape, considering,' said Thomson as he pulled up a wooden chair and sat down.

'What?' Cooper was struggling to hear anything. The blast had left a loud, high-pitched ringing sound in his ears that drowned out the world, including his own voice.

'It's a miracle he's alive,' said the captain. 'We haven't got a clue how he survived that blast. He was right over it. Another person, another time and we'd be scraping body parts off the pavement.'

'It should have been me,' said Thomson.

'Sorry?' said the doctor.

'It was my job. Keith was standing in for me.'

'Someone must be looking down on you.'

'Him too.'

'Yes. Him too.'

'What's the damage?'

'Apart from all the scratches and abrasions on his face, two toes and a finger.'

'What about his hearing?'

'Temporary. It'll come back.' The doctor turned to his patient and spoke loudly and slowly, hoping the AT could read his lips. 'You're holding up well. I'll be back in the afternoon.'

'Have you got any more painkillers, Doc? This headache is killing me.'

The doctor pulled a brown bottle out of his coat pocket and placed them on the bedside table. 'Don't overdo it. They're addictive.'

Cooper held up a thumb from a hand wrapped in a bandage. Blood stained the white material where a little finger used to be. 'Okay, Doc.' The doctor left the room and shut the door quietly behind him.

'You lucky bastard,' shouted Thomson, unconsciously mimicking Cooper's loudness. Cooper was staring hard at Thomson's lips, trying to decipher the words coming from his mouth.

'I know. Should be dead.'

'Feeling okay?'

'Every bone in my body is aching. And my head feels like someone's hitting it with a hammer all the time. I just want someone to put me out of my misery.'

'Hasn't stopped you talking.'

'What?'

'Nothing.' Having a conversation was becoming too difficult. Cooper picked up the latest edition of *MAD* from the pile of magazines on his bed. Thomson picked up a copy of *Shoot!* that featured George Best on the front cover. Thomson wasn't a big football fan. But with the banter at an end, he had nothing better to do than catch up on a sport he didn't particularly care for.

The two men quietly flicked through their magazines. Cooper was grateful to have some company and Thomson was happy to sit there taking a break from the madness outside. Twenty minutes passed before Henderson popped his head through the door. 'Hello, Sir. Hope you're feeling well.'

'What?' shouted Cooper.

'He can't hear you, Jock,' said Thomson as he folded up his magazine and put it down on the bed.

'Hope you're feeling well!' shouted Henderson, raising his voice by a couple of decibels.

'Thanks!' shouted Cooper.

'We've got a job, boss,' continued Henderson, his voice returning to its usual volume.

THIRTY-FIVE

It was Thursday. Which meant it was meet night. The day the UVF leadership got together to talk about their plans. McGuigan dreaded the meetings. They were a bore. Always a lot of big talk and little action. Filled with rants and grievances. But McGuigan felt obliged to turn up. Just to make sure, at the very least, that no stupid decisions were being made without his knowledge.

McGuigan had parked his car opposite the house. The rain was heavy and small bombs of water pounded the roof, drowning out the music on the car radio. The Special Branch man pulled out his flask of whiskey and took a sip. He wasn't in a rush to get out.

The front door of the house opened and Dorothy walked out with her umbrella already open. Bingo, no doubt, thought McGuigan, as he watched her stride down the street. She'd only walked thirty yards when a blue Vauxhall Victor pulled up beside her. She looked nervous as she opened the door and slipped inside. The car didn't move. What's going on here? McGuigan wandered out into the torrential rain, pulled up his raincoat collar and made his way down the street, keeping to the opposite side of the road. When he came level to the Vauxhall, he was lucky to find himself shielded behind a plumber's transit van. He peeked round the side. The man was furious and lashing Dorothy with venomous words.

* * *

The water was bouncing off the woman's umbrella in a synchronised display like tumblers in a circus show. Although her head was obscured, O'Mahoney could tell it was Dorothy. Her long slender legs gave her away. No other girl in Derry had legs like that. The IRA man pulled alongside his informer and flung open the passenger door. 'Get in!' he shouted.

Startled, Dorothy lifted the umbrella above her eyeline. Damn. It was that cocksucker. She quickly closed the umbrella, leapt inside the car and shut the door. She was half drenched, mascara running down her cheek, her hair wet and stringy.

O'Mahoney switched off the engine but left the wipers on. The flimsy rubber strips on the iron rods were whipping back and forth trying to clear the water from the windscreen. But the rain was winning the battle. The road ahead was just a watery blur.

'What do you want?' asked Dorothy.

'I want to know why you've been telling me lies.' Dorothy knew where this was headed. The whole Thomson thing had been an almighty fuck-up. She had answers. Excuses. But would this bastard believe her?

'I can explain.'

'Can you?'

'He came down with a flu.'

'Are you fucking kidding me?'

'It's the honest truth, Liam. On my mother's grave, God bless her soul, the bastard came down with a fucking flu.'

O'Mahoney scrutinised her face. He was an expert in detecting the lie. The twitch of an eye, the dilated pupils, the tightness of the lips. But there were no traces of one on this woman's face. The honesty wasn't going to get in the way of what O'Mahoney had been longing to do. He raised his hand and slapped Dorothy hard across the face. She screamed. 'You better have something for me,' said O'Mahoney through gritted teeth.

'He's Duty-One on Thursday.'

'You better not be taking me for a ride. A slap would be the least of your worries.'

'Thursday.'

'Thursday?'

'I've seen the roster,' said Dorothy, her hands trembling.

'Okay,' said O'Mahoney with a smile and cheery voice. His demeanour changing from tormentor to friend quicker than the blink of an eye. That volatility scared Dorothy. He was a fucking maniac. 'You can go now.' Dorothy opened the door and tumbled out onto the pavement. O'Mahoney's Vauxhall pulled away and disappeared behind a curtain of heavy rain.

'Bastard,' she murmured to herself. She needed to get out of this. Some way, somehow.

* * *

McGuigan watched as the man raised his hand and brought it down on Dorothy's face. The Special Branch man was tempted to run over, pull the bastard out of the car and give him a good beating. But he thought better of it. A good poker player never showed his hand too early. There was something more to this than met the eye. What have you got yourself into Dorothy? He can't be your lover. Although if he was, it would be completely understandable. Your husband is a putrid human being. Any other woman would have left him by now. But lovers don't hit their woman like that. So who is he?

Dorothy climbed out of the car and slammed the door shut. McGuigan got a good look at the driver's face as the man searched over his shoulder for oncoming traffic. McGuigan didn't recognise him. But the detail of his face was lodged in McGuigan's memory bank. The car sped off and Dorothy looked around to see if anyone had spotted her. McGuigan slid behind the van and stayed there until Dorothy's click-clacking high heels faded away into the distance.

THIRTY-SIX

Danny Dwyer ripped off the Mars Bar wrapper and took a big bite. His colleague, George Allen, was in the back of the caravan making a pot of tea. As he poured the hot brew into a mug, he glanced over his shoulder and caught Dwyer stuffing his face. 'Hope you've left one of those for me.'

'Don't worry. There's two left.'

Allen plodded into the front office with two mugs of milky tea. 'Here you go.'

'Thanks, George.'

'Quiet today.'

'What do you mean? It's quiet every day.'

The two customs officers had worked together in the tiny space for over year. A mundane routine had quickly set in. Arrive at work by 7 a.m. Then a mug of tea, preferably with chocolate biscuits. Followed by a slow read of the newspaper. Out on the road to lift the barrier for the occasional farmer that passed by their way. More tea. The crossword. Lunch. Sleep. More snacks.

By 3.30 p.m., their heads about to explode with boredom, they'd resort to constantly checking watches, restlessly waiting for the next shift to take over at 4 p.m. It was a dreary job but one that paid relatively well.

'What did your missus pack for lunch today?'

'Tuna. You?'

'Chicken. Swap ya one.'

'Okay. I like chicken.'

'Have you finished your paper?'

'Aye. You?'

'Aye. Let's swap then.'

The border between Northern Ireland and the Republic was a long and porous boundary which was dotted with crossings. Some checkpoints had small huts built by the side of them. Others, like the checkpoint Dwyer and Allen manned, had to get by with a small caravan. The government wasn't interested in building costly defences for a border that was impossible to protect.

A Ford Cortina made its way up Letterkenny Road toward the Killea checkpoint. Dwyer was the first to spot the bright headlights as the car edged nearer. 'Got a visitor,' said Dwyer as he turned the page of his newspaper. 'I think it's your turn.'

'Lazy bastard,' replied Allen as he put down his newspaper, stood up and pulled his drooping trousers up over his beer belly.

'I'll put the kettle on while you're out.'

'And don't eat all the biscuits.'

Allen opened the door of the caravan and stepped into the road. He held up his hand, signalling the Cortina to stop. Which it did. Ten feet away. Why has he stopped short? Stupid ass. Allen sauntered toward the car to admonish the driver. But froze in his tracks when three masked men scuttled out with shotguns in their hands.

The customs officer put his hands up instantly. 'I don't want any trouble,' he said with a tremble in his voice.

'Behave yourself and you won't get any,' said the man leading the pack. 'Head back.' Allen turned and, with legs that had rapidly turned to jelly, shuffled back toward the customs post.

Dwyer, peeking through an oval window, was breathing heavily, unable to keep his anxiety at bay. The masked men bundled Allen inside the caravan and barged in after him.

'Hands up,' said the leader. Dwyer shot his hands in the air. His heart was beating fast. Unstoppable, like a locomotive. The leader pushed the shotgun into Dwyer's spongey belly. It was enough to startle Dwyer's bladder. Warm urine started to run uncontrollably down his leg. 'What you pissing yourself for?' asked the masked leader as a dark patch spread across the custom officer's groin. 'We're not going to hurt you.'

Dwyer's chest felt tight. He clasped his left arm as a lightning bolt of pain flashed through it. The big man collapsed in a heap.

* * *

It was midday and not a single job had been called in. Thomson inspected his watch. This was the second time an unusual hiatus had occurred in less than three weeks. It didn't make sense. It wasn't like the IRA. They didn't take days off.

'Where are the buggers?' asked Thomson.

'Maybe they've decided to give up the ghost,' said Kersey. 'Finally submitted to British rule.'

Jardine laughed. 'In your dreams. They've got us on the ropes. And they know it.'

'I must admit, it is quite odd,' said Sutton, his nose stuck in a thick book. 'There's a pattern to what they do. And this kind of tactic is out of character.' Sutton turned a page. 'Not that I'm complaining, mind you.'

Kersey picked up a pack of cards. 'Anyone up for a game of Gin Rummy?' As soon as the words came out of his mouth, the ops room phone made its familiar sound. Its call to arms.

'That'll be for me,' said Thomson.

'The universe, it seems, doesn't want you to cast your cards, Rip,' said Sutton.

'You might be right there, Al,' said Kersey.

Thomson walked over to the phone and picked up the receiver. The rest of the ATs looked on as they listened to the faint murmur on the other end of the line. 'Got it,' said Thomson as he scribbled on a pad before slamming down the phone.

'Where is it?' asked Jardine.

'Killea customs post.'

'Where the fuck's that?' asked Kersey.

'On the border,' said Thomson.

'What the fuck are they doing out there?'

'We'll soon find out,' replied Thomson.

'Be careful, Dave,' said Kersey as Thomson walked out of the ops room. Thomson didn't hear the words. Didn't hear the concern. The tiny bit of dread in Kersey's voice. But Jardine did.

'What's on your mind?' asked the captain.

'Nothing, Sir,' replied Kersey. He was lying, of course. Anything out of the ordinary always raised a red flag in Kersey's head. When it came to war, violence and scumbags like the IRA, he had an uncanny intuition. And his gut was telling him something was wrong.

* * *

George Allen was leaning against a troop carrier, his eyes drawn to the tarmac, as if somehow it held the answers to the horrible events of the last hour.

Thomson handed him a sweet milky tea in a metal cup. 'Here you go.' Allen took a sip. 'How are you feeling?'

'Like shit.'

'Tell me what happened.'

'A car drove up. I went out. You know, the usual. Check passports and that.' Allen took a big gulp of tea as his hand started to tremble.

'Take your time.'

'These three men got out. Masks on their heads. Shotguns in their hands. I literally shat myself. They forced me back into the caravan. Danny was standing there with his hands up. And then it happened.' A tear dribbled down Allen's face. He wiped it away with a porky finger.

'Go on.'

'Danny grabbed his left arm. Then he hit the floor.' Allen was struggling to contain his emotions.

'Take a deep breath.' Allen sucked in the air and held it in his lungs. 'Did any of them have a package?'

'Aye. A box. He put it in the back, under the kitchen sink.'

'Did you see what was inside?'

'No. They pushed us outside and onto the ground.'

'Did they have any wire?'

'Aye. A big spool of the stuff. They attached it to a coat hanger.'

'A coat hanger?'

'Aye. The leader, he stuck it to the door handle. When he left, he tried to pull the door shut. But the hanger got in the way. He kept on slamming the door but it wouldn't close. Got pretty angry at one point. Eventually he gave up. Left the door open. Just an inch, mind.'

'Anything else?'

'No, they got in their car and drove across the border.'

'Thanks, George.' Thomson sauntered over to the Land Rover where Henderson was waiting for instructions.

A young captain from the Cheshire Regiment was with him having a smoke. 'Any way we can help, Felix?'

'Not yet, Sir. Still figuring out the lay of the land.'

'Very well. You know where I am.' The young captain made his way back to his command post to laze around and wait for something to happen.

Thomson reached into the Land Rover, pulled out a pair of binoculars and lifted them to his eyes. He twisted the lenses until the caravan came into focus. The door was slightly ajar. He could see the coat hanger attached to the outside handle.

There was only one reason the IRA would do that, he thought. It was a makeshift aerial. Which meant the box in the caravan contained a radio-controlled device.

Thomson shifted the binoculars to the surrounding countryside, searching every nook and cranny. There was an IRA terrorist hiding somewhere, just waiting for Thomson to walk to the caravan. And when he was close enough, set off the bomb.

As he swept left, the binoculars landed on an old farmhouse, less than a mile away. Was that movement he could see inside? He pulled the binoculars away from his eyes and handed them to Henderson.

'Everything okay, boss?'

'I'll be back in a minute.' Thomson marched to the command post where the young captain was chatting with a couple of his NCOs. 'Excuse me, Sir.'

'Ah, Felix. How can I help?'

'There's a radio-controlled device in the caravan. Which means there's a handler with his finger on a trigger somewhere.'

'My men have scoured the area, Felix. If there was somebody out there, we would have found them by now.'

'Have they checked that farmhouse?' asked Thomson as he pointed toward the decrepit, old structure.

'No.'

'Can we get some men over there?'

'Unfortunately not,' replied the captain apologetically. 'That's on the other side of the border. We have no jurisdiction.'

'That's where they are.'

'Sorry, Felix, there's nothing we can do.'

'We're a bit buggered then.'

'The top brass have made it clear. Under no circumstances are we to cross into the Republic. They'll cut our balls off if we do.'

'I see. Thank you, Sir.' Thomson turned on his heel and headed back to the Land Rover.

'What's going on, boss?' asked Henderson.

'It's a radio-controlled device. And the IRA are hiding in that farmhouse on the other side of the border.'

'Sneaky bastards.'

'Call in Gus.'

'What, that wee lad from the Signals?'

'Yeah. He's got a jammer, right?'

'Aye, but no one knows if it works or not.'

'We will soon.'

* * *

The farmhouse was run-down. Cold and damp. In the living room, old, flowered wallpaper was peeling off the wall. The place smelt musky. Worn-out furniture was laid on top of a worn-out carpet. The place was owned by Jack Brown, an eighty-two-year-old farmer who'd reaped his last crop some twelve years before. The eccentric old man hated company, except for his own and that of his dog.

The kettle was boiling when he heard a knock on his door. Who the hell is that? A dark cloud loomed over his head at the thought of some do-gooder coming to visit him. Was it his daughter? No, she'd given up a long time ago. He couldn't stand her and she couldn't stand him. Probably those nosey bastards from the social services. Bloody nuisance.

As soon as he opened the door, he knew he shouldn't have. Three men with masks on their heads stood on his porch. The old farmer tried to close the door shut. But it was too late. A stocky fella wedged his foot inside and barged through.

'Who the hell are you?' shouted Brown as he was pushed backward into the living room.

'Anybody else here?' asked the stocky one.

'No, just me.' Brown realised that was a bad answer and quickly added, 'But my daughter and her family are coming soon.'

'Is that right?' The eyes peering through the holes in the mask were intense. Menacing. Intimidating.

'Yes.'

'I'm going to ask you again. Is that right?'

It was a threat and Brown didn't want to be on the receiving end of it. 'No.'

'Are you sure?'

'I'm sure. I live here alone.'

'Well, why didn't you say so in the first place?' Steve Docherty pulled off his mask and threw it on the settee. 'Don't worry, old man, we're not going to hurt you.'

Curly took his mask off too and walked over to the old farmer, stood straight, and rolled off a well-rehearsed discourse. 'We're from the Irish Republican Army, Derry Brigade. We're commandeering this place for the next few hours. We apologise for the inconvenience caused. We mean you no harm. As long as you cause no trouble for us, we'll cause no trouble for you. Do you understand what I've just said?'

'Aye,' replied Brown, taken aback by the sudden turn of events. 'Does anybody want a cup of tea?'

'Why are we taking off our masks?' asked O'Mahoney. 'He can finger us.'

Docherty laughed loudly and turned to Curly. 'Where the fuck did we dig this one up from?'

'No one's going to finger anybody,' said Curly. 'But keep it on if it makes you feel comfortable.'

O'Mahoney slowly plucked the mask off his head, uncertain it was a good idea. He looked the old man directly in the eyes. And the man stared back. 'Don't give me an excuse to come back here and kill you,' said O'Mahoney.

* * *

Corporal Gus Stevens was busy with paperwork, stuck in an office with other signallers also busy with paperwork. He'd been in Northern Ireland for three weeks and hadn't left the barracks in all that time. He was bored. If only he'd been assigned to Intelligence. At least he'd be out in the field helping the spies do their surveillance work. Or assigned to a regiment as a radio operator, patrolling the streets around the Bogside.

But alas, he'd been assigned to 321 EOD and a bunch of bomb disposal men who didn't need or value his skills.

As he finished up a report, the phone on his desk started to ring. Stevens picked up the receiver and placed it to his ear. 'Corporal Stevens.'

'You're needed,' said the voice on the other end of the line.

'Sorry?'

'Staff Sergeant Thomson needs you and your equipment up at Letterkenny Road.'

'Where's that?'

'By the border. We're sending an escort. They'll take you there.'

Adrenaline was running through Corporal Stevens' veins. After sitting around twiddling his thumbs for so long, he was finally about to see some action.

'I need my van,' said Stevens.

'Go and get it and be outside in ten minutes.'

* * *

The Ford Transit, painted in military green, pulled up behind the Land Rover. Gus clambered out onto the tarmac and spotted Thomson walking hastily toward him. 'Afternoon, Sir,' said Stevens chirpily.

Thomson wasn't in the mood for chitchat. He got straight to the point. 'Right, Gus, we've got a situation here. And you might be the man who can save my life.'

Stevens wasn't sure whether the AT was being serious or having a laugh. He chuckled nervously.

'He's not joking, lad,' said Henderson.

'Oh,' replied Stevens. 'Right.'

'There's a radio-controlled bomb in that caravan over there,' said Thomson. 'And there's a terrorist in that farmhouse over there.'

'That's not good,' replied Stevens. 'Can't you send the army in to get them?'

'They're on the other side of the border. We can't touch them.'

'Oh. I see. Well, shall we give the box a go?'

'Show the way,' said Thomson. The signaller opened up the back of the transit van and climbed inside. Equipment was lined along both sides of the vehicle. Thomson popped his head in. 'Bloody hell, Gus, you've got enough equipment in here to start an electronics store.'

'We use a lot of stuff, Sir.'

'I can see that. Where's our jammer?'

Stevens pulled a canvas off the grey box. 'Here she is.'

'Can you find a signal?' asked Thomson impatiently. Stevens pulled on a set of headphones. 'Anything?'

'Give me a minute, Sir.' Stevens turned the knob, left then right. Then left again. His eyes squinted as he searched for a sound, a frequency that betrayed the presence of an IRA bomber. Thomson and Henderson lit another cigarette as they waited patiently for the signaller to do his work.

After five minutes, Stevens removed his headphones, disappointment etched in his face. 'Sorry, Sir. Nothing.'

'That's not good,' replied Thomson.

'It might be off,' said Stevens.

'What might be off?'

'The signal will only show up when they switch on the detonation device. It might be off. I would imagine they're saving their battery. Some of these walkie-talkie things only have a battery life of a couple of hours.'

'Or maybe your box doesn't work.'

'I don't believe that's the case, Sir.'

Thomson thought hard. Ideas rushing through his head. Weighing up the different options before him.

'Jock, get me a pigstick.'

'You're not going in there?'

'Pigstick.'

Henderson rushed to the back of the Land Rover, returned a moment later with a pigstick and handed it over.

'This is what we're going to do. I'm going to walk very slowly toward the caravan. Gus, I want you to search for a signal. If you're right, they'll switch on their detonation device when they see me.'

'That's very likely,' said Stevens.

'Jock, if there is a signal, shout like buggery.'

'Right you are, boss.' Thomson took a deep breath. Pigstick in hand, he walked slowly toward the caravan. One hundred yards. Ninety yards. Eighty yards. Seventy yards. Shit. This isn't working. That damned box is going to get me killed.

'Boss,' shouted Henderson. 'We've got a signal.'

Thank God, thought Thomson, as he stopped in his tracks, took a deep breath and headed back to the van.

* * *

Curly kept his binoculars fixed on the handsome AT as he lingered at the back of the green transit van. Come on you bastard. Do your job. Make a move. I haven't got all day.

It had taken the chief bomb-maker two weeks to meticulously plan the job. First, he had searched along the border for the ideal location. Once he found the right customs post, decrepit and unimportant, he passed through it five times, checking out the two unshapely

immigration men who always seemed to be on duty. Then he staked
out the farmhouse on the other side of the border. The old man who
occupied the place lived alone and stayed mostly inside his house, leaving the fields untended to.

And then he turned his attention to the bomb. Radio-controlled.
Impossible to defuse. A device that could be set off from the safety of
the Republic of Ireland.

'Likes taking his time, doesn't he?' said Docherty as he peered out
the window over Curly's shoulder.

'He's a real chess player.'

'Should've brought a rifle. Could shoot him from here.'

'Yeah, and they'd shoot this place to bits. They wouldn't give a fuck
it was the Republic.'

Staff Sergeant Thomson started walking at a snail's pace toward
the caravan.

'Why's he walking so slowly?' asked Docherty.

'He's being cautious,' said Curly, his grip tightening on the binoculars. His heart was beating faster as the excitement inside him rose.
'This is it,' the chief bomb-maker shouted. All three men huddled at the
window, watching the AT slowly make his way toward the caravan.

'What's happening?' asked the old farmer, who was sitting on the
settee holding his dog for comfort.

'The mission's nearly over, old man,' replied O'Mahoney with a
sadistic glee in his voice. One hundred yards. Ninety yards. Eighty
yards. Seventy yards. Curly handed his binoculars to Docherty, picked
up the detonation device off the windowsill and switched it on, a red
light confirming it was active. Just a few more steps and he'd have him.
This bastard was about to meet his maker.

Thomson stopped in his tracks, turned on his heels and walked back
to the van. 'The fucker!' shouted Curly.

'Why's he stopped?' asked O'Mahoney.

'Don't worry. He'll be back,' said Curly.

'Probably shitting himself,' said Docherty.

'Come back, you bastard!' demanded Curly.

* * *

Thomson arrived back at the van. 'What have you got for me, Gus?'

'Got them.' The signaller chuckled. He pointed at a dial. 'This is the frequency they're using.'

'Little bastards,' said Henderson with contempt in his voice.

'What now?' asked Thomson.

'Well, now we jam it.'

'How do you know when the frequency is jammed? I don't want to walk out there thinking we've jammed the bloody thing and it turns out we haven't.'

'We replace their signal with ours. That's all there is to it.'

'But do you know for sure? Do you know it's been replaced?'

'To be honest, Sir, this is the first time I've done this.'

'Brilliant,' said Henderson.

'Get on with it then,' ordered Thomson, a touch of exasperation in his voice.

The signaller grabbed a dial on the right side of the box and slowly turned it until the dial on the right found the same frequency as the one on the left. 'Nearly there. Just a little bit—'

A thunderous noise filled the air. The three men jumped out of the van in time to see the caravan mushrooming into a bright orange ball of fire.

'What the—' Thomson, along with every other soldier behind the cordon, lifted his arm to shield his face from the wave of hot air that rippled out from the explosion.

Ninety-Nine ran across to the van, pointing a finger. 'Sir, over there.' Thomson turned his head in the direction of the farmhouse. Three men were running out the back toward a car. One of them, a man with shoulder-length curly hair, was shouting, spitting and swearing. 'That bloke with curly hair,' said Ninety-Nine. 'He looks a bit upset.'

'Give me your rifle,' said Thomson.

'What are you going to do, Sir?' asked Ninety-Nine as he obediently handed over his weapon. Thomson took the rifle, put the butt to his shoulder and looked through the scope. Curly Coyle came into view. Red face and twisted mouth. Thomson put his finger on the trigger. This man had tried to kill him. All it would take was one little squeeze of his finger.

THIRTY-SEVEN

McGuigan pulled up at the far end of the church carpark. It was quiet as usual. He pulled out his flask of whiskey and offered it to O'Grady. The IRA man, looking glum, declined.

'I've got good news for you,' said McGuigan. 'We're getting you out next week.'

O'Grady wasn't expecting the proclamation. The Branch man usually started the conversation with a bit of fishing. Trying to weasel out IRA plots and plans. 'You wouldn't be pulling my leg would you, Jonny?' said O'Grady.

'No. It's been stamped.'

'Where you sending us? Some fucking shithole in Scotland?'

'You're a cynical bastard, Seamus.'

'Dealing with fuckers like you.'

'I hope you like Kangaroos.'

'Fucking kidding me? Australia?'

'Aye. Land of opportunity.'

A broad grin broke across O'Grady's face. 'I hear the fishing's good down there.'

'I've heard that too.'

O'Grady's soul was suddenly lifting with hope. Imagine that. Living in a place with sun all year round. Where people got on with each other. Where no one gave a damn whether you were Catholic or Protestant. He could get a job as an electrician. He'd be good at that. Get some fishing in at the weekend. Drink a beer on the beach. Live a normal life. 'How does it work?'

'Next Thursday, at exactly 6 a.m., a van will park up outside your house. You be ready. We want to be in and out. Only one suitcase each. You hear me.'

'Yeah, I hear you.'

'In the meantime, act as normal. Don't do anything out of the usual. Don't visit your relatives. Because if they find out something's up, it'll be on the grapevine. You know it.'

'My wife…'

'I know. She'll want to say goodbye. But don't let her do it. My advice to you is to tell her the night before. Leave it to the very last minute.'

'Okay.'

'Good. Next Thursday. 6 a.m.'

O'Grady repeated the instructions. 'Next Thursday. 6 a.m.'

'Now, have you got any parting gifts for me?' said McGuigan.

'They're going to kill one of those bomb disposal men.'

'What?'

'The man put a detonating cord around a volunteer's neck.'

'Thomson.'

'You know him?'

'I encouraged him to do it.'

O'Grady laughed, 'You're a fucking troublemaker, McGuigan.'

'How are they going to do it?'

'They've already tried twice. The bomb at the Londonderry Arms was meant for him. And the one up by the border. That was meant for him too. He's a lucky bastard. He should be six feet under by now.'

McGuigan was puzzled. 'How do they know?'

'Know what?'

'How do they know he's going to be the one taking the job?'

'I don't know.'

McGuigan thought for a while. Perplexed. Trying to figure out the puzzle. 'Are you involved, Seamus?'

'Aye. I'm making the bombs.'

'Can you keep him alive?'

'No. They're committed.'

'What about a bit of fiddling?'

'You're asking me to take a big risk, Jonny.'

'You'll be out of it soon, Seamus. What have you got to lose?'

'Fucking everything.'

'Try your best.'

'I'm not promising anything.'

'And what about the other thing? The big one,' asked McGuigan.

'Ha. Wondered when you'd get to that. Bet you've been creaming in your pants every night.'

'I must admit. You got me excited, Seamus.'

The IRA man reached inside his coat pocket and pulled out a scrappy piece of folded paper. McGuigan pulled it open. It was a map of Loughermore Forest. An X had been scribbled on one of the tracks that riddled the woods. 'It's an old, abandoned farm building. There's a basement round the back. We covered it in rocks and shrub.'

McGuigan pulled out a brown envelope and slapped it on O'Grady's lap. It would be the last payment. And a nice juicy one at that. McGuigan didn't begrudge giving the money. O'Grady had been worth every penny.

The IRA man hid the envelope away in his coat pocket without looking inside. He knew it was a good amount. The envelope was thicker than normal. McGuigan held out his hand. O'Grady looked at it disdainfully. 'No need for that.'

'Drop you off at the bus stop?' asked McGuigan as he turned on the engine of his BMW and reversed out of the carpark.

'Aye. I don't feel like fishing today.' O'Grady looked out of the window. Was Australia real? Would it really happen? One week. A lot can happen in that time.

THIRTY-EIGHT

The connection was bad. But even though Jean's voice was faint, her rambling monologue made Thomson smile. 'I saw Maureen today,' said Jean. 'She was a bit teary. Robert is being sent to Ireland.'

'He's an AT,' replied Thomson. 'We all get sent to Ireland eventually.'

'Doesn't make it any easier on the people left behind.'

'How's Andrew and Karen?'

'We had a bit of a moment today. I was rummaging around in the drawers looking for a stamp and I found the life insurance policy. Andrew comes into the room and sees me reading through it and he starts crying. He thought you'd died.' Thomson laughed. 'It's not funny, Dave.'

'No, it's not.'

'I thought the kids were fine. But they must be worried deep down. I had to give him a hug for ten minutes and reassure him you were okay.'

'Is he there now?'

'No, he's out playing in the woods.'

'Just tell him Dad is fine. Nothing's going to happen.' Jock Henderson walked into the ops room. He spotted Thomson on the phone, lifted his wrist and pointed at his watch. 'Darling, I've got to go. I'll call you later.'

'Be careful.'

'I will. Love you.' Thomson put the receiver on its hook. 'What's up, Jock?'

'The captain wants everyone in the shed, boss,' replied Henderson.

'What for?'

'Says he's got a little present for us.'

'Let's have a nosey.' The two men walked out of the ops room and covered the short distance across the parade ground to the shed. The other ATs, along with their number twos, had got there before them and were huddled around what looked like a diver's suit.

'Someone going swimming?' asked Thomson.

'It's a bomb suit,' replied Jardine.

'What does it do?'

'Not sure, to tell the truth,' said Jardine.

'Looks like a space suit,' said Sutton. 'Reminds me of a phrase. What is it? *Ad astra per aspera.* Through adversity to the stars.'

'Very romantic,' said Kersey.

'We'll look like astronauts walking down the street,' chuckled Sutton, puffing on his pipe.

'There's one thing for sure,' said Kersey. 'That thing won't protect you from a blast.'

Jardine laughed. 'At least it'll keep your body parts all in one place.'

'Maybe that's what it's for,' said Thomson flatly.

'How novel,' said Sutton. 'A walking body bag.'

'I think those old men at RARDE are taking the piss,' said Kersey.

'Who wants to try it on?' asked Jardine. The ATs kept quiet. There wasn't an awful lot of enthusiasm for this modern-day suit of armour. 'Come on, Rip. You're always up for a laugh.'

'Aye. I suppose I am.' Kersey bent forward, grabbed the top part of the suit with both hands and pulled it off its stand. 'Bloody hell. It's heavy. What's it made of?'

'There's armour plating underneath the fabric,' said Jardine.

Kersey turned to his number two. 'Think I'm going to need your help on this one, Brian.' Colby took the suit off Kersey and held it up so his boss could slide his arms inside. He then made his way round to the back and zipped the suit up. 'Now the helmet.' Colby grabbed the round sphere and placed it on Kersey's head. It was heavy and clunky.

Thomson laughed. 'You look like you're off to a fancy-dress party.'

'Fucking feel like it,' said Kersey, his voice hardly audible through the thick plastic visor.

'All you need now is a jousting stick and horse,' said Sutton.

Colby lifted the helmet off Kersey's head. Even though the Royal Marine hadn't moved, his hair was drenched with sweat. 'I'm not wearing that,' he said.

'No choice,' said Jardine. 'Orders from the top.'

Kersey snorted back. 'Well, if the bombs don't kill me, that fucking thing will.'

THIRTY-NINE

Curly held a loupe magnifying glass to his eye and inspected the bomb. It was a clever piece of work. A Seamus classic. Designed to dupe the handler. Curly could see the scenario in his mind. Thomson waiting, looking at his watch to see if the soaking period was over. It's safe, he would say to himself. He'd go inside the shop. Walk into the storeroom with its hundreds of boxes. He'd start searching. Slowly, carefully, patiently. But what he wouldn't realise is that the timer would still be ticking.

O'Grady had taken an ordinary alarm clock and slowed it down. He'd loosened a couple of nuts and lengthened the hair spring. And by doing so, made certain the minute hand took four hours to move around the face instead of one.

Curly inspected the device one last time.

'Good work, Seamus,' said Curly as he tossed the loupe glass to his bomb-maker. 'Whatever gave you the idea?'

'A grandfather clock my old ma owned. Was always running too fast. Until I worked out a way to fix it.'

'You're a fucking genius.'

'I wouldn't go that far.'

'This is the one that's going to do the job,' said Curly as he left the flat with a grin on his face and a spring in his step.

'Let's hope so.'

O'Grady put the glass to his eye and scanned the device. He examined the moving pieces, the tangle of wires that only he could make sense of and finally lingered on the one tiny flaw that nobody else could see.

* * *

Saturdays were expectedly slow. But by 10 a.m., the IRA were usually up and about, busy planting their bombs.

Thomson looked at his watch. It was 3 p.m. and not a single job had been called in. The ATs had managed, for the first time ever, to finish their game of Rummy. After the card game, they had a good natter, sharing war stories, jokes and friendly banter. By midday, they'd run out of things to say and found themselves sitting around and just waiting. Everyone's eyes on the phone in the corner, willing it to make its shrill sound.

'This is the third time,' said Kersey.

'Third time what?' asked Jardine.

'Third time this has happened,' said Kersey.

'I believe your calculations are correct,' said Sutton.

'Always seems to happen when you're Duty-One, Dave,' said Kersey.

'I was just thinking that myself,' said Thomson.

'Just a coincidence,' laughed Jardine.

The words ran dry again as the ATs resorted to staring at the phone. When it started ringing, there was a collective sigh of relief in the room.

'Thank fuck,' said Kersey.

Thomson sprung from his chair, plucked the receiver from its hook and placed the receiver against his ear. 'Yes…okay,' he said into the phone. 'I'm on my way.'

'Where is it?' asked Jardine.

'SPAR,' replied Thomson through a smile.

'Lucky you,' said Sutton.

* * *

'We should be back in time for an early dinner, boss,' said Henderson as he put his foot on the accelerator, as if somehow that would speed up the proceedings.

Thomson lit up a cigarette and wound down his side window. The sun was high in the sky, shining for once. It would be an effortless job. The one that every AT wanted. An easy notch on the belt. *It was about time*, thought Thomson. It was the third month of his tour and this was the first time he'd been called out to the SPAR

By the time they got there, Mr Simmons, the owner of the supermarket, would have done the hard work for them. As he did every Saturday. The IRA would put their bomb in the shop and he would take it out. Dump it on the street. All Thomson would have to do is put a few rounds of shot into the suspect device and the whole thing would be over.

As the Land Rover turned into Rosemount Road, Thomson could sense that something was amiss. Troop carriers, Land Rovers and armoured vehicles jammed up the street around the SPAR supermarket. Among the military vehicles was a white civilian ambulance with its blue light flashing.

'What's going on here?' asked Thomson.

'A bloody ambulance?' said Jock as he pulled up behind a troop carrier.

Thomson scurried out of the Land Rover and made his way to the infantry command post where a captain from the Scots Guards was waiting patiently. 'Afternoon, Sir,' said Thomson raising a salute. The captain took a quick look at the insignia on Thomson's arm.

'Afternoon, Felix.'

'What's the situation, Sir?'

'The IRA have shot the owner.'

'Dead?'

'No, he'll live.'

'Is that him in the ambulance?'

'No. He's been carted off to hospital already. That's an old lady.'

'They shot an old lady?'

'Heart murmur. Poor old dear was in the shop when it happened.'

'What about the bomb?'

'What bomb?'

'The owner. He normally puts the package in the street.'

'Not this time, Felix.'

The actions of Mr Simmons had finally caught up with him, thought Thomson. The IRA had finally lost patience.

'The woman in the ambulance. Can I speak to her?' asked Thomson.

'She's in no state,' replied the captain. 'She's suffering from shock. Medics have pumped her full of sedatives. But she was with a friend.' The officer pointed to an old lady with purple-tinted hair, talking to a plain clothes detective.

'Thanks,' replied Thomson as he headed over to his witness. *Trust my luck*, he thought to himself. *This is supposed to be the easiest job in*

Londonderry, and the one day I get it, the whole thing goes pear-shaped.
Thomson approached the detective. 'Do you mind if I talk to her?'

'Go ahead,' replied the detective.

'Hello, dear, my name's Dave.'

'I'm Betty,' replied the old lady, her hands shaking.

'I'm here to take care of any explosive devices, Betty. Make sure
this building doesn't get blown up. I need to find out what you saw.'

'It all happened so fast.'

'Try to remember, dear.'

The old lady took a sip of her tea as she searched her brain for some
details of the incident. She held up a finger as a fragment popped into
her head. 'Lorna was paying for a loaf of bread. And some butter, I
think. Then these two men came in with masks over their heads.'

'Were they carrying anything?'

Betty scoured her mind. 'One was carrying a box.'

'Just one?'

'Yes, I'm certain. One box.'

'And the other man?'

'He was carrying a shotgun. Ordered Mr Simmons to come out
from behind the counter. Mr Simmons was swearing blue murder.
Giving the man a right earful. And then it happened.'

'What happened?'

'He shot Mr Simmons in the knee.' The old lady's bottom lip quiv-
ered as she recounted the events.

'Take another sip of tea, Betty,' encouraged the Detective.

Betty took a big gulp, composed herself and continued. 'Then, when
Mr Simmons was screaming on the ground, he shot his other knee.' A
tear ran down Betty's cheek. 'It was terrible.'

'What did they do with the box?' asked Thomson.

Betty searched her mind for a few moments. 'I saw the man disappear in the storeroom. That's where he put it.'

'How long was he in there?'

'I don't really know. But it seemed a long time. Ten minutes. Maybe longer.'

'Is there anything else you can remember, Betty?'

'No. That's about it.'

'Thank you, Betty. You've been a great help.' Thomson gave the old lady a gentle squeeze on her shoulder, nodded his appreciation to the detective and walked back to the Land Rover.

Jock Henderson had prepared a Thermos of hot tea. He twisted off the top and poured it into a cup. He handed the brew to Thomson. 'What's the lay of the land, boss?'

'They've put a bomb in a box and planted it somewhere in the storeroom.'

'We going to let it soak?'

'What else is there to do?'

* * *

The two hours passed quickly. It was time. Thomson had considered using the wheelbarrow, but the doorway of the SPAR was an inch too narrow. He'd have to go in there.

'I'll get the bomb suit,' said Henderson.

'I'm not using that,' said Thomson. 'It'll just get in the way.'

'If you say so, boss,' replied Henderson, a hint of condemnation in his voice. Rules were rules.

'Get me a pigstick and a pair of wire-cutters.'

Henderson quickly found the equipment and handed it to Thomson.

Ninety-Nine and his men jumped into action and scoured the buildings, looking for anything suspicious. An open window, a flapping curtain, a head bobbing up and down.

Thomson lumbered slowly toward the supermarket. The captain from the Scots Guards, two NCOs by his side, kept their eyes glued to Thomson as he walked past them. The AT glanced over. They were the eyes of bystanders watching the condemned man heading for the gallows. He could feel their sympathy and their dread.

Thomson focused his eyes back on the SPAR. His heart was beating a little faster now, as it always did, as step by step he got closer to the job. He reached the front door, pushed it open and walked in. There was blood on the floor where poor Mr Simmons had been shot. Cornflakes from broken boxes of cereal were scattered over the tiles, soaked red from the blood.

Thomson walked into the storeroom. Shelves and shelves of boxes lined both sides of the room. Two hundred boxes. At least. The one he was looking for was hidden among them.

Thomson took a deep breath. This was going to take a bit of time. Be meticulous. Start at the door, work your way down the room and make your way back. His hands reached for the first box on the bottom shelf and gently pulled it out. What if it was a mercury tilt? No, the bomb-maker didn't have enough time. Thomson lifted the flaps as lightly as he could and peered inside. Cans of pineapple. There was a box behind that one. He pulled that one out too. Bars of chocolate. Thomson pulled out one box after another. Slowly. Methodically. Taking his time.

Two hours in and he'd only managed to get halfway down the storeroom. Other men would have lost patience. They would have rushed a few of the boxes. Thrown a bit of caution to the wind. In a hurry to get the ordeal over and done with. But Thomson wasn't one of those men. He could control his anxiety. Focus his mind. Calm his heart.

Three hours in. Two-thirds down. Box after box. Shelf after shelf. Still no sign of the package. Thomson was starting to get a little anxious. Three hours was too long to spend looking for a bomb. The hairs stood up on the back of his neck as he imagined the clock ticking away, getting closer and closer to detonation point. But it wasn't a rational thought. If it was a timer, it would have blown by now.

Almost four hours in. The far end of the storeroom. Just the top shelf to check out. Thomson climbed a stepladder, pulled out a box and opened it. Toilet paper.

And then he saw it. Tucked in behind. The box he'd been looking for. It wasn't like the other boxes. Different colour. Sitting at a slight angle. Smaller.

Thomson took a deep breath, grabbed the box by the sides and gently pulled it out. He slowly climbed down the stepladder until his feet found the hard surface of the storeroom floor. His hands were trembling ever so slightly. Thomson opened the flaps. Inside the box was four blocks of explosives, a detonator and wires connecting everything to an alarm clock.

Beads of sweat sprouted, like germinating seeds, on the AT's forehead as he examined the device. His mouth dropped. Time had run out. Literally. The long hand of the clock had made contact with the wire attached to the detonator, completing the electrical circuit.

It should have gone off. The SPAR Supermarket should have been blown to smithereens. He should be dead.

Thomson examined the mess of wires. It wasn't like the movies. There were never blue and red wires. Just black. Terrorists didn't colour code their work.

He quickly snipped the wire that appeared to connect the battery to the detonator. Something inside told him it was the right thing to do. It wasn't normally a decision he would make in haste. In normal circumstances, he would take his time. Be extra diligent about what he was cutting. Checking to see if there was a secondary device. Making sure there was no booby trap.

Thomson examined the clock, squinting his eyes and edging his face in closer. He couldn't believe his luck. There was a sliver of luminous paint on the second hand. Whoever had made the bomb had been sloppy. They hadn't scraped away all the paint. That tiny sliver was enough to stop the two pieces of metal connecting. The circuit couldn't be completed. Which meant no connection and no explosion. The AT sat on the floor and let out a huge sigh of relief. That was close. He looked up at the ceiling. 'Thank you, Lord.' He was an atheist. But even so, the words felt appropriate. Either luck was on his side or a hand from a higher power had intervened.

FORTY

Keith Cooper, dressed in his civilian clothing, was wedged into a wheelchair. A bandage had been wrapped around his left hand and another around his left foot. The visible reminders of his near-death experience.

As he was wheeled into the ops room by his number two, he suddenly felt out of place. His role here was defunct. No more calls. No more late nights. No more heroics. He would miss it.

'You're out,' said Thomson.

'Can't keep me locked up,' said Cooper.

'How's your hearing?' asked Jardine.

'Fine. Still got a high-pitched whining sound ringing through my head. Bit like listening to Rip all day.'

'See that mouth of yours is still working,' said Kersey. 'I paid that doctor a lot of money to sew it up.'

The banter brought a crack to Cooper's lips as he let out a chortle. 'I don't know where you get them from. Do you write them down in your notepad?'

'So I guess your adventure here is over,' said Sutton. 'Back to Ithaca.'

'Hounslow, actually,' said Cooper.

'Very similar places,' smiled Sutton.

'When are you off?' asked Thomson.

'Shipping me out this afternoon.'

'Not on that stinking ferry?' asked Jardine.

'No. I'm getting the VIP treatment. They're flying me out on a Hercules. MacIntyre insisted on it. Signed it off and everything.'

'Lucky bastard,' said Kersey with a grin.

'You *are* a lucky bastard,' said Thomson. Cooper nodded. A deferential acknowledgement of the good fortune that had befallen him.

Jardine held out his hand. 'Well, you survived the tour, Keith. Have a safe trip home.'

Cooper took it. 'Thank you, Sir. Just sorry I couldn't see it through to the end.'

'I bet you say that to all the girls,' said Kersey, raising a collective chuckle.

FORTY-ONE

The bungalow on Brandywell Road was set back forty feet from the main road. The streetlamps along the pavement weren't bright enough to illuminate the number on the front door. Curly had initially walked past the place. But backtracked once he realised the house numbers were going the wrong way.

It was a new safe house. Jimmy was being extra diligent. Mrs Hogan had been raided a couple of days previously. Too many touts were gobbing off just to make a bit of money. Mrs Hogan had nothing to say, of course. She had been kept in the dark. Didn't even know the names of the men drinking tea in her living room.

Curly walked to the front door and gave the coded knock. Barry Behan opened it up and invited him inside.

Steve Docherty and Jimmy Brett were sitting around the coffee table in the living room.

'I'll leave you to it then,' said the owner of the house as he disappeared into the kitchen where his wife was waiting for him.

'Take a seat, Curly,' said Brett.

Curly took a seat next to Docherty.

'Three times now,' said Brett.

'We've been unlucky,' replied Curly.

'Two times has a whiff of coincidence about it. Three times smells like a rat.'

'What are you saying?'

'We haven't got rid of our pest problem.'

'The circle of knowledge is very small,' said Docherty. 'Only five people knew about this mission. Me, Jimmy, O'Grady, the young lad McFaddon and you. Now I know it's not me. Jimmy knows it's not him. And I kinda figure that you're on the straight and narrow. So that leaves O'Grady and McFaddon.'

'McFaddon's new,' said Brett. 'So he couldn't have been involved in the previous leaks. That leaves O'Grady.'

'It can't be O'Grady,' said Curly. 'He's one of us.'

'He knew about the bomb factory,' said Docherty.

'That was Twomey,' said Curly.

'Maybe Twomey was innocent,' said Brett.

'Innocent? You killed him.'

'Aye. But maybe I killed the wrong man.'

'Fuck me,' said Curly.

'We're going to put some Dickers on him,' said Brett. 'See what turns up. But in the meantime, keep him out of the loop. You hear me.'

'Yes, Jimmy,' replied Curly. If the traitor was O'Grady, it would be a malignant betrayal. If he was the one, Curly would have no hesitation in taking a razor to O'Grady's throat.

* * *

The baked beans were bubbling away nicely in the pan. Janine O'Grady wasn't a very good cook. But she could do the basic stuff. A breakfast fry-up. Egg and chips. Baked beans on toast. She grabbed a wooden spatula and stirred the pan, scraping up the haricots that had stuck to the bottom. Done. She switched off the gas and poured the beans onto the slightly burnt toast she'd prepared earlier. 'Your dinner's ready,' she shouted as she placed the plate on the small dining table in the living room.

'Thanks,' said O'Grady, who was having a quick snooze on the threadbare settee. He stood up, walked the ten feet to the table and slumped himself down. 'Ketchup?'

'You don't need ketchup. The beans are bloody drowned in tomato sauce.'

'Not the same, is it?'

Janine marched out of the kitchen and slammed the bottle of ketchup in front of him. She took the seat opposite and watched him pick at his food.

'What's going on?' she asked, her piercing eyes boring through him. 'Nothing.'

'I know you, Seamus. You've been moping around for the past few days. Biting your nails. Stuffing shit down your face. Something's eating you up.'

She knew him more than he was comfortable with. He wanted to tell her. Had to at some point. Maybe now was the time. If he left it till the night before, how would she react? She'd be shocked, that was for certain. She was a Republican through and through. Her family had a deep history with the movement. But she wasn't that involved herself. She often complained about the IRA. Too many scumbags had been allowed to join and some of their acts were inhumane. Utterly despicable.

Should he tell her now? Would she understand? Play ball? Up sticks and go with him? Or would she tell him to bugger off? She was close to her mother. Would she choose her over him?

I'll tell her, he thought. 'I've been working.'

'You what?'

'I've been working. For the Branch.'

'Are you fucking kidding me?' Janine was about to go into a rage. Her face burning red.

'Keep it down. The neighbours will hear,' pleaded O'Grady. The walls in the terraced house were paper thin. If someone on the other side put a glass to their ear and placed it against the plaster, they'd be able to hear a baby breathing. Janine bit her lip and unleashed her hand across his face.

'You bastard!' she muttered through gritted teeth.

'Calm down.'

'How could you betray us?'

'I didn't betray you.'

'You betray the cause, you betray me.'

O'Grady sat up straight. This hadn't gone as planned. 'I've betrayed God.' Janine was caught off guard. She, like O'Grady, was a devout Catholic. She went to church with her mother three times a week. Went to confession every Wednesday. Without fail. Looking for penance for her venial sins. Placing them before the divine mercy for pardon.

'I'm going to Hell, Janine. Do you understand?'

'What you're doing. You're on the side of righteousness. God will forgive you.'

'No he won't. I've killed innocent people. Where's the righteousness in that?'

'God forgives all your sins. Even mortal ones.'

'I couldn't do it anymore, Janine. I wasn't the good guy. I was the bad guy. An evil little bastard. I needed to redeem myself. I needed to. Please.'

Janine slumped back in her chair. 'Fucking hell, Seamus.'

'They're giving us a way out. They're going to put us in a protection programme.'

'What the fuck is that?'

'They send us away. Give us new identities. New jobs. New lives.'

'But what about my family? My friends? I can't leave my mother.'

'If we don't go, they'll kill me. It's only a matter of time.'

'What if I say no?'

'Then I stay too. There's no point going if I'm not with my family.'

'But this is our home. Always has been. Always will be.'

'This isn't my home,' said O'Grady with a twisted mouth. 'I just happened to be born here. It's not home. It's fucking Hell.'

'We have our problems, but it *is* home, Seamus. There's no bloody place else.'

'You know, Janine, I was seven years old when my mother sent me out to get a loaf of bread from the corner shop at the end of our street.'

'What's that got to do with anything?'

O'Grady glared at his wife. 'Let me finish.' Janine sat back in her chair and folded her arms. 'When I got there, it was closed. So I ventured up the road where I found a shop that was open. I picked up a loaf and took it the counter. The shopkeeper looked down at me and asked me where I was from. When I told him I was from the Bogside, he told me to keep my money and get out of his shop. An old woman was standing behind me. Started shouting at me. "What the fuck are you doing in here you little Catholic bastard?" I walked out of the shop and she followed me. "Fuck off, you Catholic bastard. Fuck off. Go back to where you belong." And then a man, a fucking bystander, walked over and punched me on the side of my head. I made a run for it. I knew if I didn't, I'd get the beating of my life. I didn't stop running until I got to the Inn.'

Janine unfolded her arms and leant forward across the table. 'You're talking twaddle, Seamus. What's the fucking point?'

'The fucking point is that this is not our home. It's our prison. The Protestants don't want us here and the IRA have convinced us that the shitty piece of land we've been herded into is worth fighting for. But it's not. It's a shithole. Full of murderers and scum and power-hungry militants who believe they can treat us any way they fucking want to. It's worse than shit. It's a nightmare. And we've convinced ourselves the place is normal. Think about our kids. What future do they have? None. They'll be sucked into this shit of misery.'

Tears were running down Janine's cheek. She started shaking uncontrollably. It was as if a prophet had touched her head and given her the gift of insight. She was caught in two minds. She didn't want to leave. Her mother was getting old. She'd never see her again. But she didn't want to see her husband shot in the head and dumped in a ditch. She loved him, despite his flaws. He'd left her no choice. In sickness and in health. Till death do them part. Holy vows that can't be broken. Husband first. Family second.

'The kids will fucking hate you,' said Janine. 'They have a life here.'

'No, they won't. They'll move on.'

'Where do they want to send us?'

'Australia.'

'Australia? That's the other side of the bloody world, Seamus. It's too far.'

'It doesn't matter how far it is. We can never come back here.' Janine started crying, the reality of the situation sinking in.

'Okay. We'll do it.'

Seamus stood up, made his way round to her side of the table and gave her a hug. A tight hug. One that let out all the tension, stress and pent-up emotion. She reciprocated and wrapped her arms around his large girth.

'When is this happening?'

'Thursday. We're being picked up Thursday.'

'Shit. Two days.'

'You can't tell anyone. Not even your mother. We travel quick and we travel light.'

Janine felt sick to the stomach. How could she leave without saying goodbye?

* * *

Jason McEvoy and his three Dickers were playing on their bikes down the street from where O'Grady lived. Instructions had been given. Watch O'Grady's every move. Make sure you're not made. Anything out of the ordinary, let us know.

Jason took these assignments seriously. Each job was another opportunity to prove his value to the IRA. He wanted to be a volunteer. Do the real work. Fight the fight.

The front door to O'Grady's abode opened. He stepped out but was pulled back by his wife. He swung around and fell into an embrace. A long hug. An entanglement of emotion.

That's not normal, thought Jason. *What's going on there?* O'Grady managed to break away and let out, what seemed to Jason, some reassuring words. O'Grady made his way down the street in the opposite direction to the Dickers. The wife looking on. Worried. Once O'Grady had disappeared around the corner, Janine O'Grady went back inside her home, slamming the door shut.

'Shall we get after him,' said one of the young Dickers.

'You three tail the fat man,' replied Jason. 'I'm going to hang around here for a while.'

'Right you are, Jason.'

'Keep your distance.'

The three young Dickers rode off on their bikes in pursuit of O'Grady. Jason, on his Raleigh Chopper, dismounted. He leant against a lamppost and kept his eyes peeled on the O'Grady house. *What's up, Mrs O'Grady? What's got you so emotional?*

* * *

The bomb factory was normally a ten-minute walk from the Bogside. But O'Grady was in no hurry to get there and slowed down to a snail's pace. He was jittery. And that was not good. He was terrible at hiding his feelings and was worried that McFaddon, or God forbid, Curly, would pick up on his nervy signals. 'Keep it together, Seamus,' he said to himself. 'Only one more day to go.'

He came to Lecky Road and, as he turned the corner, caught a glimpse of the boys on the bikes. *Are they following me? Stop it, Seamus. You're being paranoid. They're just kids fucking around.*

O'Grady reached the flat, climbed the stairs and gave a coded knock on the door. McFaddon opened up. 'Morning, boss,' said the apprentice.

'Morning,' replied O'Grady flatly.

'Can I make you a mug of tea?'

'Aye, Donal. That would be grand.' The young volunteer disappeared into the kitchen while O'Grady edged over to the living room window. He pulled open the thick curtains three inches. Just enough to be able to spy on the street below. The kids on the bikes were hanging around on the corner. Maybe they were following him. The thought of it sent a shiver up his spine. *Get it out of your mind, Seamus. You're seeing things that aren't there.*

* * *

Janine smoked her cigarette. It was the first one she'd had in three years. Fucking Australia. It might as well be the fucking moon.

Tears welled up in her eyes. How could she leave without saying goodbye to the people she loved. She'd never see them again. The thought horrified her. Seamus's words sprung into her head. 'You can't tell anyone. Not even your mother.' Janine stubbed out her cigarette. Fuck Seamus. I'm not leaving without seeing my mother. I won't tell her anything. As far as she knows, it'll just be her daughter popping around for a chat. Yes. I'll pop around. Just for half an hour. What harm can it do?

Janine stood up, grabbed her coat and walked out the front door.

Jason McEvoy watched on as she walked hurriedly along the street. He slung his leg over his bike and followed her.

* * *

'Here we go,' said Mrs Gallagher as she put the pot of tea on the living room coffee table.

'Thanks, Mum,' said Janine.

'Do you want some biscuits?'

'No thanks, Mum. I'm trying to lose weight.'

'Get out ya,' said the old woman. 'Lose any more and you'll be a stick.'

'Go on then. Just one.'

Mrs Gallagher disappeared into the kitchen and returned a minute later with a plate piled up with chocolate digestives. 'Got these yesterday down at the Co-op. 10p off.'

'That's not one.'

'Tuck in, dear. I know you like the chocolate ones.' Janine couldn't contain her emotions. This is why she loved her mother. Selfless. Always putting her family first. A tear ran down Janine's cheek. 'Hey, what's up?' Mrs Gallagher pulled out a hankie from her sleeve and handed it to her daughter. 'There, there.'

'I'm sorry.' One tear suddenly turned into a flood. Janine's mascara melted into black streams that ran down her face.

Mrs Gallagher stood up and dragged her daughter to her feet. 'Janine, what's happened?'

'Nothing, Mum. Nothing.' The old woman put her arms around her daughter. Janine snuggled her face into her mother's bony shoulders. She wanted to tell her everything. Tell her that this would be the last time they'd see each other. But she knew she couldn't. It would be too dangerous. For both of them. 'I've got to go.'

'You can't like this. Stay here and we'll talk it through.'

'I can't, Mum.' Janine pulled herself away and ran to the front door. Mrs Gallagher chased after her. But there was no stopping Janine. She was bereft. 'I love you, Mum.'

'Janine, come back. Janine!' Her pleas fell on deaf ears. Janine was halfway up the road, running and bawling. Inconsolable.

Jason McEvoy saw it all. Spied them through the window. It was all very unusual. He didn't know what all this commotion meant. But he knew it was important. He followed Janine on his bike. She was still blubbing when she put her key in the front door and disappeared inside her house.

Jason smiled to himself. What would Docherty make of all this?

✳ ✳ ✳

The blue Vauxhall pulled up to the corner where the Dickers had been waiting patiently. The front window on the passenger side of the car wound down. Docherty poked out his head and locked eyes with Jason McEvoy. 'Anything?'

'I'm not sure,' replied Jason.

'Not sure?'

'I saw something, but it might be nothing.'

'Get in.'

Jason leant his bike against the wall, opened the back door and climbed inside. Liam O'Mahoney, who was sitting behind the steering wheel, adjusted his rear-view mirror to get a better view of the teenager.

'What did you see?' asked Docherty.

'I followed his wife.'

'Your mission was O'Grady.'

'The other three followed him.'

'And?'

'He walked to a place in Columbcille. Stayed there all day. Then walked home.'

'So why did you follow the wife?' asked O'Mahoney.

'She was very emotional. They had a big hug on the steps.'

'That's what husbands and wives do,' said Docherty.

'No they don't. Not like that,' replied Jason.

'What happened next?' asked O'Mahoney.

'Then I followed her to her mother's,' said Jason. 'She fell apart. Crying her eyes out. Hugging and sobbing. Her mother was trying to calm her down. Gave her a big hug. But she ran out of the house, snot and everything. Ran all the way home. Very upset she was.'

'What do you think they were talking about?' asked O'Mahoney.

'No idea.'

'You did well, Jason,' said Docherty as he handed over a fiver. Jason grabbed it appreciatively.

'Is there anything you need me to do, Mr Docherty?'

'No, you can go.' Jason jumped out of the car, mounted his bike and led his gang of Dickers down a side street.

'What does it mean?' asked O'Mahoney.

'I don't know. But I think we need a little conversation with our friend Seamus.'

'Want me to pick him up?'

'Yes, I do. The sooner the better.'

'Where shall I bring him?'

'The farmhouse.'

'Right you are.'

'Drop me off at the Inn,' said Docherty. O'Mahoney turned the ignition and headed toward the Bogside Inn. He knew why Docherty was heading there. He was going to have a powwow with Brett. Get instructions.

* * *

The kids were tucking into their fishfingers and beans. Janine and Seamus were sitting across from them, watching them eat. This would be the last dinner they'd have in the house. They hadn't told the kids yet. Wouldn't tell them until they were in the van. Best that way. No chance of their impending escape getting out.

There was a loud knock on the front door. Seamus and Janine gawked at each other with anxiety in their eyes. Seamus stood up, made his way to the door and opened it. O'Mahoney was on the other side.

'Liam,' said Seamus.

'We've been bounced,' said O'Mahoney. Seamus was taken by surprise. He was in a fix. When you were bounced you had to go there and then. No excuses. Shit.

'Right you are.' He looked over to Janine. She looked like she was about to cry. 'I'll see you later, love.' He walked out the door and closed it behind him.

A blue Vauxhall Victor was parked outside his house. 'In the back,' said O'Mahoney as he took his place behind the steering wheel. Seamus opened the back door and slid inside. Curly was at the far end of the back seat.

'Curly,' said Seamus. 'Must be a big job?'

'It is.'

O'Grady wanted to throw up.

FORTY-TWO

It was still dark outside when she woke up the two boys. They were grumpy. The oldest one moaned. 'Why are we getting up so early?'

'We're going somewhere,' was all she could tell him. She was worried. Seamus still wasn't back. She had an ominous feeling in the pit of her stomach. *Come on, Seamus. Please come back. Please. I can't do this without you.*

She spent the next hour getting the kids washed, dressed and fed. Then she took care of herself. She packed two small suitcases. One filled with clothes for the family. Just enough to get them by for the next few days. The other bag she filled with toiletries, toothbrushes, a couple of hairbrushes, the few bits of jewellery she'd got from her mother and her make-up.

Once she was done, she sat the kids down in the living room and tried to explain a bit more about what was going on. 'We're leaving Londonderry,' she told them. 'Your dad has to go to Australia. And we need to go with him.' Janine looked at the clock. It was almost 6 a.m. She was nervous and fiddling with her fingers. *Where are you, Seamus? Oh God.*

She heard a van pull up outside and, a moment's later, a knock at the door. She jumped out of her seat and peeked through the curtains. It was the Branch men. 'Come on, boys. It's time to go.'

She opened the front door and was faced with a copper with bright-orange hair. 'Mrs O'Grady,' said McGuigan. 'Are you all set?'

'He's not here.'

'What?'

'Seamus. They came for him last night. Said there was a job. But he hasn't come back.' Janine couldn't help herself. She started to cry.

'Come on,' said McGuigan. 'Let's get you out of here. We'll look for Seamus once we've got you safe.'

McGuigan bundled the family into the back of the van and slammed the door shut. He made his way round to the front and climbed into the passenger seat.

'All set?' asked McBride from behind the steering wheel.

'Let's go,' said McGuigan dourly.

* * *

As soon as the farmhouse came into view, O'Grady's worst fears were confirmed. Two thugs came out of the house, dragged him inside and planted him on a chair facing the wall. Darragh Quinn, the commander of the nutting squad, walked in the room. O'Grady had only met the man once before. But he knew why he was there. This was it. The end of the road. They'd sniffed him out and now he was going to pay the price.

'Do you know why you're here?' asked Quinn.

'No,' lied Seamus.

'You've been working.'

'No.'

'You can make this easy for yourself. Tell us.' Seamus kept his eyes focused on the wall in front of him. 'Did you know your wife went to see her mother?' Seamus's heart started to race. *Was this true? Or was he making it up? I told her not to. Fuck me. Those kids. They were staking me out. They know. Shit. They know.* 'Quite a commotion it was. Tears all over the place. Why do you think there was so much emotion, Seamus?'

'I don't know.'

'It was like, you know, it was the last time they'd see each other. A farewell.' Seamus started to tremble. The inevitable was starting to loom large in his head. 'Tell us what's going on, Seamus,' continued Quinn. 'Make it easy for yourself.'

Seamus stiffened his muscles and tightened his lips. Quinn moved around the chair until he was facing Seamus. He pulled a leather glove over his right hand and then unleashed a sharp, short punch to Seamus's nose. His beak exploded with blood and his eyes started to tear involuntarily. 'Are we really going to play this game, Seamus? You know very well it's going to get worse. Save yourself the pain and come clean.'

'She's innocent,' said Seamus. 'She only found out two days ago. Don't punish her.'

'If you give us what we need, Seamus, we'll leave your family out of it. That's a promise. Now…start speaking.'

Seamus let everything out. A huge release of pent-up misery. Like therapy. Healing and soothing. His guilt was dissipating with every word spoken. His soul shining brilliantly with truth. Nothing was left out. He told them when he started working for the Branch, how he was recruited, the information he'd given them, the people he'd betrayed.

When they asked about his handler, he didn't hesitate. Jonny McGuigan. Detective Inspector. After three hours of interrogation, Seamus was spent.

Quinn left the room and returned a moment later with Brett, Docherty and Curly following behind. Seamus couldn't look them in the eyes. Kept them firmly fixed on the ground.

'You, of all people,' said Brett. He glanced sideways at Docherty. Not a word left his mouth, but his eyes gave a very clear order. Docherty walked behind O'Grady and pinned his shoulders to the armchair with his two large hands. O'Grady panicked. He knew what this meant. He had to break free. Get out of there. He kicked his legs ferociously and pushed forward. Docherty's grip was almost broken. Quinn rushed in and punched O'Grady hard in the stomach. The pain bent him over. His body became limp. His vision blurred. Brett pulled a plastic bag from his coat pocket. He walked over to Seamus, placed it over the traitor's head and tightened it around his neck. Seamus struggled to get free. Docherty held on tightly. Seamus's face turned purple, his head thrashing from left to right, his mouth desperately trying to find air. His eyes were popping out of his head.

Within a minute, O'Grady's squirming body became limp, the life drained from his bulky frame.

Brett kept his grip on the plastic bag for another minute, partly to make sure O'Grady was dead and partly to prolong the pleasure he took from suffocating the man.

'He's dead, Jimmy,' said Docherty.

Brett let go of the bag. 'Dump him in the park. I want those Proddie bastards to know we got their snitch.'

'Do you really want to do that?' asked Quinn. 'A body means a murder investigation. No body means a missing person. Nothing for them to cling onto.'

'I'd normally agree with you Darragh. But this is different. I *want* them to know.'

'What about the wife?' asked Docherty.

'I want the traitorous bitch dead too.'

* * *

A light mist hung over the park. It was 6.30 a.m. and the grass was covered in dew, which glistened as the sun broke through the thin layer of clouds and caught the watery globules with its rays.

Tom Denny, a seventy-five-year-old pensioner, was up early to take Millie, his overweight black Labrador, for a walk and a bit of much-needed exercise. The park was empty. Tom liked this time of day. It was the only time he felt he could enjoy peace in a war-ravaged city.

As they found the middle of the park, Tom unclipped the lead from Millie's collar. She looked up at her owner, uncertain of what she was supposed to do. 'Come on, girl,' said Tom as he picked up a stick from the ground and waved it above the dog's head. Millie wagged her tail. Tom launched the stick into the air with a fling of his right hand toward a cluster of bushes. The Labrador rushed off excitedly after it.

Tom looked on as Millie disappeared behind the bushes. She didn't reappear. Come on, Millie. Find the stick. The Labrador remained out of sight. Tom shook his head, put two fingers in his mouth and whistled. 'Come on, Millie.'

The Labrador started barking. Tom marched toward the bushes. Before he could get there, Millie appeared, running toward her owner with an object in her mouth. She reached Tom and dropped a brown shoe in front of him. What's this? Tom walked around to the other side of the bush. The dog lead slipped from his hand as his body capitulated to shock. In front of him was the dead body of a man slumped against a tree. A plastic bag covered his head, the face purple.

* * *

Crowds gathered in the park as Seamus O'Grady's body was lifted onto a gurney and placed in the back of an ambulance.

Jonny McGuigan looked on. Was he responsible for this man's death? That last favour was perhaps one too many. O'Grady must have slipped up. Played the wrong move at the wrong time. Suspicion within the IRA was easy to arouse and, when it happened, their paranoia became acute. Irrational. But sometimes the absurdity of their random finger-pointing would lead to a lucky break. With a little bit of violence and a little bit of questioning, someone like O'Grady would fold pretty quickly, the beans spewing from his guts.

As McGuigan imagined the moment O'Grady struggled to find air, his lungs bursting, he started to wonder how much information they squeezed out of him. They would have asked about his handler. Name. Rank. Division. That wasn't good for McGuigan. He'd worked hard to stay under the radar. To pull the strings with an invisible hand.

Now he was exposed. He'd be hunted. He'd have to watch his back every minute of the day. Be on his toes. Perhaps he needed to change his appearance. Dye his hair black. No, that would draw ire from the boys at the station. Better to die at the hands of an assassin than look like a pillock.

The Special Branch man took out his flask of whiskey, screwed off the top and took a swig. Here's to you, Seamus. Hope Hell's not as bad as they say. I'll probably see you sooner than you think.

FORTY-THREE

It was Saturday lunchtime and the Gainsborough Arms was filled with a thick smog of cigarette smoke. Orangemen crammed into the small space, chatting loudly over each other and gulping down their drinks.

McGuigan could hear the hum of the crowd from fifty feet away. He reached the quaint front door with its pretty tinted glass and gold gilded type. Inhaling deeply, filling his lungs with fresh air, he opened the door and walked into the smoke-filled room.

Drew McBride was sitting in his usual place. On top of a bar stool at the far end of the pub. McGuigan barged his way through the crowd, apologising along the way as beer spilled from glasses. No one complained. They knew who he was. You didn't want to start anything with Jonny McGuigan. You'd come out on the wrong side of a good beating.

'The usual?' asked McBride as McGuigan pulled up the stool next to him.

'Aye.'

McBride shouted over to the barman. 'Ronnie.' The voice caught the barman's attention. Drew McBride was a VIP in this bar. And when he shouted, his order took priority. 'A wee Bush on the rocks and another Guinness for me.' The barman nodded, acknowledging the order.

'They got O'Grady,' said McGuigan.

'I heard.'

'Fuckers put a polyethene bag over his head.'

'Sorry, boss.'

'He wasn't a relative. You don't have to say sorry.'

'Still, he was working for you. Have the family been told?'

'RUC are handling it.'

'You were a cat's whisker away from getting him out. Just bad luck.'

'He fucked up somehow.'

'Look, I've heard something.'

'What would that be?'

'The word on the street is they're gunning for a senior Branch man. A tall, wiry fella with ginger hair. I'm guessing that's you.'

'Who'd you hear that from?'

'A couple of low-level bog wogs on our payroll.' McGuigan tapped the bar with agitated fingers. 'Maybe you should consider a transfer. Spend a couple of years in London.'

'I'm not doing that, Drew.'

The barman placed their drinks in front of them. McBride took two large gulps of his Guinness before planting the glass back on the wood. McGuigan knocked his whiskey back in one.

'Another one?' asked McBride.

The seed of a thought started taking shape in McGuigan's head. He couldn't let these bastards hunt him down and shoot him dead. Not without a fight. What did the paras say? *The best form of defence is attack.* And he knew exactly how to throw the first punch. 'No, I'd

better be off.' McGuigan headed out the door. He needed to make a
call to Ebrington barracks.

* * *

It was mid-afternoon and the traffic into the camp was starting to
build. Sentries stood guard at the entrance in steel helmets and shrap-
nel-proof jerkins, automatic rifles strapped to their wrists.

The young private, not yet eighteen, checked the Special Branch
identity card in McGuigan's outstretched hand. The soldier recognised
the orange-haired copper behind the wheel. He was a regular. Always
meeting with top brass. 'Morning, Sir.'

'Morning,' replied McGuigan.

'What's your business, Sir?'

'I'm here to see Staff Sergeant Thomson, 321 EOD. He's expecting me.'

'Thank you, Sir.' The sentry handed back the identity card and
nodded to one of his fellow sentries to lift the barrier. McGuigan gently
pressed his foot on the accelerator and headed toward the bomb disposal
ops room.

* * *

McGuigan held out his hand and Thomson took it. 'Good to see
you again, Dave.'

'How can I help you, Jonny?' asked Thomson.

McGuigan took a seat at the heavy wooden table in the middle of
the room. Thomson took the seat opposite, curious as to why the Special
Branch man had gone out of his way to set up a meeting. 'We've got a
problem.'

'Every day is a problem.'

'This one is very specific and one *you* should know about.'

'Sounds personal.'

'It is.'

Thomson sat back in his chair and folded his arms. 'I'm listening.'

'The little stunt you pulled with the detonating cord.'

'What about it?'

'It's got someone at the top of the Derry brigade very angry. So angry they want you dead.'

Thomson laughed. 'They'll have to get in line.'

'The thing is, they know your timetable.'

'Timetable?'

'They know which jobs you'll get called out on.'

'That's not possible.'

'Everything is possible. This base has more leaks than a baby's nappy. Dave, they stop everything just for you.'

The penny dropped. Those abnormally quiet days now made sense.

'How do they know?'

'Haven't got a clue.'

'We need to report this.'

'To who?'

'The brigadier.'

'He's going to ask you questions, Dave. He's going to ask why they're targeting you. What's so special about *you*? What are you going to tell him? That you put a detonating cord around a man's neck, threatening to blow his head off. And because of that, the IRA are after your sorry arse? He'll throw you in the stockade.'

The words from McGuigan's mouth were like bullets piercing Thomson's mind, leaving little holes of doubt and dread. 'What would you suggest we do?'

'Get on the front foot,' replied McGuigan through gritted teeth. 'Attack them before they attack us.'

'I don't get you.'

'I know where they're hiding all their explosives. We can booby trap the fucker. Kill the people who are trying to kill you.'

'You're out of your mind.'

'Or maybe I've got my head screwed on and I'm showing you a way to get out of this place alive.'

'I've only got two weeks to go.'

'Two weeks is just enough time to get killed.'

Thomson leant forward and pushed his face into McGuigan's personal space. 'What's in this for you?'

'We're two peas in a pod, Dave. They're after me too.'

The ops room phone made its familiar sound, bringing the conversation to an end. Thomson stood up slowly, walked over to the table in the corner and picked up the receiver. McGuigan could hear a garble on the other end of the phone, like a duck quacking for bread. 'Thanks, I'm on my way.'

'Are you in?'

'Sorry,' said Thomson as he left the room.

FORTY-FOUR

A stolen car had been abandoned on Bishop Street near the city centre. The IRA had called the RUC an hour earlier to let them know they'd planted a bomb in the boot. The terrorists liked to tip off the authorities because the chaos caused by a shutdown was greater, in many ways, than the bomb itself.

The crowds had already gathered at each end of the street, standing on tip-toes to get a better view of the theatre unfolding in front of them. The Green Howards had set up a cordon to keep them at bay.

'The wheelbarrow's ready, boss,' said Henderson.

'Send it in,' replied Thomson. Henderson pushed a steel lever and the robot moved slowly forward. 'It wouldn't win the hundred metres dash, would it?'

'More of tortoise than a hare,' chuckled Henderson.

The wheelbarrow took more than five minutes to reach the car. It was equipped with a camera, shotgun and a mechanical arm with a detonation cord in its pincer. Thomson stood behind the closed-circuit TV and scrutinised the pixels on the screen. 'Let's get a look inside, Jock?' Henderson craned the camera to get a good view of the interior. 'Nothing. Let's take the boot off, shall we?' With a twiddle of the controls, Henderson manoeuvred the robot's arm and laid a length of detonating cord along the seam of the boot.

Thomson, with the firing device in his hand, took a good look at the crowd. Everyone's eyes were on him. Watching with anticipation. He was the ringmaster in charge of the show, and it was about to start. 'Pull it out.'

Henderson withdrew the robot to a safe distance. 'Good to go, boss.'

'Firing,' shouted Thomson, flicking the switch.

The detonating cord exploded, breaking the boot open and leaving it ajar by a couple of feet.

'Okay, Jock. Send it back in.' The corporal put the robot into forward. Thomson kept his eyes committed to the screen. As the wheelbarrow approached the boot he could see a package in the back. A cardboard box that had been wrapped up with brown masking tape. 'There's our bomb.'

'Shotgun, boss?'

'Yep. Let's give it a blast.'

Henderson loved this bit. It was the only time he got to play bomb disposal man. He tilted the arm of the robot and pointed the shotgun at the box inside the boot. 'Tell me when, boss.'

'When.' Henderson pulled a lever. The shot ripped the box apart.

'Another one,' said Thomson. Henderson obliged.

Thomson examined the screen. A cloud of gun smoke shrouded his view. As it dissipated into the air, Thomson could make out the contents inside the box. A clock, wires and what seemed to be plastic explosives. The shotgun had done a nice job of smashing the circuit apart. 'I think we're safe to go in.'

'Shall I get the bomb suit out?'

'If you must.' Thomson didn't see the point of the suit. It wouldn't save your life. But after several ATs had flouted the rules and refused to wear the suit out in the field, orders were reissued from on high. The suit *must* be used. Any AT that disobeyed the orders would be reprimanded. No one knew what the castigation would be and they weren't prepared to break the rules to find out.

Henderson pulled out the various parts of the bomb suit and attached them, bit by bit, to Thomson's body. 'This thing weighs a ton,' moaned Thomson.

The last piece of the suit was the helmet. Henderson lifted it above Thomson's head and lowered it gently until it fit snugly into the neck of the suit.

'All set, boss,' said Henderson.

'Hook and line, Jock.' Henderson fetched the grappling hook and placed it in Thomson's gloved right hand. With a knuckle, he tapped the helmet twice. That was the sign to go.

Thomson walked slowly toward the car. Condensation was already starting to build up on the inside of the helmet's visor. Damn, I can hardly see. The bulky suit was making it difficult to walk freely. It was an unholy ordeal.

Thomson's breathing became heavy. Partly because of the exertion, partly because of the anxiety. He looked around at the surrounding buildings. They had an ominous halo around them. The sun caught something shiny and the glint irritated Thomson's eye. What was that? Could it be the sun catching the glass of a scope? If McGuigan was right, he was literally a walking target. A sniper could have his sights on him right now, watching him through cross-hairs. Ready to pull the trigger at any moment. The glint caught his eye again. Thomson was waiting for the bullet that would take him out. Splatter his brains across the street. *Get it out of your head, Dave*, he thought. *You'll drive yourself nuts. Just focus on the job.*

Thomson was out of breath by the time he reached the exposed boot of the car. He studied the device. The circuit had been broken. But that counted for nothing. For all he knew, there might be a secondary device hidden below. The IRA had done it before, so he wasn't about to take any chances. Thomson slipped the hook securely under the box and walked back slowly to where Henderson was waiting for him. The crowd looked on silently. A bit puzzled. This was the first time anyone had seen a bomb suit. It was like something an astronaut might wear.

The sweat was running down Thomson's face. His visibility was reduced to blurred figures through the condensation. Henderson rushed over to the AT and guided him to the Land Rover. 'Get this fucking thing off me,' shouted Thomson.

'Right away, boss,' replied Henderson as he pulled the helmet off.

Thomson sucked in the fresh air, desperately trying to get oxygen into his lungs. His head was wet from sweat. 'Have we got a towel?'

'We don't run a hotel service here, boss,' chuckled Henderson.

'That was fucking awful.'

'Let me see if there's a spare rag in the back.'

'Get this off me first.'

Henderson pulled off the different parts of the suit until the staff sergeant was peeled back to his normal attire. Thomson took a deep breath. A hundred pairs of eyes were watching his every move. Under normal circumstances, they would be invisible. But today, Thomson was flustered. As he scanned the crowd, his eyes caught a mop of curly hair. The man underneath it was smirking at him, a wicked smile filled with ill intent. Was that the same man from the border?

'Here you go, boss,' said Henderson, holding out a rag covered with grease.

'What?' said Thomson, distracted by the man with curly hair.

'The best I could find.'

Thomson turned to Henderson, grabbed the tattered cloth out of his hand and dabbed his neck and face.

'What about the bomb?'

'That can wait.'

'Are you okay, boss? You seem a bit rattled.'

Thomson didn't hear Henderson's words. He was caught up in his own anxiety. Get a grip, Dave. He looked back into the crowd. The man with the mop of curly hair had disappeared.

* * *

Curly Coyle watched as the corporal stripped the bomb suit off Thomson's body. The staff sergeant was drenched with sweat, breathing heavily, his face betraying anxiety and stress.

He doesn't look much, thought Curly. *Looked like a clown walking around in that ridiculous suit. Is this really the man we're up against? The man who had the temerity to put a detonating cord around my brother's neck? Doesn't look the sort. More of a fall-in-line type of man. A sheep rather than a wolf.*

Curly stared at the staff sergeant, willing him to look up. And he did, catching the chief bomb-maker's gaze. There you are, soldier boy. Take a good look. Because I'm the fucker who's going to get you. Put you in the ground. Curly smiled, hoping to tease a reaction from the bomb man. But Thomson was distracted by the corporal handing him a rag.

Time to get out of here. Curly Coyle slipped away through the crowd, more determined than ever to get his man.

FORTY-FIVE

Thomson was on his fifth pint. His nerves frayed. The old saying, ignorance is bliss, popped into his head. But he wasn't ignorant. He now knew, thanks to McGuigan, the IRA were out to kill him. Nausea was rising in his throat at the thought. It was one thing to be targeted as an anonymous British soldier among many. But to be targeted as an individual, by name and number. That was a different thing altogether. It was personal. Which meant the IRA would be more determined, more precise in their plans.

The door clattered open as Kersey barged into the ops room. 'What a fucking day,' said Kersey, pulling up a barstool next to Thomson. 'Running around like a monkey.'

Thomson nodded sullenly and took a gulp of his beer.

'You alright?' asked Kersey.

'Yeah, fine,' replied Thomson.

'You've got a face like a sour pig.'

'Been a long week.'

'Need an ear?'

'No. Just a beer.'

'Watch those. They get you pissed.'

'It's okay. I've got the day off tomorrow.'

'Lucky you. Maybe you should get out of camp. Might cheer you up.'

Thomson wanted to tell Rip about his predicament. He trusted him. Felt more courageous with him around. He was a big brother who looked out for you. But what could Rip do? What would the point be of dragging him into this mess? It would only complicate matters.

'Can't hang around,' said Kersey. 'Duty-One tomorrow and I need some shut-eye.' Kersey slapped Thomson on the back and headed out the door.

Thomson slugged down the remainder of his beer and slammed the glass on the counter. 'Fuck.' Do something, Dave. He had to get ahead of this now and deal with the consequences later. Sitting around moping wasn't going to solve anything. Thomson made his way to the ops room phone, a renewed determination in his stride. He picked it up and made a call to the base exchange.

'Hello,' the voice on the other end of the line said.

'Can you put me through to Strand Road police station?' asked Thomson.

* * *

It was still dark outside when Thomson climbed out of bed. He checked his watch. 5 a.m. After washing his armpits, brushing his teeth and combing his hair, he pulled on a pair of jeans and a sweater.

He pulled a khaki canvas bag from underneath his bunk, unzipped it and peered inside. A final check. Everything he needed was in there: a couple of detonators, a coil of wire, cutters, torchlight and duct tape.

A last-minute thought entered his head. The mouse. He reached over to the bedside table, grabbed Kersey's toy rodent and put it in the back pocket of his jeans. *All set*, he thought as he headed out the door.

McGuigan was already parked up outside the Sergeants' Mess. Waiting. Thomson climbed into the passenger seat and slipped the canvas bag between his legs.

'Morning,' said McGuigan as he glanced at the bag. 'Got everything you need?'

'Yeah. Where we going?'

'Into the woods.' McGuigan started the engine and drove out of the camp. The sun was just beginning to rise and the streets were starting to come alive. The obedient soldier inside Thomson wanted to tell McGuigan to stop and turn the car around. But it was too late. They were on their way.

Thomson, at the point of no return, was wondering what the hell he was walking into.

FORTY-SIX

I t was a full Irish. Bacon, sausage, egg, beans and black pudding, with two slices of toast on the side.

Brett picked up his knife and fork and launched into the breakfast. As he did every morning at O'Brien's cafe. At 6.00 in the morning, the place was filled with workmen filling their stomachs with fatty, greasy food before heading off for an arduous day's work on a building site. It was hard to hear yourself speak above all the noise. A continuous hum of chattering men, the sound of bacon frying, the clatter of cutlery hitting ceramic plates. The odd burst of laughter.

Brett had secured himself a table in the corner. Curly Coyle was sitting across from him, sipping hot tea from a mug. He wasn't much of a breakfast man. He was there because Brett had summoned him for a chat.

Barry Behan was keeping watch outside the cafe, smoking a cigarette and scouring the street for anybody who looked suspicious. Anyone who had a whiff of Military Intelligence or Branch about them. Curly watched the Scotsman through the large glass-paned window. He was a scary figure. The silent, calm type that could turn violent in an instant. Brett noticed Curly's interest in the bodyguard. 'Not much gets past him.'

'What?' said Curly, taken by surprise.

'Behan.'

'Oh. Yes.'

'I saw him take two bastards down. Killed one and put the other one in a wheelchair. Doesn't mess about that boy.'

'I'll remember that.'

Brett took a sip of his tea and looked at Curly pensively. 'O'Grady was your mate.'

'He was,' replied Curly.

'You must be cut up.'

'I am. I knew him for a long time. He was like a brother.'

'We never really know anybody, do we?'

'Guess not.'

'You didn't know him at all,' reflected Brett. Curly looked down at his tea, an ache spreading in his stomach. 'But what's important to me, right now, is you understand.'

'Understand what?'

'Understand that he was not of the same feather. He was not like me and you. He was a traitor. A dirty little tout who sold us out. Sold *you* out.'

'I get that.'

'Do you?' said Brett raising his voice. 'Explain to me how.'

'I feel betrayed.'

'Is that it?'

Curly's temperature started to rise. He didn't deserve this treatment. His loyalty was beyond doubt. He spoke through a trembling voice. 'He got what was coming to him.'

'He deserved worse.'

'If you had given me a gun, I would have put a bullet in his skull myself.'

'What about a polythene bag?'

'A polythene bag?'

'Not your cup of tea?' pressed Brett.

'No.'

Brett stared into Curly's eyes, trying to get a glimpse into his soul. He leant back in his chair and wiped his mouth with a paper serviette. 'Don't get me wrong, Curly. I'm not angry at you.'

'Good to know.'

Brett picked up his mug of tea and took a large gulp. 'What's the damage?'

'We're shutting down everything he knew about. The flat in Columbcille has already been decommissioned.'

'What about the dump?'

'We're going out there today.'

'Seems like you've got it all under control.'

'I have.'

'You'd better get to it then.' That was Brett's way of saying fuck off, we're done here.

Curly got up from the table and left the cafe without saying a word. The dump was front of mind. What if O'Grady had spewed his guts to the Branch?

FORTY-SEVEN

McGuigan navigated the BMW along the small, bumpy track that weaved through a forest of pine trees. 'Sure you've got the right road?' asked Thomson.

'Hope so,' replied McGuigan.

'Hope so? You've been here before, right?'

'Nope. This is the first time.' As they turned a corner, the old, crumbled building came into view. 'This is it.' McGuigan parked up the car and both men stepped out. They stood statue-still for a while, giving their ears and eyes time to pick up any unusual sights and sounds, any evidence of human presence.

'All clear,' muttered Thomson.

McGuigan made his way to the back of the ruin. Thomson grabbed his canvas bag and followed closely behind. They came to a pile of bricks covered by branches, shrubs and thorns. 'It's under that,' said McGuigan.

Thomson opened his bag and pulled out a pair of thick gloves and put them on his hands. 'Let's get to it then,' said Thomson as he started ripping the thorns off the top of the pile. Once the barbed plants were cleared, McGuigan cleared the branches and the bricks. Beneath all the debris was a metal door. The Special Branch man was excited. He grabbed the handle. 'Stop.'

'What?' said McGuigan.

'It could be booby-trapped. Stay still.' McGuigan froze as Thomson rummaged through his bag to find a torch. He switched it on and ran it across the gap between the door and the ground, looking for wires that might trigger an explosion. 'Lift it gently.' McGuigan did as instructed. 'Okay, it's clear. You can open it.' McGuigan pulled the door up until it was vertical and then let it fall backward onto the ground. The metal made a thunderous clang.

As the two men peered into the dark basement, a pungent smell wafted under their noses.

'Can you smell that?' said McGuigan.

Thomson sucked in the air through his nostrils. 'Fuel oil.'

The two men descended into the cavern below. Thomson shone his torchlight beam around the room. The light landed on barrels of fuel oil, fertiliser bags and jars of ammonium nitrate. 'What's that in the corner?' asked McGuigan.

Thomson swung the light around and picked out a large tarpaulin that was covering something sizeable. The AT walked over and gently peeled it back to reveal a massive stash of plastic explosives, small packages that had been neatly stacked in columns.

'Jackpot,' said McGuigan.

'That's a shitload of explosives,' said Thomson.

'How much?'

'Over a ton. Maybe a ton and a half.'

'That's a lot of death.'

Thomson held the torchlight between his teeth. He rummaged around inside his canvas bag and pulled out a detonator, a few feet of copper wire and an Eveready battery. He got to work, quickly assembling a booby trap. Even though it was cool in the basement, beads of sweat sprouted from Thomson's brow. His heart was racing, but his fingers moved slowly, meticulously piecing the bomb together. Was he really doing this?

Fifteen minutes later and the bomb was ready. Thomson pulled out four packets from the middle of the stack of plastic explosives and placed his device inside, replacing the packets on top so his handiwork remained hidden. A short length of copper wire, with a noose at its end, was sticking out. Thomson put his hand in the back pocket of his jeans and pulled out the toy mouse. He inserted the toy into the noose, tightening the wire around the rodent's neck. The AT gently positioned the furry lure so it looked as natural as possible. 'Done,' said Thomson, an air of pride in his voice.

'A fucking mouse?' said McGuigan.

Thomson smiled. 'The most dangerous mouse you'll ever meet.'

* * *

The two stolen Ford Transits travelled along the A6 half a mile apart. Docherty and Curly were in the lead, O'Mahoney and McFadden in the rear. At 7 a.m., the road was quiet. Sparsely populated by cars heading into the city and tractors heading the opposite way toward the fields.

'How the hell did you find this place?' asked Docherty.

'I just went for a ramble one day,' replied Curly. 'Stumbled upon this old building and thought that would be a good place to hide a shitload of bombs.'

Docherty laughed half-heartedly. 'What if O'Grady told them about it?'

Curly looked out the window. He had the same concern. O'Grady had been on the inside. He knew everything about the IRA setup.

Where the factories were located and who was running them. But despite his knowledge of the IRA bomb-making apparatus, it seemed that he had kept it mostly to himself.

After O'Grady's execution, Curly was certain that all the factories would be raided. But they weren't. He had managed to clear out the bomb-making facilities and find new ones without any trouble. It occurred to Curly that maybe O'Grady was drip-feeding information to the Branch men. Giving them enough to feed their hunger without emptying the kitchen cupboard. That way he would be able to protect himself. Hide his identity. Stay alive.

Did O'Grady tell them about Loughermore? *No*, said Curly to himself. O'Grady was the only other person who knew about the location. If the dump had been found, O'Grady would've been outed. It was a secret too dangerous to tell. The dump in the forest was safe. Curly was absolutely sure of it.

Docherty persisted. 'What if O'Grady told them about it?'

'We'd know by now,' said Curly.

Docherty tightened his lips and kept his eyes on the road.

'Turn left here,' said Curly.

Docherty switched on his left indicator and turned onto Baranailt, one of the only two roads that led to Loughermore Forest.

They soon came to a crossroads and a Give Way sign. Docherty came to a halt and looked left and right for oncoming traffic. A BMW came to a stop on the other side of the crossroads. *The car looked out of place*, thought Curly as he scrutinised the driver who stood out with his flash of bright-orange hair. Next to the red nut was a man whose face was partly hidden by a gleam of sunlight on the windscreen. But despite the sun's reflection, the man seemed familiar. Curly couldn't place him.

There was no traffic, so Docherty put his foot on the accelerator and cut across the intersection. Curly looked down into the BMW as the van sped by. The man with orange hair caught his gaze. The man next to him, the one that seemed so familiar, was looking the other way.

* * *

McGuigan had managed to find his way out of Loughermore's wooded spiderweb and was driving along Baranailt Road, heading back toward the city centre. He pulled up at a crossroads. A Ford Transit had stopped on the other side. McGuigan looked left and right and was about to cross the intersection when Thomson made a proclamation. 'That's him.'

'Who?' asked McGuigan.

'The man with the curly hair.'

McGuigan kept his foot on the brake and focused his attention on the men in the van.

'That's the IRA man I saw at the border,' continued Thomson.

The van shot across the intersection toward them. As it passed by the BMW, Curly Coyle peered down at McGuigan from his elevated perch. McGuigan reciprocated with his own flinty-eyed gaze. *So you're the one*, he thought. *The man causing all the problems. Well, not for very much longer, sonny.*

* * *

The pub was dark but strangely warm and welcoming. An old pub made with old wood and occupied by old men. Thomson waited in a corner alcove, a couple of spent pint glasses in front of him. A moment later McGuigan appeared with two pints of lager in his hands. 'Here you go.'

'Thanks,' said Thomson, putting the glass to his mouth and taking a big gulp of fizzy beer. It was their third pint. The alcohol had gone to Thomson's head and steadied his nerves. 'Where are we?'

'Bushmills.'

'Where they make the whiskey?'

'Aye. Good whiskey it is too. Always a good place to drop off for a drink after a hard day at work.' McGuigan raised his glass. 'Here's to a job well done.'

'It's not done yet.'

'It's done, believe me. And I'm grateful for your help, Dave. Not many people would stick their necks out like that.'

Thomson took another gulp of his beer. 'You know what they say, when you stick your neck out, it's easier for them to chop off your head.'

'You're worried?'

'No, I'm not worried. I just don't feel good about what we've done. It doesn't sit well with me, Jonny.'

'The rules are different out here, Dave. If we played with a straight bat, we'd be trampled over. What you did today was a good thing.'

'Good might be too strong a word.'

'Don't carry a cross, Dave. You'll get splinters in your back.'

Thomson couldn't help but laugh. 'You have a strange way of putting things, Jonny.'

'Come on,' said McGuigan. 'Drink up and I'll take you back to camp.'

Thomson stood up and followed McGuigan out of the pub. His mind was racing. What if they spotted the booby trap? They'll know we're onto them. And that will make them more determined than ever to get their man. Thomson felt his hands go clammy. If the IRA survived his booby trap, he wouldn't stand a chance.

* * *

McFaddon and O'Mahoney cleared away the debris above the stash, while Curly and Docherty watched on.

'You can help,' complained O'Mahoney.

'You're doing just fine,' replied Docherty.

Once the debris was cleared, Curly flung open the metal door, switched on his flashlight and ventured into the basement, the other IRA men following like sheep.

'We'll put the plastic in one van and the rest in the other,' instructed Curly.

'Which one shall we take?' asked McFadden.

'Take the plastic,' replied Curly, pointing to the corner where the blocks of explosive had been stacked and shrouded in tarpaulin.

O'Mahoney ripped off the sheet. 'Careful,' said McFadden. 'That's fucking explosives.'

O'Mahoney smiled sarcastically at the young bomb-maker. 'You sound like a little girl.'

'Maniac,' murmured McFadden under his breath. An object on top of the pile caught his attention. He let his eyes get accustomed to the dark and make sense of the blurry shape. 'Fuck, there's a mouse.'

'What?'

'Look.' McFadden fixed his torchlight on the small rodent.

O'Mahoney leant over to take a closer look. 'I think it's dead.'

McFadden pushed the rodent gently with his torchlight. 'I think you're right.'

'What are you two fucking around with?' shouted Docherty from the other side of the room.

'We found a dead mouse.'

'Of course you fucking did. We're in the fucking countryside.'

'What do you want me to do with it?'

'You can fucking eat it for all I care,' said Docherty.

Curly wasn't amused. He was here to do a job. Not lark around. These men were acting like fools. And fools got you killed. He marched over to McFadden and O'Mahoney, his face filled with enmity. 'Can you two stop fucking around and get this stuff out of here.'

O'Mahoney reached over and grabbed the mouse by the tail. A glint from the copper wire wrapped around the rodent's neck caught Curly's eye. Shit. Someone's been here. The man in the BMW. Could it have been the bomb disposal man? Surely not. O'Grady. He told them.

Curly watched in horror as O'Mahoney lifted the mouse in the air. 'Nooooooo—'

A flash of intense-white heat rolled over the chief bomb-maker, melting the flesh on his body and incinerating his bones.

FORTY-EIGHT

Kersey stood over the crater where, he presumed, a farm building once stood. It was a big hole. Twenty, maybe twenty-five yards in diameter. Bricks had been flung two hundred yards in every direction. Two transit vans had been thrown onto their sides, crushed and mangled by the force of the blast.

Colby arrived at Kersey's side with a mug of tea. 'Thanks,' said Kersey as he took a sip.

'What do you want to do, boss?' asked Colby.

'Don't think there is anything to do.'

'What's it all about?'

'I've no idea. If I was to hazard a guess, it's an IRA stash that's gone up.'

'That's some hole. Must have been some stash.'

'Yeah. Lucky it was in the middle of a forest. Would have caused some serious damage in a built-up area.' Kersey handed his mug of tea to Colby and shuffled down into the crater. 'I'm going for a shufty.'

The AT scoured the ground looking for anything unusual, clearing bricks out of the way with both his feet. If people had been near the blast, they would most likely have been vaporised. But an explosion – even a big one like this – was a strange and unpredictable beast. It could be pitiless, cremating all organic matter in its way. But it could also show pockets of restraint, like a god exerting its magical privilege, leaving traces of humans who dared to be in its presence.

Kersey moved up the crater to where a ring of debris had formed. A burnt boot caught his eye. He picked it up. The leather was tough and had managed to survive the firestorm. As his eyes wandered to the right, he spotted a blackened hand sticking up through the rubble. Kersey walked over to take a closer look. He noticed something caught between the thumb and forefinger. Is that a mouse? No, it's a toy mouse. Lucy!

* * *

McGuigan pulled his car up to the kerb outside the camp gate. He held out his hand and Thomson took it. There was no need for words. Everything they needed to say to each other had been said. Thomson climbed out of the car and slammed the door shut. The BMW pulled away.

Thomson watched on as the BMW turned the corner, an ominous feeling welling up inside. Was this the end of it? Were the fading tail-lights of McGuigan's BMW an allegory of a crisis thwarted? Or was it just the portent of trouble to come? Thomson put the dark thoughts out of his head, walked up to the camp's sentry post, flashed his ID and strolled slowly toward the Sergeants' Mess. He felt dirty and needed a shower.

A Land Rover pulled up beside Thomson just before he reached the entrance of the mess. Kersey stuck his head out of the window and looked Thomson up and down. The staff sergeant's jeans and boots were muddy. 'What have you been up to?' asked Kersey jovially. 'Digging up a field?'

'Just a walk in the country.'

'A walk in the country? Did you see any mice?'

'What?'

'Just ribbing you, Dave.'

'Where have you been?' asked Thomson.

'Just got back from Loughermore Forest where I found a big bloody hole in the ground.'

'Anyone injured?'

'Fancy a beer? I'll tell you all about it.'

* * *

It was an unusually quiet night for 321 EOD, and as such, the ops room had its full complement of ATs. Kersey switched on the TV and turned the channel to the BBC. The newscaster announced the explosion in the middle of Loughermore Forest. Jardine and Sutton watched on, their mouths agape, bewildered by the announcement.

'You might get a medal for this,' said Captain Jardine.

'I didn't do anything,' replied Kersey.

'What's that got to do with the price of bread?'

'I wouldn't accept it,' said Kersey.

'Good on you,' said Sutton. 'A warrior is defined by his scars, not his medals.'

'Maybe a BEM,' said Jardine.

'More like an OBE,' said Kersey. 'Because that's all it is, a bit of entertainment for the toffs at the top.'

'You're a cynical bastard, Rip,' said Jardine.

'And may long it last,' said Sutton.

Thomson walked into the room.

'Ah, the prodigal son,' shouted Rip. 'How was your day?'

'Just hanging around mostly.'

'Have you seen this?' said Captain Jardine pointing at the TV screen. 'The IRA, it seems, is doing our job for us.'

Thomson fixed his eyes on the TV. Footage from a helicopter showed the damage caused by the explosion. The staff sergeant feigned surprise. 'Bloody hell.' He could feel Kersey's eyes locked on him.

'Fancy that beer, Dave?' said Kersey.

The two men walked to the bar at the far end of the ops room. Thomson climbed onto a barstool while Kersey moved around to the serving side and took command of the beer tap.

'Something not right about Loughermore,' said Kersey.

Thomson kept his mouth shut. He didn't want to engage in the conversation. Because if he did, he'd have to lie. And he wasn't very good at that.

'Must have been a big dump,' continued Kersey. 'At first, I thought maybe the stupid bastards put a spotty teenager in charge. You know what the IRA are like. They're happy to put babies in charge of stuff that's too big for them.' Kersey handed Thomson a pint of Carlsberg, took another glass and poured his own. 'But then I thought, nah. With a stash that big, they're not going to put some little knacker in charge. Doesn't make sense.'

'A lot of stuff doesn't make sense over here.'

'I agree with you, Dave.' Kersey reached into his pocket, pulled out the charred toy mouse and flung it on the bar. 'I found this. In a dead man's hand.'

Thomson choked on his beer. 'Fuck me. How the fuck did that survive?'

'I don't know. You tell me.'

Thomson took a deep breath and leant back into the cushioned back of the barstool. 'It's a long story, Rip.'

'That phone isn't ringing, so I guess we've got time.'

In some way, Thomson was relieved he'd been found out. Keeping the secret bottled up inside, even though it had only been for a day, was weighing on his mind. On his soul. Kersey had shaken the bottle and popped the cork and all Thomson had to do was let it all gush out. And gush out it did. He told Kersey everything. The life and death situation at the Droppin' Well. The decision to put a detonating cord around the terrorist's neck. The news from McGuigan that the IRA had put a target on his back. The worry that his wife would be made a widow by lousy IRA men with a lousy grudge. The plan conjured up by the Special Branch man to thwart the terrorists. And the booby trap he'd laid for the man with the curly hair. The man who would have him dead.

Thomson hardly took a breath as he blurted the details of his misdeeds and misdemeanours. Kersey resisted the temptation to interrupt and instead let Thomson get to the end.

'Why didn't you say something?' asked Kersey.

'It was my problem. I'd stepped over the line and I couldn't walk it back.'

Kersey picked up the blackened mouse and threw it toward Thomson, who caught the toy in his right hand. 'Told you that little bastard would save your life.'

'What should I do? Talk to MacIntyre?' Thomson had an overwhelming urge to cleanse himself further of his grubby dealings. He wanted to tell someone in authority. Make his misdeed official.

'Don't be daft,' said Kersey. If I'd been in your shoes, I would have done exactly the same thing.'

'I don't think so.'

'No doubt a fucking about it, Dave. We play it clean and they play it dirty. But if your neck's on the line, you have the right, in my book, to play it dirty back. You only have one life. No one's going to turn around at your graveside and say, "we're sorry he's dead but at least he was a decent fella who didn't break the rules". Fuck that. I take my hat off to you, Dave. You stuck it to the bastards.'

Kersey held out his hand and Thomson took it.

'My advice,' said Kersey. 'Keep it to yourself and take it to the grave with you.'

FORTY-NINE

The bubbles in the pint of Guinness were sinking to the bottom of the glass. Brett watched them, reflecting on the string of mishaps that had stricken his unit over the past few months. 'Did you know,' said Brett, 'that Guinness is the only beer where the bubbles go downward?'

'No, I didn't,' said Behan who was sitting beside the commander at the bar, nursing a cup of black coffee.

'It's because they mix nitrogen with the carbon dioxide.'

'You learn something new every day.'

The noise outside was getting louder as the motorcade of four hearses, followed by a large crowd of Bogside residents, reached the Inn and turned right onto Lecky Road. Brett craned his neck to get a look. 'I'd better make an appearance.' The commander knocked back his Guinness and slammed the empty glass on the bar top.

'Another?' asked Byrne.

'No,' said Brett.

Byrne swept up the glass and put it in the sink. The Bogside Inn was empty. The doors kept closed out of respect for the fallen. Which made it the ideal place for a clandestine meeting.

'Give it to him, John,' said Brett. Byrne reached under the counter, grabbed two pistols and placed them on the counter in front of Behan. A Webley .455 and a Browning MK1.

'Untraceable,' said Byrne.

Behan picked up the Browning and slipped it into his coat pocket. Byrne picked up the Webley and put it back in its hiding place beneath the counter.

Brett climbed off his stool and, without uttering a word, walked out of the Inn where he joined the entourage of mourners making their way to St Columba's Church.

* * *

The last two weeks of Thomson's tour had passed without major incident. Just a string of hoaxes interspersed with the occasional clock bomb.

And now it was over. He'd survived the four months. Thomson's last day in Northern Ireland coincided with the funeral of the men he'd had a hand in blowing up. The irony of the day hadn't slipped his attention. He'd be climbing to the top deck of the ferry as they were being lowered into the ground.

He felt elated. His tour was over and he had survived. Jean and the kids were waiting for him at home. *She must be excited*, he thought. He was excited too. He couldn't wait to hold her in his arms again.

The ops room was empty. The rest of the unit had been called out on jobs. But Thomson had managed to say his farewells over the previous few days. He'd miss the crew, that was for sure. On a tour like this, bonds were made that would last a lifetime. Rip, especially, would stay in his heart for ever. The mentor, the friend, the man who gave him courage.

Thomson picked up his mug of tea and swallowed the last of the brew. It was his sixth cup. That morning's predilection for tea had increased partly because of his excitement at leaving and partly because there was nothing else to do except drink something hot and milky.

The ops room door swung open and Jock Henderson walked through it.

'Jock,' said Thomson as he put down his mug and stood up.

'Boss,' replied Henderson. Thomson walked over to his number two and smiled. Henderson smiled back. 'You're off then?'

'Yeah. It was a pleasure working with you, Jock.'

'It's been an honour working with you, Sir.' Henderson moved forward and embraced Thomson with his arms. Thomson hesitated for a moment before wrapping his arms around the Scotsman. Men didn't hug in the army. But he could make an exception for this man. They had formed a close bond. Thomson liked the short, wiry Scotsman. His doggedness. His humour. His loyalty.

The hug was brief. But both men knew how much it meant. They had been through remarkable times together.

Thomson held out his hand and Henderson took it. 'Have a safe trip back, boss.'

'Take care of yourself, Jock.' Henderson turned on his heels and walked out of the ops room, tears welling up in his eyes. Soft bastard, thought Thomson, a tender smile spreading across his face. He picked up his suitcase, looked around the room briefly and walked out the door. The Q car that had been assigned to take him to the ferry was waiting outside.

The driver spotted Thomson, rushed over and grabbed the suitcase from his hand.

'Afternoon, Staff,' said the young soldier. 'Let me help you with that.'

'Thank you.'

The driver took the suitcase and slung it in the boot. Thomson, who would normally climb into the front passenger seat of the car, was feeling antisocial and so climbed in the back. He didn't want to engage in small talk on the way to the ferry. He wanted to indulge in his own company for once. Keep his thoughts to himself.

'All set, Staff?' asked the driver.

'Yes. All set.' The driver pulled away. Thomson felt strange. *One minute you're deep in the action*, he thought, *and the next you're an outsider. Just a casual observer. It would be a smooth ride back from here.*

* * *

The Gainsborough Arms was full to the rafters. Everyone's eyes were on the TV. Today was the funeral of the four IRA men who had lost their lives at Loughermore Forest and BBC Northern Ireland were beaming the images live. The Catholic community was out in force. Over a thousand people walked behind the four hearses carrying the coffins of the fallen heroes, each draped with the tricolour flag.

The security forces were out in strength too, determined to stop the IRA from giving their dead brethren a pistol salute.

'They'll be out soon,' said McBride, who was sitting at the bar next to McGuigan.

'I don't know why the squaddies try and stop them,' said McGuigan.

'You've got to try.'

'Fucking no point,' said McGuigan. 'They're going to do it anyway. All it does is create more angst.'

Eight men dressed in paramilitary garb, their faces covered by black Balaclavas, appeared out of the thick crowd. They marched quickly to the side of the hearses, pulled out their pistols and fired four shots each into the sky. The security services tried to swarm in but the hostile crowd made sure they were held at bay. The eight men, palming their weapons off to accomplices in the crowd, melted away as quickly as they had appeared.

'Fucking told you so,' said McGuigan as he took a sip of his whiskey.

The newscaster, with her posh English accent, gave a running commentary of the events. Four photographs of the dead men were flashed up on the screen. She read out their names and gave details of where they were from. Patrick Coyle from Meenan Drive, the Bogside. Steve Docherty from Kerrigan Close, Brandywell. Donal McFaddon from Curlyhill Road, Strabane. And Liam O'Mahoney from Farndreg Estate, Dundalk in the Republic of Ireland.

McGuigan froze. He recognised O'Mahoney's face. But he couldn't place him. Where the fuck do I know him from? He searched the database inside his mind for scraps of information.

Dorothy!

He'd seen him that night inside the blue Vauxhall with Dorothy. All the disparate cogs in McGuigan's head clicked together to reveal a fully formed picture. The Special Branch man put his hand into his pocket, pulled out a couple of pound notes and slammed them on the counter. 'I've got to go.'

'Go where?' asked McBride as McGuigan walked out of the pub.

* * *

Robert Campbell was out of the house. Dorothy didn't know where. Didn't care. He was probably down the pub with his cronies getting pissed and making stupid little plans. The longer he stayed out, the better. Hopefully she'd be fast asleep by the time he crawled into bed in the early hours of the morning.

She lay back into the settee with a whiskey in her hand watching the IRA funeral on TV. Every time O'Mahoney's face flashed on the screen, she smiled. A grotesque gratification rose in her stomach. 'Hope you suffered,' she said out loud to the TV.

But despite the fact that O'Mahoney was now out of her life, Dorothy was miserable. The IRA had already replaced him. A tall, sinewy man with a deep Y-shaped scar in his left cheek. Probably from a beer glass. Scarface was already pestering her, threatening her with violence and harm if she didn't comply with his demands.

A knock on the door interrupted her thoughts. She leapt up from the settee and peered through the curtains. Jonny McGuigan was at the door. What the fuck did he want on a Saturday afternoon? She ruffled her hair, made her way to the front door and opened it.

'Dorothy,' said McGuigan.

'Jonny,' replied Dorothy. 'Robert isn't here.'

'I'm not here to see him. I'm here to see you.' Dorothy moved to one side and let the Special Branch man through the wooden door frame. McGuigan made himself at home in an armchair.

'Can I pour you a drink?' asked Dorothy.

'No, I'm good.'

Dorothy switched off the TV and took her place on the sofa. 'How can I help you?'

'I know.'

'Know what?'

'I know you've been supplying the IRA with information.'

Dorothy's heart started to race. 'I don't know what you're talking about, Jonny.'

'It only clicked when I saw his face on TV.'

'What are you talking about?'

'I saw you with him. You got into his car. I thought maybe he was a lover. Good for you, I thought. A step up from that shitty husband of yours. He hit you. That made me mad. I wanted to drag him out of the car and give him a beating. I didn't. It wasn't my business. But I was never going to forget his face after that.'

Dorothy started crying. 'I had no choice, Jonny.'

'Everyone's got a choice.'

'No, they don't. That bastard drugged me and took photos of me. He had me over a barrel.'

'You could have come to me.'

'You'd have gone to my husband. And if he'd found out…if he'd seen the photographs, he'd have fucking killed me.'

It was true. McGuigan would have told her husband. And it was most likely that Robert Campbell would have given her a brutal beating. Perhaps even smashed her skull in. He felt a pang of sympathy for Dorothy. What a shit life. And it wasn't going to get any better. The IRA had their hooks embedded in her. And they weren't about to pull them out. They would keep coming at her as long as they thought she was useful.

'Have they replaced him?' asked McGuigan.

'What do you mean?' replied Dorothy.

'Has anyone approached you since his death.'

Dorothy held a hand up to her mouth. Determined to keep the sobs contained. Tears streamed down her cheeks.

'Dorothy!' shouted McGuigan as he grabbed her forearm to the point of stopping the blood flow.

'Let go of me.' McGuigan released her arm. 'A man approached me at the bus stop two days ago.'

'His name?'

'He wouldn't tell me.'

'What did he want?'

'He wanted to know the last day.'

'Last day?'

'Thomson's last day.'

'Did you tell him?'

'Yes.'

'When is it?'

'His car was arranged for 2 p.m. today.'

'What did this man look like?'

'Tall. Skinny. Has a deep Y-shaped scar on his right cheek. Someone must have smashed a glass…'

McGuigan stood up and looked down on Dorothy. If it was a man sitting there instead of her, he would strangle the bastard there and then. But it wasn't a man. It was a woman. A woman who he knew. A woman he felt sorry for. She'd got caught up in a shit show she had no control over. 'Listen to me, Dorothy. They're never going to leave you alone.'

'And what am I supposed to do?'

'Leave. Go to London.'

'I can't do that.'

'Yes you can. Leave that fucking pig of a husband. Start a new life. Get a job. A woman like you will have no problems getting work. Just get yourself out of this shit. Or I promise you, you'll end up dead.'

McGuigan marched out of the house and climbed into his BMW. He looked at his watch. There was no way he could get to the ferry on time. But he'd try.

FIFTY

B arry Behan had made a habit of being early all his life. Meetings, football matches, trains, buses, blind dates. Even at the moment of his birth, he was early. By two weeks.

Thomson was expected at the ferry terminal at around 4 p.m. So Behan made sure he got there three hours earlier. That would give him time to scout the area. Work out where the security forces were positioned. Pick the best place for the hit. Make plans for a stealthy escape.

The Browning pistol was tucked into the inside pocket of his raincoat. Easy to pull out. Fire at close quarters. In a crowd. The noise of the gun would cause panic. Confusion. People would be screaming and scurrying around in all directions. Providing the perfect cover for his escape.

Barry Behan was calm, his heart rate pumping at fifty-five beats per minute. And it would stay that way. That's why he was so good at this game. Nothing got him flustered. He would remain calm-headed throughout.

He looked at his watch. One hour to go. Behan made his way to the small cafe near the entrance. It would be the ideal place to view the field of combat. He'd see the target coming from fifty yards away. And once Thomson walked into the main hall, he would move in for the kill. It would be like a duck shoot.

* * *

The Q car stopped outside the ferry terminal. They had arrived half an hour later than planned, the delay caused by a broken-down lorry on the Glenshane Pass. Thomson pulled himself out of the vehicle and walked toward the back of the car. The driver got there first, opened the boot, pulled the suitcase out and planted it on the tarmac. 'Here you go, Staff,' said the driver.

'Thanks.'

The driver jumped back into the Q car and sped off. Thomson picked up his suitcase and walked toward the entrance of the ferry terminal. He wondered who he'd be sharing his cabin with. The memories of the Irish navvies on the way over flashed into his mind. Hopefully the company would be better on the way back. And if it wasn't, perhaps he'd spend the night on the deck smoking cigarettes and taking in the sea air. He wasn't sure he'd be able to sleep anyway. His mind was buzzing at the thought of getting home. There was no more thought of bombs running through his head. No stress-induced cortisol pumping through his veins. That was all over now. His job done. All he could think of was Jean and the kids. God, he'd missed them. It wouldn't be long now. Just a ten-hour trip across the water. He could almost feel them in his arms.

As Thomson entered the main hall of the terminal, he felt a swelling in his bladder. A result, no doubt, of the six mugs of tea he'd drunk earlier. The staff sergeant looked around for the nearest public toilets. They were on the other side of the hall. His bladder was giving way.

He needed to get there quick. Thomson walked quicker than a Gurkha march, suitcase swinging furiously in his right hand.

* * *

Behan spotted Thomson walking into the terminal. He pushed his half-finished coffee to one side, casually stood up and walked out of the cafe.

The plan was to move in close behind Thomson and shoot him at close quarters. But the staff sergeant was racing away from him at a hare's pace. It didn't take long for Behan to realise where his target was heading. The loo. That was fine. It was a better place to finish him off than in the open. More discreet.

Behan stretched his neck above the crowd, keeping his eyes on Thomson's back. The staff sergeant rushed into the toilets with Behan on his heels.

* * *

Thomson put down his suitcase, unzipped his fly and rushed to the nearest urinal. *That's a relief,* he thought as his bladder was finally allowed to do its job. Once he'd finished urinating, he shook his manhood a couple of times and zipped up. He turned and made his way to the sink where he caught his reflection in the mirror. Badger eyes stared back at him. You're a mess. Thomson suddenly became aware of a figure standing behind him. He twisted round in time to see the man pull a Browning MK1 from his raincoat. Death was at his door in the most unlikely of places.

Instinct took over. Thomson grabbed the pistol with both hands and tried to wrench it out of the assailant's hand. The Browning fell to the floor. But out of nowhere, a massive fist smashed into Thomson's nose, knocking him on his back. The bomb man could only watch through watery eyes as Behan stooped down and picked up the pistol.

The door to a cubicle creaked open and a chubby man in a sharp suit shuffled out, unaware of the struggle that had been taking place outside. He looked up and, seeing Thomson bleeding on the floor, stiffened. Behan didn't hesitate. He shot the accidental intruder in the forehead. The force of the bullet knocked the man backward into the cubicle, splattering the walls with brains and blood.

Behan brought the pistol around and trained it at Thomson's head. 'You've been lucky. But I guess everybody's luck runs out eventually.' Thomson closed his eyes. *Was this the way he was going to die? A bullet instead of a bomb? He thought of Jean. I love you.*

Bang.

FIFTY-ONE

The atmosphere in the room was tense. McGuigan was sitting in his chair with a straight back, his hands resting on his knees. Opposite him, across an old wooden table, was the chief superintendent seated between his two most senior officers.

'What a cock-up,' said the chief superintendent. 'What the hell happened?'

McGuigan needed to keep the wolves at bay. Give enough information to keep the grey-haired men mollified. But no more than necessary. Too many words got you in trouble and too few got you fired. 'We think he was IRA.'

'What was he doing at the ferry?'

'Making a hit.'

'But why *this* man?'

'We don't know.'

'Since when have the IRA gone after low-level people?'

'Maybe it's a new tactic.'

'What the hell were *you* doing there?'

'I got a tip-off.'

'From whom?'

'I can't tell you.'

'You *will* tell us,' interrupted the officer to the right of the chief superintendent, his face flushing red.

'I heard it from my tout,' said McGuigan with a sneer. 'She's put her life on the line to get me this information. And I'm not giving her up to anybody. Not even you. Her name stays secret.'

'Is that right? Let's see how you feel when you're kicked off the force.'

'Are you threatening me?'

'Let's calm down, shall we?' intervened the chief superintendent. 'Whitehall has taken an interest in this case. The man was an English businessman. I guess when someone from the mainland gets shot, they sit up and take notice.'

'That's not surprising, is it, Sir?' said McGuigan disdainfully. If only they knew, he thought. The poor English businessman was in the wrong place at the wrong time. But the death, although tragic, was a blessing in disguise. He had become the perfect diversion. A shroud pulled over the *real* story. A cover for the incident that would be more difficult to explain away.

McGuigan had managed to get to the ferry terminal in good time. He saw Thomson being dropped off. He was late.

The AT hurried inside and the Branch man dashed after him. And that's when he caught sight of the assassin. A tall, sinewy man. Walking through the crowd. Casually and calmly. Shrouded by a veneer of ordinary. But the attempt at normality was betrayed by the Y-shaped scar on the man's face. It was the beacon that McGuigan had been looking for. The tell-tale sign of a cold-blooded killer. The IRA hitman followed Thomson, pretending inadequately not to. Moving in, getting ready to make his kill.

McGuigan tore across the terminal floor, dodging in and out of people, knocking one woman to the ground. He had no time to apologise. He had to get to the toilets. The pop of a firearm resounded through the air. Damn. Too late. McGuigan's right hand pulled the pistol from its holster as he glided through the entrance of the toilets.

Behan was standing over Thomson, his Browning pointed at the soldier's head. McGuigan lifted his pistol with two hands, aimed at Behan's skull and let off a round. The tall IRA man wavered for a brief moment before lurching forward and hitting the floor. Dead.

Thomson opened his eyes. Had he been shot? He hadn't felt anything.

'Are you okay?' came a voice from near the entrance. Thomson recognised the flash of orange hair. It was McGuigan, a pistol smoking in his hand.

'Not really.'

McGuigan looked over toward the dead man in the cubicle. Sirens sounded off in the distance. 'We need to get you on that ferry. Before the police arrive.'

FIFTY-TWO

Life as an instructor was as mundane as ever. But Thomson was thankful. Boredom can be a gift, he thought. He was enjoying his old routine. Dinner with the family every evening. Shopping on a Saturday. He'd even managed to get down to Croydon and make it up with his old man.

Thomson kissed Jean on the doorstep of their house and gave her a hug. It lasted longer than it normally would. After Northern Ireland, ordinary moments were cherished more. A higher value attached to them.

As Thomson took his usual route to camp, he smoked more cigarettes than he usually would. The nicotine addiction had grown while he was in Northern Ireland, a natural consequence of the amplified stress. He thought about the people he'd left behind.

Jock Henderson had left Londonderry a week after Thomson. Six months after that, he left the army altogether. They lost touch.

Thomson heard on the grapevine that Dorothy Campbell had mysteriously disappeared. One day she simply didn't turn up to work. Apparently, all her clothes had been cleared out of her cupboards at home. No notice. No note. No indication of anything untoward. Her husband was baffled. He thought she was happy. The police were called in to investigate. But the trail went cold quickly, and the police, even though they kept a missing person's file open, didn't pursue the case for long.

Keith Cooper was posted to Germany. But retired for health reasons a year later. The bones in his body didn't stop aching. The fact he'd survived a bomb blast at such close quarters had confounded scientists and medical experts. He should have died. And they wanted to know why he hadn't. He was continually subjected to examinations and tests to try and work out the inexplicable phenomena.

Rip rejoined the Royal Marines and was sent to Dhofar a year later. He took part in a hearts and minds campaign to repel a communist insurgency against the Sultan of Oman. While on the way to meet a village elder, his Land Rover was ambushed on an open stretch of road in the desert. The waiting rebels tore into the vehicle with heavy machine guns, killing everybody inside instantly.

Thomson got drunk in the mess the day he heard the news. Kersey was like a brother. And the loss was hard to bear.

Rip's body was shipped backed to England where he was given a Royal Marine send off in Portsmouth, home of the Corps.

Alan Sutton left the army and pursued a career in academia. He had more of an appetite for studying the classics than dismantling bombs. But he was quite often called back as a guest lecturer at the School of Ammunition.

Captain Jardine retired from the British Army and made his way back to New Zealand where he started playing rugby again, and eventually, when his knees got too stiff, became a referee.

Janine O'Grady and her kids, according to the intelligence grapevine, moved to Australia. She married an Aussie man and started her own hairdressing business. She never returned to Londonderry, even when her mother passed away.

Jimmy Brett was eventually caught and indicted for a laundry list of crimes. He was sent to Long Kesh for life. But a life sentence for Jimmy Brett was different from other men. He only spent three years in jail. A fatal heart attack made sure of that.

Michael Coyle was released early. He served ten years of a fifteen-year sentence. Once he was released, he left Ireland for ever. He travelled to Asia and became an English teacher.

Jonny McGuigan stayed in Londonderry, despite the offer of a transfer to Special Branch in London. He climbed into his car one morning, turned the key in the ignition and died in the resulting explosion. The IRA had finally caught up with him. Thomson wasn't close to McGuigan. Their relationship was one of convenience. But he would be for ever in the Irishman's debt. So on the day of the Detective Inspector's funeral, he raised a glass of Jameson's whiskey and gave thanks.

And Thomson? Well, the staff sergeant was awarded the British Empire Medal for gallantry. During his tour in Northern Ireland, he'd dismantled more than thirty explosive devices. He brought his family along to Buckingham Palace to attend the ceremony. Prince Charles was expected to hand out medals to an array of armed forces personnel. Andrew was delighted when it turned out to be the queen pinning the medals on soldiers' chests. When it was Thomson's turn to step up and stand in front of Her Majesty, Karen shouted, 'That's my Daddy.' The audience silently chuckled. Even the queen seemed to crack a smile.

* * *

Thomson reached the gates of the camp. Security was tighter than it had been before. The IRA were now targeting military sites on the mainland and all bases were on high alert. Two Gurkha soldiers scrutinised Thomson's ID before lifting the barrier and letting him through.

From the gates, the AT turned left and came to the large patch of neatly mown lawn in front of the school. The small wooden sign, with the words KEEP OFF THE GRASS, had been given a fresh lick of paint. In the past, Thomson would have followed the strict instructions. He would have kept to the pavement and walked around the neatly manicured lawn. But Ireland had changed him. Ever so slightly. All the molecules in his body had moved to create a slightly different version of himself. An imperceptibly different version. Make no mistake, he was still a man who played it by the book. A disciple of discipline. But now, after the tour, a few pages had been torn out.

Thomson walked across the grass and, smiling at the crows stamping on the ground, saved himself a minute. Maybe a bit more.

THE END

AUTHOR'S NOTES

A book set in the period of The Troubles is bound to stoke contro-
versy. Even though the events in this novel occurred almost fifty
years ago, they still touch a raw nerve among many whose lives were
touched abhorrently and indelibly by the conflict.

To this day, The Troubles give rise to deep passions. The perspectives of the people embroiled in the conflict, as you might expect, differ
greatly. Acute bias exists depending on which side people were on.

In writing this book, I have tried to give an insight into the circumstances that led to The Troubles. I touch on the blatant social injustice
and religious discrimination that was endemic in Northern Ireland. I
open a window into the deadly excesses of the British Army, who exac-
erbated the problem and contributed to the rise of the IRA.

But this is not a book about the rights and wrongs of the conflict. It's
a novel. A story which has been inspired by my father. A bomb disposal
man who was posted to Northern Ireland in 1973, at the height of the
bombings. It is through the eyes of a British soldier that we view the
events that unfold. I'll be honest. It is one-sided. That is not to say there
aren't other valid perspectives of what happened. As they say, there's
always two sides to a story.

That said, I have endeavoured to write a book that is authentic. A book that gives people an accurate view of the practices and protocols followed by the British Army. A sense of how the IRA operated. A feeling of the deep distrust between Catholics and Protestants.

In the story, there are many firsts. The wheelbarrow, the bomb suit and electronic countermeasures were introduced during my father's tour of duty.

No one has ever written a novel about the brave men from 321 EOD before. Many action writers like to put the more glamorous SAS at the heart of their stories.

But *The Bomb Man* is more than just a story. It is a tribute to a rare breed of men who were thrust into a conflict they were not prepared for.

I want to thank the following people for their feedback and contribution to the book: Pat Brett, Seanie Boyle, Stephen Mangham, Jonathan Daly, Jonathan Holburt, David Greig, Reuben Sinclair, Sally Foo, Irene Gomez and Tal Adams (who fact-checked places, dates, names and events).

And a special callout to Heather Daly, who became my editor. Heather pushed me to tighten up my writing, build more depth into my characters and improve the overall structure of the manuscript.

Printed in Great Britain
by Amazon